FRIEND

OF THE

FAMILY

FRIEND

OF THE

FAMILY

Natalie Bates

ATHENEUM

New York   1988

Atheneum
Macmillan Publishing Company
866 Third Avenue, New York, N.Y. 10022
Collier Macmillan Canada, Inc.

Library of Congress Cataloging-in-Publication Data
Bates, Natalie.
   Friend of the family.

   I. Title.
PS3552.A8275F74   1988   813'.54   88-10499
ISBN 0-689-11984-4

10 9 8 7 6 5 4 3 2 1

Printed in the United States of America

For John Rechy

Acknowledgments

I would like to thank the following people:

My husband, John, and my children, Jenna, Chris, and Georgina, for their patience, support, and inspiration.

All of the participants in John Rechy's writing workshop from October 1979 until October 1985, especially Joan Gurfield and Ross Drieblatt, whose insights and considerate suggestions helped this book grow.

And my friends in NSA, especially Mrs. Kazue Elliot, Miss Ramona Sinclair, and Mrs. Anulka Kitamura, for their personal guidance and encouragement; and Daisaku Ikeda and George M. Williams for giving me a beautiful vision and hope for the future.

LOS ANGELES, CALIFORNIA

March 1973

1

MICHAEL IS beautiful. Even after ten years of marriage, he can still take my breath away. Especially in moments like this. Unguarded, nude, he leans in front of the bathroom mirror, his pale gold skin taut as a boy's. Whistling to himself, he lathers his face with sandalwood soap. His blond hair, darkened by moisture, is combed straight back from his high forehead; his seawater green eyes gaze at his reflection. Catching sight of me in the mirror, he smiles.

"Let's see you."

I spin slowly for him. "What do you think? Not too much?" I tug at the neckline of the too-tight black jersey.

"No. It's terrific. I knew that sweater would look great."

"You don't think it's a little . . . ?" I'm five years younger than Michael, but two pregnancies have taken their toll. "Maybe something prim and wifey?"

"No." Michael studies me. "Stay with that. Give Asher something to think about." He mimes a kiss before turning again to the mirror.

The razor glides along Michael's jaw. He leans into the mirror; muscles move under the skin of his broad back; in the cleft between his firm, narrow buttocks there is soft, blond down.

"And what about you?" I whisper. "Give *you* something to think about too?" I wrap my arms around his waist, press into his back. "I've been missing you."

His body jerks. "Careful!" He frowns at the drop of bright blood welling on his chin.

"Oh, I'm sorry. Is it bad?"

"No, no, it's okay." He pulls away from me, dabbing at his chin. "It's getting late. I wonder where David is."

I gather wet towels off the floor. "He said he'd stop at the bakery and pick up the bread. I'm sorry I made you cut yourself."

"It's okay, it's nothing." He plugs in his hair dryer. His hairbrush follows the course of the dryer over his sleek head.

"Should I go and fix the salad?"

"Great," he shouts over the buzzing.

Because I'm still standing, hand on the doorknob, he switches off the dryer and turns to me. He smiles. "It'll be a terrific evening. Don't worry. Asher'll be crazy about you!" His lips kiss the air.

The living room, ruthlessly cleaned by Michael, over-flowing with cut flowers, looks like a hotel lobby. The usual clutter—books, toys, loose pages of Michael's half-finished screenplay—has been shoved inside the window seat. A yellow-and-blue plastic cowboy is hiding between the sofa cushions. I leave him there. I move the tufted hassock closer to the fireplace to cover a frayed spot on the carpet.

In our cramped yellow kitchen, washing a small mountain of spinach, I remind myself that this dinner might be worth it—if Asher agrees to invest in the movie theater, if he gives Michael and David sole rights to exhibit his library of old films—obscure old films rarely seen—we might make enough money to do some of the things we've talked about.

Like redecorate this house.

I turn off the uncompromising overhead light and switch on a small pink table lamp. In the year we've been living here, this house has stolidly refused to become a home to me. I feel as out of place here as our furniture. In our New York apartment the stocky, overstuffed sofa and chairs were warm and comforting. Here, bleaching in the Southern California sunshine, they've become gloomy, stodgy, uncompromisingly oppressive. The little nicks and frayed places, unapparent in the soft gray light of Manhattan, glare like wounds.

Michael's plan is to throw everything out. A garage sale, he says—that's what they do here. Every weekend sofas and tables and kitchen stoves appear on the sidewalks in front of houses, as though they belonged to families evicted from their homes during the Depression era. We'll do everything in white, Michael says. Rice-paper shades on the windows to replace the lovely old brocaded drapes, bare bleached floors instead of the richly intricate Persian rugs.

Michael seems to have glided into the California "lifestyle" with no bumps. He happily discarded his tweed jacket and Shetland sweaters for loose Hawaiian shirts and bleached-out jeans. He's taking tennis lessons. He works at getting a tan.

While I stay as pale as the day we arrived, and stubbornly cling to my high heels and city dresses.

The spinach is unimaginably gritty. I rub each leaf under the running water. The bottom of the sink is covered in muddy sand.

Maybe Michael is right. If the house looked different, I might feel better. Especially since I seem to spend so

5

much of my time inside. Not white, though . . . soft pastels. And pale, thick rugs. Japanese prints, a low Japanese table. If my surroundings were lighter, prettier, I might be able to paint again. Watercolors . . . more delicate than anything I've done in the past. Perhaps I'd come to like the gaudy hibiscus and bougainvillea if I tried painting them. If the house was cool and tranquil and beautiful, Michael might stay home, start writing again. All day, writing at the low table . . . happy and loving. I could set up my easel in the living room, in front of the picture window. At noon we'll take a break. Make love. Afterward, I'll fix us lunch and we'll eat it off a tray in bed. . . .

"Hi, Annie." David saunters into the kitchen, long spears of French bread under his arms. He kisses me on both cheeks. "Hi, sweetie. What's up? You look like you could use a few glasses of wine." His gypsy-black eyes assess me. "Everything okay?"

"Sure."

"Unconvinced." He rolls up his sleeves and moves to the sink. "I'll fix the salad, you relax."

I hug him. His tall, compact body feels solidly reassuring in my arms. Despite the curling black hairs and knotted veins, his hands are surprisingly delicate. His touch on my back is gentle.

"Pretty." He touches the jade beads around my neck with one finger.

"You think I look all right? The sweater was Michael's idea."

"He has good ideas."

I laugh, pleased. I always feel better when David is around. He's become Michael's closest friend. They met at a screenwriting workshop just after we moved to Los Angeles. They wrote a screenplay together, and when they failed to sell it they started on a new venture. With our small savings and borrowed money, they bought a crumbling old burlesque house. Together they're rebuilding it as an art-movie theater specializing in revival films.

David waves a pink bakery box at me. "Where are the kids?"

"Already tucked in, thank God."

"I got them a surprise."

"Sweet of you."

"It'll keep till tomorrow." He begins to tie an apron around his waist. "Come on, let me do that."

"You're very dear. But you'd better go tell Michael you're here."

David grins. "He's going to give me hell for dressing like this." He's wearing faded jeans and a rumpled gray sweater. His curly dark hair is rumpled too; long tendrils brush his eyelids. "I figured one of us ought to look artistic."

"Artsy or not, he'll make you comb your hair," I call after him.

The buzzing of the hair dryer grows loud, then soft again, as the bathroom door closes behind David.

Maggie and Oliver Turner, recent transplants from England, and our neighbors as well as the only other friends I've made here, are late as usual. Asher, the guest of honor, arrives before them.

Wally Asher is a slender, graceful man of about thirty, with close-cropped brown hair and a broad and angular face. He's dressed in the style of a college boy circa 1930—soft-collared shirt and argyle sweater over baggy flannels. His smile as he grips my hand is brilliant. His blue eyes are coolly appraising.

"Wonderful to meet you, finally. Mike and Dave talk about you all the time."

7

I return his smile, but his greeting has thrown me off balance.

"I thought you barely knew him," I whisper to Michael as he sweeps past me, escorting Asher into the living room.

Out in the kitchen, I mix margaritas and arrange hors d'oeuvres on a platter.

Asher frowns slightly at the tray of drinks I offer. "Juanita Hansen is another one," he's saying. "A gorgeous creature. She was a slave to heroin the whole time she was doing the Keystone comedies." He sips his margarita as if he were performing an arduous duty.

He sits in the maroon velvet chair by the fireplace; Michael sits in the rocking chair opposite, and David sprawls against the hassock.

Fingering my jade beads, I perch on the sofa across the room. I nod, smiling a spectator's smile.

"*Very* rare footage," Asher says. His voice purrs; he has a miser's narrowed eyes. "My father spent most of his life gathering this collection. I couldn't possibly allow—"

"Sorry we're late, darlings," Maggie calls from the front hall.

When she hugs me I can smell scotch mingled with her perfume. Oliver's smile is particularly lascivious. They must have been fighting.

"How are you, beauty?" Oliver says. He kisses me loudly on the mouth. "What a lovely thing you've got on." As he strokes my shoulder his arm deftly brushes my breast.

"We've been waiting for you." I duck out of his embrace. "Come and meet Wally Asher."

"Lead on." He smiles good-humoredly. Oliver is big and sandy-haired, bearded, hearty and clumsy as a bear, with a bear's misleading cuddleliness. He grabs a drink off the coffee table, grins at Michael and David, and flops on the sofa, waving in response to Michael's introductions.

Maggie smiles brilliantly around the room. "Lovely to see you!" Her beautifully tailored white linen slacks and shirt transform her raw-boned lankiness into slim elegance. She blows Michael a kiss and signals me to follow her out to the kitchen.

"Bloody hell!" She kicks the kitchen door shut. "What a bastard he is!"

"Oliver?"

"The whole bloody weekend with the little bitch! Some kind of Women's Primal Consciousness Raising retreat. Orgy, more like. Damn him and his *research*. . . . Where's the scotch?"

I hand her the bottle.

"You look smashing, love." She pours whiskey into a juice glass. "Cheers, darling. Let's have a marvelous evening. I haven't been out of the house in days."

Tomorrow she'll phone me and I'll listen with appropriate indignation while she tells me the details of her husband's latest infidelity. Now I simply tell her how beautiful she looks.

"Not bloody likely." She runs both hands through her thick auburn curls.

"Oh, yes." Her thin face, with its delicate pallor, the heavy-lidded chestnut eyes, the small drooping mouth give her the look of a world-weary child.

"You're so lovely," I tell her. "I wish I could wear the kind of clothes you do."

"Rubbish," she says, drinking. "If I had tits like yours, I'd be wearing what you've got on." She drops into a kitchen chair. "Fucking Oliver and his fucking tarts. And still—can you believe it?—he writes me love poems." She giggles, her anger sliding abruptly into fuzzy-voiced affection. "Dirty ones."

I recap the scotch bottle. "Let's go in now. They'll think we're talking about them."

"Who's the chap in the armchair?" she asks, uncapping the bottle and refilling her glass.

"That's him—I told you. Wally Asher. We're supposed to be charming him."

"Charm *him*? He looks a bit of an iceberg."

"What's keeping you two?" Michael appears in the kitchen, the empty margarita pitcher in his hand. He squeezes Maggie's waist. "Aren't we gorgeous?"

"And you." She slides her arm around him and pats his behind. "Lovely bum. What a lovely old man you've got, Annie," she sighs.

I put a tray of cheeses in her hands. "Go inside and be charming," I say, laughing. "That's what you're here for."

My grandmother's silver gleams a dull, greenish-black in the peach-colored candlelight. Michael had asked me to polish it, but all those swirls and convolutions defeated me before I'd begun. I thought I saw Asher wipe his fork surreptitiously on his napkin before beginning his salad.

He sits at the head of the table, flanked by Michael and David.

"Barbara La Marr," he says, "billed as 'The Girl Who Was Too Beautiful.'"

"*The Three Musketeers*," Michael says quickly.

"That's right. Very good." Asher beams a smile at him. "She had style. Kept her cocaine in a solid gold box on her grand piano. Never slept more than two hours a night. She said she had lovers by the dozen, like roses."

"Like roses, eh?" Maggie refills her wineglass. She and Oliver have finished a bottle of Beaujolais between them and started on another. "Like *weeds*."

Oliver leans over and, lifting her heavy hair, kisses the back of her neck.

The room is too hot. The lace tablecloth was a mistake; from my place at the foot of the table I can see the ragged edges of an old Burgundy wine stain peeping out from beneath the centerpiece of lilies and fresia.

Asher is talking animatedly; his spinach salad rests untouched on his plate. "*Wolf Song*, for example. My father spent a fortune to have the print restored, and still about half of it is disintegrating." He stabs the air with his fork. "As it is there are very few of her early films in showable condition."

"That was . . . who?" Michael asks humbly.

"Velez. Lupe Velez."

"Oh, of course." Michael is deeply apologetic.

"A fabulous beauty, Lupe Velez. No one ever knew how to use her right."

"Wait . . . !" I lean forward eagerly. "I've heard of her. She committed suicide, didn't she? Got all dressed up and invited people over, but then died in the bathroom with her head in the—"

"The details of her death are unimportant. She was a beautiful woman. Tragic." Asher's voice is ice.

"I've seen her in the Tarzan films," David says.

Asher's frigid eyes release me. "She was desperate." He turns enthusiastically to David. "Weissmuller was a beast to her, she worshiped him. . . ."

I gather up the salad plates.

When I serve the saffron-scented bouillabaisse, Asher's conversation falters. He stares wordlessly into his bowl.

11

I feel drowned in shadows. It seems to me the candle-light illuminates only Asher's end of the table. He hasn't touched his food. "Don't you like bouillabaisse, Mr. Asher?"

"I'm allergic to shellfish."

"Have some bread, then, Wally." Michael thrusts the basket toward him. "It's homemade, Annie made it."

"She's a wonderful little baker." David looks at me, his eyebrows raised in amusement. "This is as good as any French bakery."

"Really?" Asher helps himself to a large chunk of bread. "My father used to bake bread. He said it helped him remember his mother. My grandmother was a fabulous lady, she looked just like Olive Thomas in *Tomboy*. . . ."

"I had no idea you were so talented, Annie." Oliver helps himself. "What a treat."

"I baked bread for you. I baked *scones*." Maggie's words slide into each other. "You said you loved them. Swine."

Oliver pats her hand affectionately. "Perhaps you'd like to powder your nose, my love?"

"I'll give you a help." As I leave the room, Maggie drooping against my shoulder, Asher calls after me, "Your bread is excellent, Mrs. Morrow."

"Annie," Michael says.

When we return the men have moved into the living room. Maggie reclines, pale and sleepy, on the sofa. I serve dessert and coffee.

David and Michael are speaking earnestly of their devotion to cinema classics, the plans they've made for the safekeeping of the films.

I hear Asher's refusals growing weaker, hear the beginnings of agreement in his voice.

"Presented through the courtesy of Wallace Asher," David says.

"One print," Michael says. "It'll stay in the safe till the show. I'll run the projector myself."

I freeze on the threshold of the living room. Michael can't possibly be planning to be at the theater running the film every night. He's already promised me that the long hours he's spent working on the theater, sometimes through the night, will end as soon as they're ready to open.

"Why don't you come see me tomorrow and we can work out the details?" Asher says. He smiles slowly at Michael.

Michael feels my eyes on him. He looks up and winks at me.

No, he won't work at the theater every night. That was just part of the sales pitch. He doesn't want to leave me always alone.

When the guests have gone we celebrate with cognac in the kitchen.

David piles dirty dishes into the sink. ". . . for my love is wild as the wind . . ." he sings in a cracked tenor.

"It was a fabulous dinner, sweetheart. Thank you." Michael's lips are warm on my neck. "Did I tell you how beautiful you look tonight?" His hands move over my hips.

"Now, children, no necking in the balcony." David throws a playful arm around both of us.

"Damn," Michael laughs. "You've got wet hands." He blots at his silk shirt with a dish towel. "I'd better go put on a sweatshirt."

"My turn." David hugs me. "You don't mind wet hands, do you, Annushka?" He kisses my forehead. "As soon as we get our first box-office bonanza, we'll take you out somewhere wonderful."

"That would be fun."

I like David's attentions, his flattery. They don't make me uncomfortable, the way Oliver's flirting does. There is

13

something reverential in David's affection that makes me feel noble and beautiful.

"Why don't you find yourself a girl and get married again?" I ask because I love to hear his faithful answer: "If I could find someone like you, I would."

David had been married, briefly and disastrously, at nineteen. He never talks about it, but Michael's told me that his wife had been spoiled and demanding.

Poor David. I return his hug and kiss him gently on his full lips.

"I can't leave you two alone for a minute," Michael teases. He's juggling a stack of dirty dishes and cups. "Let's get to work."

Outside, the street is sleeping; our kitchen is a bright island of warmth. We clean up, the three of us, laughing, comfortably tired, sipping cognac.

Michael brushes up against me as he moves around the room. He touches my hair or my back. When he looks at me his eyes are warm and thrilling.

It's been so long since Michael and I have made love. He's been exhausted from strenuous working hours, or else numbed by the dozens of worries attached to launching a theater. But tonight he's happy and relaxed. Already I can feel a joyful, expectant fluttering deep in my stomach. I increase my attentions to David to compensate for wanting him gone.

The last dish has been stacked in the cupboard; we're sitting at the table, finishing the cognac.

Yawning, I put my arm around Michael's shoulder. "You must be beat," I say pointedly to David. "Thanks for all your help. Will we see you tomorrow for breakfast?"

His face darkens, he frowns at Michael. "You didn't tell her about tonight."

Michael flushes. "I thought it might spoil the evening," he mumbles.

"You're planning to work tonight?" I stare at him. "Why didn't you tell me?"

"It's lousy," David says. His eyes are sympathetic. "We've got to get that extra row of seats out of there—the fire inspector's coming at nine in the morning."

"You could have told me." I pull my arm away from Michael's stroking hand. "I thought you'd stay with me. I cooked a whole dinner . . . that Asher never said one word to me . . ." I'm ashamed of the tears choking my voice. And of my anger.

"Don't be mad," Michael whispers. "You know I'd stay if I could." He holds me tight, kisses my neck, my cheek. "You've been so wonderful about everything, don't ruin it now. As soon as we have the theater rolling, we'll take off, have a weekend. . . ."

David looks at his watch.

"You're fabulous," Michael tells me at the front door.

"I love you, Michael," I say.

I move around the living room replacing the books, the toys, the comforting debris of our everyday life.

The bedroom is cold. Our bed, with its neat, pale sheets and perfectly plumped pillows, is colder. I take a book of short stories into the living room and sit in the scuffed oak rocker. In New York we'd kept this rocker in the bedroom between the rickety iron bed Michael's mother had lent us and the window. When the children were babies, if they were having a fretful night, I'd rock them in this chair while Michael, propped up in bed, read his plays to me till the baby fell asleep.

The fire is dying; it responds feebly to my proddings. I

15

wrap my bare feet in an ancient brown cardigan of Michael's.

I'll wait here till he comes home. He's my best friend. He'll be able to tell me why it is that the happier he becomes, the lonelier I feel.

2

I WAKE UP startled, my heart racing. The living room is chill and silent. The book I was reading has fallen to the floor; I take it in my lap and smooth the creases.

A soft scraping of a key in the lock, and Michael crouches in front of me.

"What is it, sweetheart? Are you crying?"

"I think I was dreaming. . . . What time is it?"

He strokes my back. "Come to bed. I'll make you some tea." He tucks the soft, worn quilt around me. Smiling, touching my hair: "You know what Maggie says—tea'll cure anything."

We sip sweet tea, the bedside lamp holds us in a circle of pink warmth.

"I had a bad dream, I think. I can't remember—"

"Would you like me to read to you till you fall asleep?"

I curl against him and close my eyes. "You must be so tired."

"I'm okay."

His voice murmurs, the words of the story blur into a drowsy ripple of sound.

In the Japanese maple outside our bedroom window a mockingbird begins his raucous dawn song. Michael sleeps, his arm, warm and heavy, flung over me, hand cupped around my breast.

When I was a child my father used to sing me to sleep. He would sit by my bed and sing very softly "Has Anybody Seen My Gal?" and "Who's Sorry Now?" Old songs. He'd end up with the "St. Louis Blues." My mother would come to my bedroom door in her apron. She wouldn't say "Ethan, your dinner's getting cold." She'd just stand there. And he would wink at me and add on another chorus.

I wake alone; a note on Michael's pillow reads, "I've taken the kids out for breakfast so you could have a good long sleep."

The bedroom door eases open. Robin's round blue eyes peek cautiously out of his small face. "You're awake!" He tumbles onto the bed; his kisses are sticky. "We've been waiting so long for you to wake up."

Frowning in deep concentration, Emily carries in a tray. "I made the coffee. It's probably horrible." She wobbles the tray onto my knees. "You don't have to drink it."

"Thank you, darling. It smells wonderful."

As she bends to kiss me her skinny brown braids, tied up in knotted shoelaces, sweep my cheek.

Michael brings toast and jam. "Have a good sleep?"

The bedroom window shows a patch of milky-gray sky. A cozy cloudy day. A New York day. "What a nice morning."

"It's not morning anymore, Mommy," Robin corrects gently. He nibbles my toast. Michael shares my coffee. Last night's sadness has retreated to its hiding place. I smile at them, grateful and happy.

"Did you get all your work done last night, darling?" I

18

trace the line of Michael's jaw, down his neck, across his wide shoulder.

"Just about. David's meeting with the fire inspectors now."

"I thought they were coming at nine."

"So did we." He reaches across the bed and pulls Emily onto his lap. "Don't look so glum, peaches, we'll go in a little while."

"Daddy's taking us to the hobby store." Robin smoothes the pillows behind my head.

"Why didn't the inspectors let you know they'd be late—you could have stayed with me. . . ."

"I know." Michael kisses my hand. "Those guys are a pain, they never show up when they say they will."

"If you knew that, they why did you go rushing off?" My voice has risen into the querulous tone I hate.

"Mom? Mommy?" Robin stands on the bed and puts his arms tight around me. "We're going to the hobby store, I'm getting a plane . . ."

A metallic sun has appeared low in the sky; the dove-colored clouds are dispersing. This will be another blazing day of relentless sunshine after all.

"You could have gotten up early . . . done the work this morning."

"Can we go now, Dad?" Emily squirms on Michael's lap.

"Annie." His sigh is burdened.

Unreasonable tears rise in my throat. "Why didn't you wake me up, then? I could have gone to breakfast with you."

"Honey . . ." Inside its sweetness, the word hides a thin sharp blade of anger.

"I *told* you the coffee was terrible." Emily slides off Michael's lap. She jerks the tray off the bed.

19

"No, it was wonderful, Em."

"We were trying to give you a treat." Michael holds his head stiffly, his voice is tight.

My anger makes me feel ugly and foolish; I force it into stillness before I speak. "It *was* a treat. It was lovely to have breakfast in bed. Thank you."

The three of them stand by the door. Their hands are linked, they are looking at me with closed faces.

"It was a *wonderful* treat." My smile feels askew. "I don't like to be left behind, that's all."

"We won't be long, Mommy," Robin says.

"Wouldn't you like me to come with you?"

Michael tells the children to wait for him in the car. He comes to sit beside me on the bed. "What is it?" he says. "What's bothering you?"

"Nothing. You didn't have to go out last night."

He shakes his head slowly, staring into my eyes. "What's *bothering* you?" His voice is quietly patient; the coiled anger seems apparent only in his rigid back and clasped hands.

"You *choose*, Michael. Every time. When you could be with me, you choose to be somewhere else."

"It's not by choice, Annie. Jesus!"

"You're always away. . . . I get lonely. . . . I hate it here. . . ."

"I don't know what you want me to do. . . . I'm doing this for us. . . ."

Too demanding. Too dependent. Other wives. Find something to do. Start painting again.

Michael has said all this before, sometimes calmly, sometimes scolding. Today there's a newness to the words; his anger seems to have fresh power. It frightens me.

"I'm sorry, Michael."

"I just don't know what you want me to—"

"I'm sorry. Darling. Don't listen to me—"

"I've been trying—"

"I know. I've just felt lonesome. Left out—"

"It won't be for much longer." He strokes my hand. "I hope you can understand. God, I hate these scenes."

"I know you do. I'm sorry. I love you."

"I love you too." He sounds exhausted.

"You must be so tired, you hardly slept. I could take the kids—"

He stands abruptly. "No. I promised them. They're waiting."

"I could come along."

"Why don't you stay here and relax? Take a bubble bath—enjoy the quiet."

The door closes behind him.

Desolation swallows me.

I stare out of the window at the silent street. No children playing on the brown-green squares of lawn, no cats prowling the small, careful gardens. The yellow and pink stucco houses are painted on the blank sky. A white car moves slowly down our street, pauses at the corner, turns, is gone. The afternoon stretches to the horizon. Empty.

I'm alone. It seems he never wants me to go with him now. Why?

A dangerous thought stirs. I have to quiet it. Searching for chores to fill this dangerous, empty time, I move from room to room. The house defies me with its smug orderliness.

The garden, too, is primly neat—no weeds, nothing to be tended.

I dial Maggie's number. No answer.

I snatch my paint box from the shelf in the closet where it's been since we arrived in Los Angeles. The paints inside look cracked and dead, the brushes are stiff. In

New York I painted every day—the roofs and towers I could see from our tenth-floor window; the Riverside Park playground half buried in snow; the daffodils growing in the littered medians along upper Broadway. I sketched people on the subway, wobbly charcoal drawings, smeared by the jostling of the train.

Michael came with me on those sketching expeditions. Sometimes we'd have lunch at a cafe near Central Park and go to the Metropolitan Museum. He'd tease me when I became transfixed by a Turner or a van Gogh. When we lived in New York we were together almost all the time.

I close my paint box and return it to the shelf. I can't paint in this city. Too much light. Too many colors. The climate saps my energy.

In the kitchen I pour a beer and open my stained copy of *The Joy of Cooking*. I'll plan this week's dinners. Will Michael be home to eat them? I'll make sure he is—I'll choose elaborate meals, dishes that will require long and careful preparation. I scan the lists of recipes.

The sound of the doorbell floods me with grateful relief. Maggie! She'll have new stories about Oliver. Maybe she'll suggest a window-shopping trip to Beverly Hills, or sherry at the English tearoom near the beach. As I unlock the door I lean out of the window to smile at her.

A boy is standing on our porch. Eighteen or nineteen years old, he's very thin, very pale. His blond, nearly white, hair is long; he pushes it away from his forehead with nervous impatience. His feet move restlessly on the doormat.

I open the door halfway. "May I help you?"

His head jerks up, he stares at me. Behind rimless glasses his light eyes appear magnified. Stunned.

"Are you looking for someone?" I ask.

He moistens his pale lips; his eyes move to the house number written beside the door. "Do you live here?"

"Yes. Who are you looking for?"

The boy turns abruptly. He takes the porch steps in one leap. His shoulders hunched, his hands in his pockets, he walks rapidly away down the street. At the corner he seems to waver, seems on the point of turning back, then breaks into a sprint and disappears.

In the kitchen I feel chilled and weakened. As if I'd narrowly escaped from some disaster. Only later, when I'm cooking our dinner, when Robin is coloring at the kitchen table and Michael is sprawled on the living-room floor helping Emily piece together a model airplane, do I feel safe again.

"Something funny happened today," I say when we're sitting at the kitchen table finishing dinner. "A boy came to the door."

I can feel Michael's eyes on my face. The children look at me expectantly.

"Well, that's all, really. He . . . he didn't know who he was looking for."

"Why is that funny, Mommy?"

I falter into silence. What *had* happened? A shy boy who'd mistaken an address and then gotten embarrassed.

"What did he want?" Michael rises to clear the table. "Was he collecting for something? You shouldn't open the door to strangers when you're home alone."

"No. It was nothing. He just seemed odd."

Michael shrugs. "Well, God knows there are plenty of odd people in this town. Who wants ice cream with their pie?"

Michael washes the dishes. He puts the children to bed. Then, grinning, he flops onto the sofa. "The hell with work," he announces. "Tonight I'm staying home." He pulls me down beside him.

23

"Oh, I'm so glad." I hold on to him tight. His back feels so broad and smooth under my hands, his warm, clean scent is so familiar. He'll take away this troubling darkness. "Let's go to bed," I say.

"In a little while." His smile is loving. "You're so beautiful. I like to look at you."

In bed Michael rubs my feet and legs with perfumed oil. He massages my back.

"I love your hair," he says. He tangles his fingers in it and tugs gently. "Let's not fight anymore." He kisses my eyes, my neck.

I press myself close against him. His hands stroke my back, slowly.

"You know, I love you," he murmurs.

"I love you too." I kiss him; his mouth is soft. His hand on my back moves more slowly.

"Annie." A whispered sigh.

My head is resting on his chest; I move my hand lower on his body.

"So . . . sweet . . ." His belly rises and falls with a gentle, steady rhythm. His hand slides off my back and rests, palm up, on the blanket beside me. He's asleep.

The scent of night-blooming jasmine filters through the open window. Michael's sleeping flesh seems to give off a feverish heat. I kick the covers away. Michael mutters incomprehensible words. I fling my pillows to the floor, press my face against the cool sheet. The squat, staring alarm clock reads three-fifteen. My body aches with longing. "He's exhausted," I murmur out loud. Like a gentle mother, I stroke his hair, kiss his forehead. But my anger won't be soothed. I squeeze my eyes shut.

The boy's face appears instantly, as if summoned. I see again the platinum hair, the pale eyes. There was some-

24

thing besides shock in his eyes when he looked at me. There was anger there too. And hatred.

Why this, from a stranger?

Michael stirs, sighing.

3

I WAIT ON one of the park benches circling the sandbox. I've asked David to meet me here on his lunch break. Across from me a sleepy-eyed woman rocks an infant in a carriage. Another mother holds an unread magazine while her anxious eyes travel the playground from swings to slides to sandbox, following the exuberant dartings of her three-year-old. Except for the grainy intensity of the light and the few palm trees, this could be Riverside Park in New York. The same cozy monotony of motherhood, the same sweet lassitude warms this park too; the women bask in it like cats in the sun.

"Mommy! Watch me slide."

My head jerks up, I lift my hand to wave. Someone else's child is calling to his mother from the top of the tallest slide.

Michael was with us that day when Emily toppled off the slide in Riverside Park. Early October, the maples along the parkway auburn, the hot-chestnut man in the ice-cream vendor's usual spot just outside the playground fence. Michael had run to Emily, scooped her up, and kissed her tears away. Try it again, he told her. Daddy will wait here and catch you if you fall.

The boy on the slide is very blond and pale; an involuntary shudder passes through me. What's keeping David?

A middle-aged man in a business suit wanders into the park. He sits on a bench slightly removed from the play area. In his somber clothes he's like a bare tree in a flowering orchard. Maybe he's drawn to the park for the same reason I am. I feel safe here.

A fawn-colored dog led by a young man wearing khaki shorts and sandals passes my bench. The dog wants to stop and inspect the bench; the young man jerks him sharply away. A small girl reaches for the dog; her mother pulls her back, scolding.

Maybe David's not—

Walking toward me across the basketball court, David keeps his eyes down, head thrust slightly forward, hands in his pockets. His striped T-shirt, faded jeans, and torn sneakers are like those worn by the little boys playing in the sandbox. When I call he waves and breaks into a trot.

"Sorry I'm late." He drops down beside me. David has the tense, balanced grace of a swimmer. "I've been unpacking candy all morning." He bends to kiss my cheek. He smells faintly of chocolate and soap.

I return his kiss. "You smell like Robin. I'm glad to see you."

"Lunch." He hands me a lumpy, foil-wrapped bar. "I have no idea what these are—their wrappers fell off. Cosmic Chews, Starbursts. Whatever happened to good old Hershey bars? Let's see . . ." He unwraps a bar and takes a bite. "Nuts . . . caramel . . ." he chews ponderously ". . . and something unidentifiable. How's yours?"

"Tastes like an eraser."

David laughs, and the brotherly brown eyes, the wide, affable mouth, the frizzy dark curls suddenly seem unfamiliar.

"This is great." He stretches and yawns, throwing his arms up over his head, arching his back. His T-shirt pulls out of his jeans, exposing a ribbon of smooth tawny skin. "I feel like I haven't seen daylight since we bought the damn theater."

I laugh. "I feel like I haven't seen *Michael* since you bought the damn theater."

His smile is sympathetic. "I know you haven't. This hasn't been much fun for you, either." He sighs happily. "Sun! I ought to bring Robin here some afternoon. It's time he learned to play baseball. It's a cinch his dad's never going to teach him. That husband of yours is useless on the playing fields," he says. "What did he do with his childhood?"

"I think he collected bugs or stamps or something." David's brown eyes gleam amber . . . such warm eyes . . . I lay my hand on his arm. "I'm awfully glad you came today."

"Me, too. I get to have you all to myself." His gaze shifts to two small boys digging in the sandbox. "He'll be jealous." He grins. "Serves him right for being such a slave driver. That man sure loves to work! I keep telling him to slow down, but you know how he is."

"Yes. I do. I know how he is."

David leans back and closes his eyes. "He doesn't know how to relax."

"He used to. In New York." We would take picnics—pâté, a bottle of wine—up to the Cloisters . . . sit on the stone wall overlooking the George Washington Bridge, and have our supper. . . .

"He'll ease up once the theater gets going." He sits up and smiles. "We finally set the schedule last night. *Finally*. I gave in on *Jezebel*, and he gave up on the Magnani films—we're going to run *Bicycle Thief* and *Nights of Cabiria* instead."

"Magnani's his favorite actress."

"Yeah, she's great, but Michael agrees with me—her films don't really draw."

"She was my favorite actress too. David . . . there's . . . I don't know . . ." His face is so kind, so anxious to soothe. "Do you think the theater really has a good chance of making it? That money, you know . . . we were going to buy a house. We talked about the north coast, or maybe Oregon . . ."

"You'll have *two* houses! We're going to be rich—we'll be the new Shuberts, we'll have theaters all over the place." He strokes my hand. "Please don't worry." He turns to face me. "I just got a terrific idea. Since you like Magnani so much, we'll have a special screening. Just for you." He claps his hands. "Which do you want first? *The Rose Tattoo* or *Orpheus Descending*? I'll even make the popcorn. It'll be fun."

"Thanks, but I was hoping for some fun that doesn't involve the damn theater." His face clouds. "I'm sorry," I apologize hastily. "That's very sweet of you to think of. I guess I'm just not used to being apart from Michael so much. You two have worked late every night for the last three weeks."

"Not *every* night."

"Yes, every single night."

"Really?" David looks at me, then he breaks into an apologetic smile. "Yeah," he says. "I guess it has been pretty long hours." He smoothes the crumpled candy wrapper, recrumples it, and tosses it into a trash can beside the bench. "It's been rough on all of us. We almost strangled each other yesterday."

"At least you get to see him."

"Anytime you'd like to come by and help rip out seats or install plumbing, you're more than welcome."

"I've considered it, believe me." I laugh. "It isn't just that he's away so much . . ."

The mothers and toddlers are packing up to leave; the playground is filling with older kids swooping and shrieking on skateboards. The younger children scatter in alarm like frightened chicks.

"He *is* pretty obsessed with the place," David says. "But it won't be much longer, sweetie."

On the basketball court a group of five or six men have gathered to play a game. Their voices, hoarse and gutteral, rise above the children's reedy clamor.

"I know," I say. "I ought to be used to it—my mother went through the same kind of thing. My father used to work endless hours. And when he wasn't working he'd go off with his fishing buddies."

"Good thing Michael doesn't like fishing," David teases.

"Yeah—my father still holds it against him. He and his buddies took Michael up to Canada on a fishing trip once. He *hated* it. He said it was like outtakes from *The Legend of Daniel Boone* with four overweight, over-the-hill Fess Parkers."

"He told me about that." David chuckles. "Several times."

Across the park the businessman is petting the fawn-colored dog and talking to its owner.

"I guess Michael talks to you a lot."

"There's nothing like gutting a theater together to promote conversation." David frowns and glances at his watch. "Damn, I have to get back."

"You need to go already?"

"A guy's coming to show me how to install the soda fountain." He stands. "I know you get lonely, Annie. He gets lonely for you too. But it's all going to be worth it. I promise." He holds out his hand for me. "Are you leaving now? I'll walk you to your car."

We walk close together, our arms touching. David tells me that just yesterday Michael spoke about taking me away for a second honeymoon . . . soon. "I shouldn't tell you this," he says. "He probably wants to surprise you."

As we approach the bench where the businessman had been, I see the fawn-colored dog again. Tied to the empty bench, she lies with her head on her paws, her tail lowered. Her owner is not in sight.

"What's wrong?"

"That man left his dog all alone, David."

"You worry about everything, don't you?"

"Someone could steal him."

"I don't think his owner will be gone too long." He squeezes my shoulder affectionately and turns me toward the parking lot. "Have you ever thought about getting a puppy for the kids? Kids ought to have a dog."

He tells me about the dog he had when he was growing up. His voice is cheerful, his comforting arm is around my shoulder, but I feel neither cheered nor comforted.

As we near the parking lot we pass the businessman and the dog owner—walking together along the path that curves down the hill into the grove of trees beyond the baseball field.

In the cold, bright supermarket I push my wire cart up and down the neat geometry of the aisles. Aisle five: waxy apples, melons already quartered and wrapped in cellophane. Aisle seventeen: cans, bottles, boxes. Aisle twenty-one: blocks of frozen meat.

In New York, Michael carried the big straw basket and we strolled along Ninth Avenue: vegetable stands streaming colors—reds, greens, yellows; pink and silver fish on sawdust-flecked ice; sacks of red and black beans; barrels of dusty rice; kegs of olive oil. . . . Big men in stained aprons smiled and asked, "How thick you want these chops cut, missus?" When our basket was full, and as beautiful as a still life, we stopped at a bakery that smelled like mornings in Italy and drank cups of espresso and steamed milk before taking the crowded noisy bus back uptown.

Now an old woman blocks the supermarket aisle. Her face looks lost, she loads box after box of cornflakes into her cart.

Robin is already standing by the kindergarten door waiting when I pull up at the school. Relief lights his small face when he sees me.

"I thought you weren't coming, Mommy." He hands me a paper plate on which bits of macaroni are glued in a rough design. " Art project." He studies my face. "Are you tired, Mommy?"

"No, darling."

Emily and her best friend, Melissa, have disappeared, Melissa's gorgeous mother tells me, laughing, when I ring her doorbell. I circle their street twice before I spot them, crouched behind a hibiscus hedge.

"What were you doing back there, Emily?" I open the car door for her.

"Playing."

"Playing *what*?"

"Just playing." She pouts in righteous indignation. "I was just playing, Mom. Geeze."

"The light's green, Mommy," Robin urges.

We drive home in silence.

Later tonight . . . after I've fed the children and put them to bed . . . when Michael gets home . . . I'll light a fire in the fireplace, open a bottle of brandy. I know you're working very hard, I'll say. But I miss you. I miss the way we used to be. I can do . . . We were so close, and now . . .

"Dad's home!" Robin shouts.

I feel a flutter of panic—Michael's car in the driveway.

He comes out onto the porch, the children run to him.

"I thought you'd be working late." I hide my confusion behind bags of groceries.

He takes the bags from my arms, kissing me. "I came straight here from downtown. I thought we could have dinner together. Come on, Em," he calls. "I'll help you with your homework."

During dinner Michael jokes with the children. I avoid his eyes.

"You're angry," Emily says when I tuck her into bed. "Are you mad at me?" I comfort her with kisses, but her eyes stay full of questions.

"You forgot to hang up my art project," Robin whispers when I bend to kiss him good night. "Didn't you like it?"

Michael is in the living room, turning the pages of last week's *People* magazine, smoking one of his infrequent cigarettes. "Did they brush their teeth?" he asks, not looking up.

"Yes. Do you want more coffee? A brandy?"

"No, thanks."

I sit beside him on the sofa. "I saw David today."

"Did he drop by?"

"No. I asked him to meet me in the park."

Michael looks up at me. "What for?"

"Nothing. I was lonely. You weren't around."

Michael sighs, shaking his head, and returns to his magazine.

"I wanted to talk to him. About you ."

The magazine slides to the floor. Michael is staring at me.

"Michael, we're never together anymore. You're hardly ever here, and when you are—"

"You were talking to David about *me*?"

"Michael, I've been feeling so—"

"You were asking David questions about *me*?"

"Michael—"

"Goddamn it!" he explodes. "If you want to know something, you ask me! You don't drag our friends into our private—"

"I didn't drag—"

"I won't be discussed—"

"He's our friend, Michael—"

"Our marriage is between us. It's private." He paces the room. "You violate the trust between us when you—"

"Why are you so upset?"

"I don't want you talking about me—"

"—our friend!"

"—not to him, not to *anyone*."

"I need to know why it seems you don't want to be with me."

Michael stands still, his face is white with suppressed rage. When he speaks his voice is chilled calm. "This is ridiculous and depressing."

"Where are you going?" He's grabbed his jacket off the hook in the front hall.

"To the theater."

"Don't, Michael."

"You'd better find something to fill your time, Annie. All this inactivity is making a neurotic woman out of you."

The door slams behind him.

I dial David's number; my tears begin as soon as I hear his voice.

He listens to me, making small, soothing interjections.

"I've never seen him this angry," I sob. "I don't understand. That boy was angry at me too. Everything feels twisted. I haven't done anything wrong, David."

"No, of course you haven't, sweetie. What boy?"

"I don't know him, he just had the wrong address. But he scared me. I've been feeling out of focus. . . . I don't feel like me. . . ."

"What did he look like?"

"Blond and pale, with glasses. Do you know him?"

"No. But I'm sure it's nothing to worry about. Where's Michael now?"

"At the theater. He slammed out—"

"Why don't I go over there and bring him home? You two can talk things out quietly. Make up."

"I don't know if he'll come home now. He's very angry."

"Of course he will." David's voice is hearty. "We'll see you in about twenty minutes."

I feel as if I can't breathe. I wait for them on the front porch. I need the cool night air. The sky is very clear. There's no moon, but the stars are bright. I squint my eyes, and the stars become smudges of yellow pulsing against the sky. I begin to shiver.

I'll put my arms around Michael, I'll apologize, tell him that from now on I'll be stronger. Tell him he's right—I've allowed homesickness and boredom to fester into irrational fear. I'll find a way to fill my empty time . . . maybe take a class . . . French lessons or Chinese cooking.

David's red Volkswagen pulls into the driveway. David gets out alone. He runs up the porch steps, past me into the house. "Michael?" he calls. He turns to me. "He wasn't at the theater, I thought I might have missed him, I thought he'd come home." His eyes are shining with a dark urgency.

"Do you think he's had an accident?" I clutch his arm.

"No, no," he says. "Of course not." His smile is brittle. "I'm sure he'll be along any minute. I'll wait with you."

I make a pot of coffee. We wait on the sofa.

"Does Emily like her new teacher?" David asks me, staring at the window.

"Yes."

"That's good."

I refill the coffee cups. "Are you still going ahead with the Fritz Lang retrospective?"

"No, there wasn't enough interest. Was that a . . . ? No . . ."

"He might have gone to the warehouse to check on the lobby posters," David says.

"I think he mentioned something about that this morning," I offer. His fear is igniting my own. I feel something hidden in the dark waiting with us.

David stares into the empty fireplace. His laced fingers grip each other. "It's *late*," he whispers.

The ringing telephone brings us both to our feet.

"Hello, darling." Maggie's voice is slurred and jubilant. "You weren't sleeping, were you?"

"It's Maggie," I whisper to David. He begins to pace the living room.

"No," I tell her. "I'm awake."

"Something lovely's happened—oh, you weren't fucking, darling, were you?"

David's pacing stops at the front door. He goes out onto the porch. "No, Maggie. What's going on?" Through the open door I can see car headlights.

"I told you about Oliver's little bitch, didn't I? The latest one?"

"Yes, Maggie." The headlights stop in front of our house, go dark. A car door slams.

"This was the weekend he was taking her to Taos . . ."

Michael is on the porch. David has stepped forward to meet him. They whisper close together. ". . . she wasn't there, the little bitch. Oliver looked everywhere for her . . ." David has gripped Michael's shoulder. ". . . and the note said . . ." Michael turns his face away. ". . . to Las Vegas with a kid from the university. Old Oliver ousted by a schoolboy!" David's hands slice the air. "Isn't it marvelous?"

"Maggie, I've got to go."

"Why didn't you tell me I was disturbing you?" she says, petulant.

"No, no. Robin's woken up with a tummy ache. I'll call you tomorrow."

"I knew you were fucking," she mutters. The phone goes dead.

David is halfway down the porch steps; Michael stands below him, blocking his way. David thrusts him aside, strides across the lawn to his car.

Michael runs after him. He clutches David's arm; David pulls away, slams the door. Michael stands on the driveway, his arms at his side, watching David's car disappear around the corner of our street.

The darkness assumes a shape.

I leave our house and walk slowly down the long, graveled driveway to Michael. My shadow falls across him; he turns his face to me. Tears leave silver trails down his cheeks. The gravel gleams black as quicksand.

"Michael? How long have you and David been lovers?"

4

MOTIONLESS, I wait for Michael's outraged denial.

He stares into the still darkness behind me.

A square of yellow light flares in the window of our neighbor's house; a silhouette floats across the shade.

"Come inside," I whisper.

His body jerks as though he's tearing free from someone's fierce hold. He walks past me into the house.

We sit at opposite ends of the kitchen table. I clasp my hands in my lap to stop the trembling in my shoulders. He drinks brandy, gripping the glass with both hands. I can hear our breathing, the hum of the refrigerator. Numbers slide across the face of the digital clock on the yellow wall behind Michael. When I chose this color for the kitchen, I thought it would be the yellow of van Gogh sunflowers, but it's just a drab, mustardy color. Tomorrow, when this awful night has been erased by tears, relief at our narrow escape, I'll start to repaint the kitchen. Pale blue walls . . . the color of Monet water lilies . . .

Michael draws a deep, shuddering breath. He's going to convince me, deny there's anything. . . .

Why doesn't he speak?

I look into my lap; I fold a paper napkin until it comes apart in my hands. I look at the crayoned pictures taped to the refrigerator: a tiny, lopsided house surrounded by gargantuan flowers; a grimacing purple sun. Michael sighs raggedly. On the low shelf, wooden spoons standing upright in a red canister that once held macaroons. A Valentine's Day present. Or was it Christmas? Which Christmas? Sick panic washes over me. A red canister . . . a pink bow on top . . . I doled out the cookies like a miser. . . . But when? Whose gift?

Michael stands, his chair skids into the cabinet. "Jesus Christ." He prowls the kitchen, touching the cool, gleaming surfaces with the palms of his hands. "Jesus Christ."

I see myself as a stranger: a woman sitting straight and still on a kitchen chair, her eyes ravenous.

"You really believe that I . . ." His voice breaks.

"Yes," I tell him, to urge his denial. "You and David." His outrage will burn away my sickly fears.

"Annie." He whispers my name like a prayer.

My heart freezes.

Pressed against the wall, he watches me. His wounded eyes reflect the cruel shape of his accuser: me.

A thrill of horror—I run to him. "I didn't mean . . . You're a husband, a father." I hold him as tight as I can.

"You can't leave me, Annie."

I lead him to the table, we sit beside each other. "You mustn't worry," I tell him. He's pale, his mouth looks swollen. I touch his lips. "I'll take better care of you from now on."

"David—"

"No. We won't see him, we won't talk about him." I stand up, smoothing my skirt over my thighs. "Everything will be fine." I take the sugar bowl from the table and refill it carefully from the tall glass jar beside the stove.

Michael drops his head in his hands.

"You'll sell your share of the theater."

"It's not . . ." He goes to the sink, splashes water on his face. He leans heavily on the sink and says:

"It's not what you think."

I set the sugar bowl and its matching cream jug in the center of the table. "He'll buy you out." I reach for cereal bowls. Chipped. We must get new ones. "We'll move."

"I can't go away from David."

"None of us will remember this." I set the bowls on the table.

"I won't go away from him."

"Don't talk anymore."

"I was afraid to tell you. But David was right—it's better if you know." He moves toward me, his face reckless. I have to close my eyes to see him as he really looks.

"Let's not talk anymore, Michael. In the morning—"

His arms come around me. The scratchy tweed sweater he's wearing isn't his. "I *need* to tell you."

"No. You love me. You're my husband."

"Annie . . ." His tears are beautiful. "Of course I love you. More than anything."

"You see? There's nothing." I take his hands from around my waist. "Nothing." I lay out spoons, knives, napkins.

"What are you *doing*?" His voice is sharp.

"Setting the table for breakfast. This way I won't be so rushed in the morning."

"I'm trying to tell you—"

"*No*. Would you rather have pancakes or eggs?"

His fingers dig into my shoulders. "You *have* to listen."

He loves David.

"You have to understand. You have to forgive me."

He loves David.

He buries his face in my hair.

40

He loves David!

The kitchen is a blur of yellow lights. I can destroy him. I can crush his sunburned throat. Strangle the words before he says them.

I gasp for air.

I wrench myself away from him, throw the kitchen window open, gulp clean chilled air. In the darkened garden the bushes look like crouched eavesdroppers.

"You're shivering." He puts a tentative arm on my shoulder. Something has broken in his voice—he sounds small and frightened. "Come lie down on the sofa. I'll build a fire."

I let him lead me into the living room. I glance over my shoulder, looking for my husband, but there's only this boy now. He fusses over me, tucking a blanket around me, propping pillows under my head, asking in that same strained voice if I would like tea.

He sits in the rocking chair watching me. As he rocks his shadow slides back and forth over the wall; his profile emerges from the dark mass, then recedes, slides back into darkness again. One hand absently massages his throat. I slide my trembling hands between my knees.

"You know that I love you very much," he says.

Under the blanket my fingers move convulsively. I want to tear at his face, tear away the terrifying look of contrition I see there. My nails rake the skin of my thighs.

"Because he was . . . because I was never with another woman . . . I thought I wasn't taking anything away from you."

All this time . . . all those nights. Our life together. Lies!

"David always thought it would be better if you knew—"

Always! On the coffee table in front of me is the book of movie stars' portraits David gave him for his birthday.

41

Four months ago. They were lovers then. I cried because he said he had to work late on his birthday. Were they together? Drinking champagne? Lying naked under the sheets on David's brass bed?

"—but I was afraid to tell you."

He can't love a man. "You're my *husband*!"

I kick free of the blanket. He's kneeling by the sofa, struggling to unclench my fists, chafing my hands between his cold, damp palms. "You have to stay calm," he's pleading. "You have to try to *understand*—"

How has this happened? What is there so dreadful in me that would frighten him into wanting a man?

"—I need you, Annie."

When he makes love to me does he pretend I'm David? *Can* he?

He sits beside me, holds me in his arms. I can't move, I can't breathe.

He says, "I thought . . . that part of my life was over. I thought I wouldn't want a man again. . . ."

Other men!

"I thought you'd transformed me, Annie."

My mouth struggles to form words from ice. "Why did you marry me if you love men?"

He drops his hands. He stands. He moves to the door.

Knife-sharp panic pierces me. He's going to David! He'll never come back! "I'm sorry." I run to the front door to block his way. "Don't go . . ." I try to pull him to me, but he stands rigid. "Don't *go*!"

"When I met David—"

"You don't need David, you have me."

"—I couldn't understand myself—"

"I love you, Michael. Don't go away from me. It doesn't matter . . . just say you'll never see him again. . . ."

"I can't."

"Yes. Promise. You'll never want a man again. You said I transformed you. Promise me—"

"I would be lying—"

"No! You love me. You'll never want anyone else. Promise!"

"Annie—"

"I'm your *wife*!"

"Stop it. Please." He grips my shoulders.

Laughing, I open my arms to him. "Push me to the floor, Michael. Push yourself into me. Come on." Afterward we'll be calm and sweet. "Come on." I yank my sweater over my head. "*Come on.*" My hands tear at my skirt.

"Annie." He pulls me up from the floor. He holds me for a long time until my shaking is quieted. I'm amazed to hear that I'm sobbing.

5

O N THE nightstand rest a glass of stale water and the crumpled foil wrapping of the sleeping pill Michael insisted I take. I press my hands to the place in my chest where the emptiness has gathered; I wait for the pain to fill it. I feel nothing. My skirt lies folded on the dresser. Next to it, neatly piled sweater, slip, bra, panties. I don't remember getting undressed for bed. On the double dresser the mirror reflects the curdled plaster ceiling. Michael stands over me.

"You're awake." His voice is careful. He isn't naked this morning; he has a large bath towel wrapped around his waist. He takes clothes from his closet and carries them to the bathroom.

In the kitchen the overhead light still burns, anemic against the glare of daylight. Outside the kitchen window the trees are luminous—foliage painted on a stage backdrop. The breakfast table with its props already in place stands waiting.

Michael and the children come in and sit around the table. They eat toast and cold cereal. They talk. Emily drinks orange juice straight from the container. Michael turns the pages of the newspaper. They stand; the children gather their books, Michael picks up his car keys. At the kitchen door his eyes meet mine. We both look away.

When the sound of our car has faded, I take my coffee and go out onto the porch. There are no cars moving along the street. Air conditioners hum in every window of the apartment building next door. Stucco houses with rust-colored roofs bake in the sun. The houses are heavily barred—tendrils of black wrought iron crawl across their narrow windows. A police helicopter throbs overhead, circles, hovers briefly, moves on. Who are they looking for? There's no one on the street. No one could hide in this ruthless light.

I sit down on the porch steps. The wood is hot. In places the white paint is chipped and peeling; a sharp splinter of wood catches on my bathrobe. I stare at the road in front of the house. Our apartment in New York overlooked the Hudson River. Sometimes in winter the river was the same color as this road—dense gray, its surface flecked with the same metallic sparkle.

Dozens of sticky brown nuts have fallen from the palm trees opposite our house. They litter the sidewalk; already rotting in the heat, they give off a faint, sweet smell. The roses I planted along our path are drooping on their garden stakes. I fill an empty plastic milk jug from the outside spigot and douse them before I remember I'm not supposed to water when the sun is hot. My nylon bathrobe is plastered to my body, sweat trickles down my stomach.

Naked in the bathroom, I slide the mirrored medicine chest open so I won't have to see my reflection. I stand under a cold shower until I begin to shiver.

The bedroom is stifling even with all the windows open. I tear sheets and pillowcases off the bed and cram them into the laundry basket.

I was ten when I saw a Susan Hayward movie in which the heroine rushes to a hospital to see her dying lover. When she arrives she finds his bed empty, the mattress stripped, the bare pillows stacked neatly at the footboard. For months afterward I felt a sick panic whenever I had to change the sheets on my small white bed. I felt my life was in danger until I made up the bed again with fresh, pink sheets, pulled the ruffled bedspread smooth, and arranged my stuffed animals in a congenial group against the pillows.

There are no clean sheets in the linen closet. I throw the quilted bedspread over the bare mattress.

On Michael's desk his electric typewriter rests under its vinyl dustcover. The swivel chair sways slightly, adjusting itself to my weight. I slide open the middle drawer. A battalion of sharpened pencils, fine-point pens, clips, tape, scissors, half a pack of stale cigarettes, pocket dictionary. Upper left-hand drawer: typing paper, carbon. Lower drawer: his camera, empty film canisters. In the right-hand drawers: manila envelopes containing his screenplay and notes for the novel he hasn't written. A cookie tin filled with bills and receipts. I look through these. Car payments. Insurance. Dentist.

Michael's shirts hang in a starched row at his end of the closet. I push these aside—his suits and sports jackets are lined up at the other end. I slide my hand into the outside pockets: coins, a stick of gum. In the navy-blue blazer, a yellow plastic tow truck. I unbutton the first button of each jacket. Breast pockets: a folded handkerchief. Ballpoint pen. His trousers hang upside down. Their pockets are empty.

I go through his dresser drawers. Stacks of folded underwear, paired socks. T-shirts. Sweaters.

In the bathroom: electric razor, after-shave, comb and hairbrush, toothbrush.

I open the carved rosewood box where he keeps his cuff links: his class ring. A silver key chain. Collar stays. A dairy. Blank.

I open the diary to today's date. I fold down the top corner of the page.

I know where he is.

He and David are talking together, their eager faces are close.

I told her, Michael says. It's no good. She fell apart. What can I do?

David sighs and shrugs. Move out.

Tonight Michael comes home and takes the big gray suitcase down from the shelf in the hall closet. He empties his drawers. He empties his closet. He puts his toiletries in his brown leather bag. He packs pencils, manuscript, receipts, camera into shopping bags. The front door clicks shut; his car pulls away. The doors of the closet stand open. The empty wooden hangers rattle like bones.

David has already cleared a place for Michael's things. He smiles at Michael when they hang his navy-blue blazer beside David's gray suit. . . .

Maggie's phone rings eight times before she answers.

"Hell," she breathes. "What's the time?"

I tell her I need to see her.

She fumbles with the phone. I hear the small scratch of a match. "Bloody hell," she mutters.

I twist the telephone cord tight around my fingers. Slowly Maggie comes awake, her voice warms. She has to do the laundry today, she says, but we can talk at the

Laundromat. She'll meet me there, give her ten minutes to get dressed.

I should have known Maggie would keep me waiting. I move to the open doorway of the Laundromat to watch for her. A barefoot derelict in a filthy army jacket sags against a parked car.

Inside, pink and orange waves billow across the Laundromat walls. In one of the plastic chairs opposite the row of droning machines a woman sits hunched over a book. Her ample body is stuffed into a flowered dress. She holds the book inches away from her damp face, her pudgy fingers turn the pages eagerly.

I sit down next to her to wait for Maggie.

A woman with a baby slung on her back propels a laundry cart from washer to washer collecting bath towels and diapers. An elderly man stands stiffly in front of a whirring dryer; his face has a look of desperate dignity; he clutches his empty laundry cart and stares straight ahead. In the corner a blond young man and a dark-haired girl are folding sheets together—huge striped squares of maroon and gray. They smile secretively at each other.

"Hello, my darling," Maggie calls. Peering over the top of the huge wicker laundry basket she's carrying, her face is furrowed with sweet concern. She pecks me on the cheek and studies me for a moment, balancing the basket on one hip.

"Let's get our wash in and then we can have a nice gab." She sets her laundry down on an empty machine. "I'll take this one, and here's one for you. Where's your stuff?"

I stand still in confusion. "I don't have it. I forgot to bring it."

Maggie pats my arm, her magenta fingernails are brilliant against my skin. "Never mind, darlin'." She digs in her purse and brings out a compact and lipstick. "Here, love, you could use a bit of color. It'll make you feel better." She watches me while I dab my lips with her cherry-red lipstick. "Is it to do with Michael?" She moves closer. "Is he stepping out on you?"

"Yes," I whisper, in fascination at my ease in revealing it.

"Bastard. Did he tell you himself, or did you just discover it?"

The woman in the flowered dress positions herself at the dryer behind us and begins stuffing clothes into a canvas duffel bag, moving with deliberate slowness. She eyes us with the same fervent ardor with which she devoured her romance novel.

"At first I thought it was the move here"—I drop my voice—"the reason I felt so cut off." I lean close to Maggie. "But then . . . whenever he touched me, his hand felt lifeless. Whenever he talked tenderly about us, the look in his eyes didn't go with what he was saying. I kept asking him to tell me what was on his mind, but he always had something to do, somewhere he had to dash off to."

"And then he started staying out late, giving you feeble excuses." Maggie smiles knowingly.

I stare at the scuffed floor.

"So you guessed."

"Yes."

"Bastard." Maggie turns suddenly and flashes a poisonous grin at the woman behind us. "Hullo, dearie. How's *your* love life?"

The woman colors, snatches up her laundry, and lumbers away, shooting us a furious glance over her shoulder.

"We've brightened up someone's day, anyway," Maggie chortles. "Good old Oliver always loves making the announcement. 'You're so beautiful,' he says, 'I can't live without you, you're the bloody rudder on my ship of life' or some such rot, and then he drops his little bomb. 'But there's this girl, this magical creature.' He's an awful fool." Maggie's laughter is brittle. "They're all such fools. . . . Have you seen her yet? You will, you know. They always turn up. The thing is, you see, they're dying to get a look at *you*. They show up at your hairdresser's or your favorite Chinese restaurant. You know who it is right away because she's trying so damn hard not to stare. One actually rang our doorbell pretending she had the wrong address."

My breath catches in my throat. I twist the leather strap on my handbag.

"The little bitch." Maggie measures soap powder into the gaping washers. She moves with silken ease; her auburn hair sweeps her slender shoulders as she bends over the machines.

Maggie would never fall in love with a man who would rather sleep with other men. How can I tell her?

She slams the washer lids and slides up onto the counter, motioning me to sit beside her. "Do you have any clues? Do you know anything about her?"

She'll be very kind to me from now on. Sweet to Michael. Oliver will roar with laughter when she tells him.

"How long has he been seeing her, love?"

My father will—

"Here, what's wrong? You've gone all white."

My mother. Emily and Robin . . .

The buzzing in my ears becomes a roar.

"What's wrong?" Maggie's voice is far away.

"Drink this." She holds a paper cup of water to my lips. "Better now?"

My vision clears. I sip the water, waiting for my breathing to become normal again. I force myself to look into Maggie's worried face. I force my voice into steadiness.

"She's blond and young. I don't know her name. He's been seeing her for about six months."

She nods knowingly. "Well, it's no good your conking out over it. You've got to fight, my girl. Get yourself some smashing new clothes. Get your hair done. You're lovely looking, you know, but from here on in, you've got to be dazzling."

"It doesn't matter how I look," I whisper. My chest feels raked hollow.

"Of course it does. You've got to get out of your house and let the world see you. There are all sorts of men out there. Don't look so shocked, auntie. You've got to show Michael you can give as good as you get. It's a cinch to meet men—they're all over the place. . . ."

Michael with David. And me with . . . whom? Men met in bars? Married businessmen in town for a convention—lugubrious with guilt and six martinis? Or the men who lounge in doorways and whose urgent whispers hang in the air like a bad smell?

Or maybe the husband of a close friend?

"I don't want to meet men, Maggie. I want Michael." The pressure behind my eyes feels dangerous. I blink rapidly. *I will not.* Not in front of Maggie.

She puffs out her cheeks in exasperation. "You're being awfully thick, girl. Of course you want Michael. But how do you think I get Oliver back, every single time? I work at it—and damned hard too. The gym, facials, great clothes. Just about the time he's noticing that his newest true love has an unattractive bulge or bowlegs, I show up, looking absolutely fabulous, with an adoring man hanging on my arm. It doesn't matter a damn who the man is—just make sure Michael knows about him."

If I had a lover, would Michael be jealous of him? Or of me?

She has a boyfriend now, David, Michael tells him. Good, David says. That lets you off. He's cute, too, Michael says, teasing. The way he used to tease me when he let me know he found Maggie sexy. *Pretended* to find her sexy. My eyes flood with hopeless fury. I thrust away Maggie's hand with its proffered linen handkerchief. "Michael's not like Oliver. . . . You don't understand. . . . It's all a game to you. . . . Nothing bothers you. You don't know anything about pain."

Maggie stares at me. Her hazel eyes harden. She folds her hands in her lap like a schoolgirl reciting a lesson. "My best friend's name was Carol," she says. "I loved her. I used to tell her everything—all about Oliver's girls. She would always hold me when I cried. She'd tell me what a swine he was. She bought me presents to cheer me up. She was fucking him. He got her pregnant. That was the worst part, because *I* was trying so hard to have a baby. I wanted to keep their kid, but Oliver sent her and the baby away to Scotland. He still sends her money."

She looks over her shoulder as if she's afraid of being overheard. "I left him then. He went mad. He wouldn't leave me alone. He said he couldn't eat, couldn't sleep. He even threatened suicide—twice." Her smile is thin. "So I went home."

I touch her shoulder. "Don't cry, darling." She's always seemed so unclouded, so buoyant, it has never occurred to me to allow her any sorrow.

But Maggie's eyes show no sign of tears. She pushes her hair off her forehead and sighs. "Have you got a ciggy, love?"

52

I shake my head. "It must have been horrible. He was so cruel. . . . How could you just—"

"Because the affair was done with." She turns away and rummages in her purse. "There's *got* to be *one* ciggy in here—a-ha!" Triumphantly she waves Marlboro broken at the filter. Lighting it, she stands looking at me. I can't read her face, but fear pricks the back of my neck. "You'll see," she says.

"You mean you love him. That's why you went back, why you stay with him. Because you love him."

Maggie exhales smoke, stares at the pink- and orange-tiled floor. A thin trail of soap powder leads from the row of machines to the open doorway. I touch her hand; the slender gold bracelets on her wrist make a sound like a faint wind chime.

"You *love* Oliver."

"One time we were on a trip," she says slowly. "We were in Belgrade. It was November, about six in the evening. We'd just come off the train. He told me to wait for him, and he disappeared into the masses of people. He was gone for a long time, I didn't know where. I sat on my suitcase outside the station. Nothing was familiar, there were no landmarks. I didn't know the language, so even the street signs and advertisements were meaningless. It was cold. Lights had come on in the houses. People were moving along the street, on their way home. I felt invisible. Weightless. There was nothing to hold me in the world. I could have floated away over the mountains, but then I saw someone coming, and it was Oliver, and I remembered that I belonged somewhere. . . ."

She stretches herself like a cat waking up, and gives me a dazzling smile. "I've got to get this laundry finished and get home. My old man's taking me out to lunch." She laughs. "And it'd better be somewhere posh." She elbows me gently. "Look, let's go shopping this week, pick out some super outfits." She hoists the wicker basket onto her hip. "Cheer up, love. It'll all come right in the end."

The derelict has wandered into the Laundromat. He walks dreamily up to a spinning dryer, and sighing deeply, his arms spread wide, he presses himself against the warm glass window.

6

I THOUGHT MAGGIE would stay with me, at least until the children got back from school, but she's loaded her clean, folded wash into her car and driven away.

At home, silence will assault me. I begin to walk, watching my feet in their brown leather sandals rise and fall. The street, lined with shops and restaurants, slopes downhill. I pass a realtor's office with faded photographs of homes for sale taped to the glass door. An optometrist's window is filled with empty eyeglass frames. Heat rises from the deserted sidewalk. I wish I'd begged Maggie to stay. A bus, plastered with posters of bikini'd blondes, rattles to a halt on the corner. A girl's face stares from a grimy window. The bus doors open and shut, no one gets on or off; the bus lumbers on. Or I could have asked to go along with her and Oliver on their lunch date.

Would she have agreed?

How does Maggie picture Michael's "girlfriend"? What type of woman does she imagine he'd choose? Younger and prettier? Like Oliver's girls?

I walk past a parking lot, a bank, a pharmacy, until I reach a restaurant with a sign that boasts "Salad Bar. Cocktails. Happy Hour."

In the foyer a tall girl in a yellow dress readjusts the sheaf of menus under her arm and gives me a businesslike smile. "Lunch for one?" Her clear blue eyes are pitying.

"Just drinks, thank you." Self-conscious, I push aside the beaded curtain that separates the dining room from the cocktail lounge. I've never done this before—gone drinking alone in the middle of the day in the middle of the week.

The lounge is empty—it's not quite noon. The floors are carpeted in red and green plaid; the walls, also covered in plaid, are hung with reproductions of antique circus posters.

I order a vodka and tonic. It's shatteringly cold and sourer than I remember from last summer's cocktail parties. The bartender, a tanned, muscular man with wide, childish eyes, twists the dials on a radio beneath the bar and a sugary rendition of "My Funny Valentine" drenches the room. He sings a reverent, off-key accompaniment.

I smile tentatively at him.

Suppose some night I followed Maggie's advice and went looking for a lover? Suppose I put on my new dress and my highest heels and went out alone to a bar?

We used to call them "mixers," those agonizing events held every Friday night at the Teen Social Hall. The girls stood against the crepe-paper-festooned wall miming extravagant indifference. The boys paced the area between the punch bowl and the windows, staring, whispering, daring each other. When I got home my mother would always want to know if I'd been asked to dance. *Yes,* I would say, even if it was a lie. *Every dance.* I loved her triumphant smile and the way she patted my cheek, as if I'd done something especially thoughtful for her.

I sip my second vodka, fighting off a wave of queasiness. Suppose I *did* find a man at one of those bars? If he came home with me, made love to me? *You have to leave before my children wake up, but will I see you again?*

I finish the last of my drink and signal to the bartender that I'd like another, but he's lounging against the cash register talking to the hostess in the yellow dress. When she throws back her head to laugh, his eyes fasten on her breasts. She smiles and lets the tips of her red fingernails brush his palms as she reaches across him to pick up her drink order. A safari fan suspended above my head spins in the air-conditioned breeze. Who will drive me home if I get drunk? There are no convenient taxis waiting at the curbs in his city. I'd have to call someone. *Michael. Come and get me, I'm drunk at Charcoal Charlie's.*

Suppose he refused?

I pay the check and leave.

Outside, the sunlight sears my eyes. I lean my head against the cool glass of a store window. On the other side of the glass is a painting. Not an original, a lithograph, but a very excellent print. I study it, fascinated. A New England seacoast, probably Maine. A beautiful storm approaching. Deepening blue-gray sky, frantic white clouds tumbling like sea foam across the horizon. A small patch of azure in the upper right-hand corner to indicate the lost brilliance of the afternoon. Three sailboats in the foreground: one making for port, one easing along the shoreline, one heading joyfully into the wind. A weathered Victorian house stands at the water's edge; its cupolas look out over the ultramarine waters of the bay. So does the unscreened, circular front porch, on which a lone chair waits for an occupant.

I press against the glass. My breath catches in my throat.

I'll set up my easel on the porch. Paint until the daylight is used up. Eat apples and cheese for dinner and watch the sky darken. At night, curled under layers of quilts in the towered bedroom, I'll dream the past away. The memory of Michael will fade, and in the morning I'll wake up to sea sounds. . . .

A man emerges from the shop carrying a large flat parcel wrapped in brown paper. When I pass through the doorway a discreet alarm buzzes softly.

An expensive-looking woman in a dark suit sits behind a gleaming mahogany desk speaking into one of several telephones. She glances at me and holds up a manicured index finger.

For now I'll hang the painting opposite our bed so I can see it every morning when I wake up. Michael will see only a pretty picture, but I'll know it's the blueprint for my new life. When I've moved into my seacoast house, when I've left him, it will hang in my new living room—a memento of my freedom.

As soon as she's finished her phone conversation I ask the woman the price of the print in the window.

"Which one, dear?"

"The seascape."

"Which *one*, dear?" She reaches again for the phone.

If Michael were here, he'd smile his hesitant, boyish smile; he'd let his voice slide into warm familiarity. The woman would be disarmed. She'd fuss over him, bring out other prints for him to inspect. He'd wink at me; the woman wouldn't see the mockery in his green eyes. . . .

"The one with the white house and the storm. It looks a bit like a Hopper."

She cradles the phone on her shoulder, holding one hand over the mouthpiece. "It *is* a Hopper. A very limited edition," she murmurs. "Five thousand dollars." She smiles, anticipating my apologetic thanks.

The door closes behind me with a soft, metallic click.

It would be dangerous to live that close to the water. What if Robin should lose his footing on a rock, slide under the water while I had my back turned? With Michael gone there'd be no one but myself to make sure nothing happened to the children. Our children . . .

I walk past a costume jewelry shop. Another bank. A dry cleaner's, where paper-shrouded garments drift like ghosts across the window.

I'm leaving, Michael will say. I'm moving in with David. His face will be sad, but his eyes will shine with eagerness.

Our house will feel like a ruin. The children and I will eat our dinners in front of the television, trying to drown the silence. After they've gone to bed there will be endless hours to fill until I can sleep. I'll move my pillow to his side of the bed. I'll wake up in the night. Every day will be exactly like the one before. There will be no reason to put on makeup or comb my hair. David and Michael will be lying in each other's arms. . . .

An old man is peering into my face. His bald skull gleams above a tuft of feathery white hair. "Are you okay, miss?" He thrusts his face closer.

I pull away from him and plunge across the street. A coffee shop.

I sit down at the counter. The waitress hands me a menu. She's a young black woman with velvety eyes. Her smile is beautiful. Her name, embroidered across the pocket of her uniform: Sunny. She offers me coffee. Her voice matches her eyes; her accent is Jamaican, full of mysterious music. Her hands are long and graceful and strong; her fingernails are the color of seashells. It seems to me she has a deep knowledge of the heart.

I pretend to look at the menu for a long time so I can keep her near me. I wish that she would come and sit beside me, that she would stroke my face with her beautiful hands. I long to tell her about Michael.

"What do you recommend?" I ask.

"The vegetable soup is nice today," she says.

She sets it down in front of me as though it were a gift.

"What town do you come from?" I ask.

A man beckons her from the other end of the counter. She turns her wonderful smile toward him. Her hips, under the thin, tight, white dress, sway as she moves to him.

The soup is bland and watery. I crumble the packet of saltines and drink my coffee. Nearly two o'clock—Michael must have picked up the children by now. I leave the uneaten soup and a generous tip on the counter.

I find Robin and Emily eating giant hamburgers and fried potatoes at the kitchen table. With Michael.

"Big Macs, Mommy," Robin says with a happy, guilty grin.

Michael's eyes wait for my response.

I can feel pressure building behind my eyes. I retreat quickly into the bedroom.

Michael comes in and locks the door behind him. He sits beside me on the bed. "I'm sorry."

"Are you going to move out, Michael?"

He clasps his hands in his lap. "I can't give up David."

"You've already told me that."

"Do you want me to move out?"

"I saw Maggie today. She thinks you have a girlfriend. I wish to hell you did."

He passes his hand over his eyes. "What do you want me to do?" He sits with his shoulders hunched, his head bowed. The diffused sunlight filtering through the venetian blinds highlights his delicate cheekbones, his defiant chin, the undefended curve of his mouth. Wisps of blond

60

hair fall over his forehead. The back of his neck looks childishly vulnerable. "I don't want to move out," he says.

"What will we do, then?"

"I don't know. I can't give him up."

"You haven't tried."

His voice is husky with tenderness. "I love you."

7

MICHAEL IS weaving a net of comfort and consolation. He presents me with gifts: an unexpected fervent kiss, a warm, "special" glance from across the room. Evenings at home, with Irish coffee in front of the fire after the children have been put to bed.

"You know everything there is to know about me now," he says, touching my face with his fingertips, as if relearning my features.

"You look jolly," Maggie says grumpily. She's still dressed in her bathrobe, at noon. "Come in, it's so bloody bright out here." She squints in the afternoon sunlight.

"I can't stay. I have to pick up the kids. I only stopped by to tell you that I think it's over."

"What's over?" She pulls me into her dim, cool hallway.

"Michael's affair. I think it might be finished."

She grunts noncommittally.

"He's been so sweet lately. Attentive. It's almost as if I'm his ally, now that I know . . . as if he wants my help to end the thing."

Maggie braces herself against the wall. I wonder if she's been drinking. Her eyes have a misted, preoccupied cast.

"Darling," she says, "I hope you're right. But I wouldn't hang out the streamers just yet. Oliver's never as wonderful to me as when he's in the throes of a romance."

"Michael's not Oliver." I force the irritation out of my voice. Maggie looks defeated today. I suppose it's natural for her to think Michael is as incorrigible as her own husband. "I really think, I *feel*, that it's all going to be okay."

She shrugs, then smiles. "I hope so, ducky." She makes a movement toward her kitchen. "Stay for a bit. I'll make us some tea."

"No thanks. Don't you think it's possible? Men have affairs. They blow over. It happens."

"You know your own husband. If he says it's over, it probably is." Her voice is cool, flip.

"He hasn't exactly *said*. . . . But I know it's what he wants."

She lifts her hands in a gesture of weary acquiescence. "You'll know soon enough. But I wouldn't count on his lady friend relinquishing without a fight. Hell hath no fury, and so on."

"Maggie . . ." No. There's no need to tell her. Not now, when it's so close to being over. It could ruin everything, send him hurrying back to David. . . .

She gives me a quizzical stare. "What, love?"

"I'll fight too."

"Course you will." Her eyes move restlessly around the small entryway. "I suppose you'd better not keep the kiddies waiting."

"No." I feel a sudden desolation. "Why don't you come over this evening? Have dinner with us. We can have a proper visit."

She shakes her head. "Thanks. But I don't think you need company right in the middle of all this. You and Michael must have a lot of making up to do."

*　　*　　*

That night, Michael's lovemaking is gentle, hesitant. I lie very still, afraid that if he feels the hugeness of my passion, and my relief, he'll stop.

Afterward he lights a candle and we sit naked on the bed. Michael tells me how happy we're going to be. He says he doesn't know what he would have done if I'd left him.

"I almost forgot how beautiful you are"—his arm slides around my waist—"and how sweet."

I turn my head to receive his kiss.

"Sleepy, darling?"

"No. Too happy," I murmur.

I fall asleep in his arms, my head resting on his chest.

When I open my eyes in the morning, Michael, already dressed, is perched on the edge of the bed, smiling.

"I've brought you some juice." He props the pillows behind my head, first leaning down to kiss my neck. "I was watching you sleep," he says.

I run my hand along the inside of his thigh. "Where are the kids? Any chance . . . ?"

"No luck. They're plastered to the TV set—cartoons."

I open my arms to him. "Goody. They're busy, then."

"Until the first commercial, when Robin charges in here and demands a remote-controlled dump truck." Laughing, he lifts my hand from his leg and raises it to his lips. "Last night was wonderful."

I answer him with a smile.

"I want to say something to you," he says. "But you have to promise you won't get upset."

My shoulders stiffen; my smile freezes. "Yes?"

He caresses my arm. In the next room the television blares suddenly, followed by a small muffled sound. Emily shouts. The TV is silenced. Michael shakes his head. "They need their own apartment."

I smile weakly. Dread fills my mouth, tightens my chest.

"It's about David," Michael says quietly. The pressure of his hand on my arm increases. "He cares so much about you. He wants to talk to you. Apologize. You won't deny him that. You aren't cruel."

He lifts my chin so he can see my eyes. "Will you do it? It's important to me. I feel it's important for *us*. I couldn't take it if the two of you stopped being friends."

"Friends . . ."

"You'll do it, won't you? He feels so terrible."

Michael's eyes plead, his voice is humble, his hands on my arm are so tender.

"When?"

"Today. I thought we'd take the afternoon and drive to the beach—all of us. . . ."

"Michael—"

He kisses me, and I force my apprehension into a dim, barely felt tremor.

The freeway follows the curve of the shoreline. Beyond it the ocean stretches flat as sheet metal. Oil rigs rise offshore like marooned cities.

Crowded amid the picnic baskets and rubber beach toys in the backseat, listless from the long ride, the children bicker halfheartedly. Michael drives, drumming his fingers on the steering wheel in fretful accompaniment to the jazz music playing on the radio. David stares straight ahead, chain-smoking. He sips occasionally from a can of tomato juice. Wedged between him and Michael, I sit rigid, my hands clasped over my purse.

The car lurches around a curve. I feel David's shoulder stiffen against my weight. My leg presses his. His thighs, bare below tan hiking shorts, are narrow and sinewy, covered with curling brown hairs. I struggle to sit upright.

"Are we almost there, Mommy?" Robin leans over the front seat.

"Sit back, Rob," Michael admonishes. "We'll be there soon."

It was Michael's idea to bring the children. I agreed, hoping their presence might provide safety.

"I see a whale," Robin shouts. Emily snorts derision.

"I *do*! Look, David!" He tugs at his shoulder. David turns to smile at him, and his coarse, brown curls graze my cheek. His hair smells familiar. It smells like Michael's.

"One time I was on this beach," Michael says, "just before dawn. I found a baby seal. He'd crawled right up on the sand to take a rest."

A faint smile lifts the corners of David's mouth. He glances at Michael. I lay my hand on Michael's leg. "You never told me about that. When was that?"

"I wish I had a baby seal," Emily sighs. "Why didn't you bring him home, Dad?"

For the rest of the drive Michael tells the children animal stories. David gazes out of the window; the faint smile comes and goes. What is he thinking?

We turn off the freeway onto a narrow rutted road lined with scrub oaks and stunted pines, leading to a rocky beach. The parking lot is nearly empty. Michael crows, "I told you we'd have this beach to ourselves—the surf's no good here. Two miles farther down it'll be jammed."

Silently David begins to unload the car, piling his arms with beach paraphernalia. We follow him to a low grassy rise shaded by a twisted juniper tree.

"This is the best spot," he says. "We'll be out of the wind."

"Isn't this great?" Michael beams proprietarily at the chrome-colored ocean.

"Yes, very pretty. Have you been here before, too, David?"

His nod is almost imperceptible. "Do you want me to set the food out, Annie?" Without waiting for an answer, he begins unpacking the picnic hamper.

The children are peeling off jeans and shirts, stripping down to their bathing suits. "Come swimming, Mommy!" They pull at my hands.

"Mommy will come in a little while," Michael says. "She'll meet us in the water."

"I'm waiting for Mom." Emily squats stolidly at my feet.

"Me, too," Robin echoes.

"She'll come soon." Michael pulls them up. "Race you to the water! On your mark . . ." He watches them tumble across the sand. His gaze shifts to David kneeling on the blanket, arranging plastic forks and paper plates in meticulous place settings. "I'll keep the kids busy for a while," he tells me. He touches my cheek with one finger. His smile is a plea.

"Hurry, Dad!" Emily calls. "We found an oyster or something." Shrill and insistent, her voice carries on the wind. Michael pulls off his sweatshirt and jogs down the beach to where the children are crouched in the gentle surf.

David is still kneeling on the green plaid blanket between bundles of foil-wrapped food and cans of soft drinks.

"Let's go over there," he says finally. "In the sun."

He spreads his nylon windbreaker on the dry grass for me. His gestures are stiffly formal, like those of a child playing at being gallant. He takes a cigarette from his dented pack. "Thank you for agreeing to this," he says.

He pulls off his white T-shirt, folds it carefully, and lays it on the grass beside us. "I know how you must be feeling." He leans back on his elbows. The muscles of his chest and upper arms are clearly defined; fine brown hair grows over his breastbone and nipples. As he speaks his blunt fingers scratch his stubble. "I wanted to protect you. A mistake, maybe . . ." His lips are full, fleshy pink, almost vermilion; moisture glistens at their corners. "It all got so damned complicated." His broad red tongue slides across his lower lip. "I nearly went crazy. . . ." His smooth stomach rises and falls. "I always felt . . . closer to you than to him. . . ." His words are flat and shimmering, like the ocean; I feel as if I might sink inside him. "You mean so much to me. . . ." The long muscles in his thighs are tensed as though he's about to spring. "I told Michael . . ." Michael lying close beside him. Michael's hand with its strong, elegant fingers stroking the narrow thighs, following the line of curling brown hairs, moving upward, caressing, fumbling with the buttons of the tan hiking shorts. "Can't we . . . the three of us . . ." His mouth, pressing against David's, his tongue inside. "We're all grown-ups. . . ." His mouth moving. Down the broad chest, over the hard belly, moaning a little the way he does, his mouth moving lower. "Can't we—somehow?"

"No!" Michael made love to me last night. "Michael made love to me last night!"

David looks at me with startled eyes. He leans forward to massage his ankles. "He should make love to you. He loves you."

My eyes search the beach. "There! Look!" Michael and the children are crouched, digging in the sand. Robin has one arm flung around Michael's neck; Emily is grinning up at him. "Look! He's—"

"I know, Annie." David reaches for my hand. I pull it away.

"He loves *my* body."

"Yes, he does," David says, softly.

"If he liked men, I would have known about it years ago." David says nothing; he keeps his eyes hidden.

A trembling starts in my arms and legs. "Michael isn't this way. You must have done something to him. This must be *your* fault. *You* did this." David lowers his head and braces his shoulders against my words. "You forced him. He doesn't want you!" The words came faster, shriller; my heart pumps with wild exhilaration. "It's all your fault! Michael loves me! Not you! You were never my friend, you don't care about me, you used me to get him, you lied to me, I hate you!" And then in a surge of righteous fury: "Faggot!"

His head jerks up. I stand over him, my fists raised, gasping. He stares at me; his shocked eyes are like the blond boy's—full of chill disgust. "You're wrong," he spits. "I *loved* you."

The wind has risen. It urges the torpid water into waves and sends a fine spray of sand stinging across my cheeks. David turns away from me. Toward the beach where Michael is.

His hands rake the sand. "I thought you had the capacity to understand. My mistake." He flings his words like stones. He looks at me over his shoulder. His mouth is twisted with bitterness, his eyes are wet. "I thought you were different. I thought you weren't like any other woman in the world."

I feel as if I'm drowning.

"David . . ." I sink, weak-kneed, on the sand beside him. "I didn't mean it. I only want it to be the way it was before." My throat constricts. "The way I *thought* it was. Me and Michael. And you. Our friend." The congealed misery melts, tears spill over my cheeks.

He watches me cry, he makes no move to comfort me. I long for him to throw his arm around me, hug me with the old, warm ease.

When my tears have subsided he says, "You know that Michael loves you."

I bow my head.

"And you know how much I care about you."

"Mommy, look!" A shout and a small figure racing toward me with outstretched hands. I try to compose my face for Robin.

"Look, Mom—" He hurls himself against me. "See?" He waves an empty crab shell under my nose. "I'm taking him home for my collection. Will you keep him in your purse?"

"Robin," Michael calls from the water's edge, "come and see, the tunnel is finished."

Robin stands in hesitation, one hand grasping my skirt. "It's got water in it, Rob. Come see."

Robin thrusts his find into my hands, scrambles down the beach to join his father and sister.

David gives me a small, tight smile. He holds out his hand for the brittle shell. "Treasure," he murmurs. He lays it down gently on top of his folded T-shirt.

"Annie," he says softly, "nothing will change. You'll have us both. We'll be together. The three of us."

I shake my head fiercely.

"I want us to be happy. The truth is, it's up to you." He reaches for my hand. I pull away. "I've always thought," he says, speaking in the same caressing voice, "that if there was any woman in the world who could understand about Michael and me, it was you. If I could have found someone like you—"

"You'd have married her and deceived her. Just like Michael." Hot, angry tears blur my vision.

"We never meant to deceive you," he says.

I rub my sleeve across my eyes. "If you loved me, if you cared about me, you'd leave my husband alone."

"I do love you. And I love Michael." He draws his knees up and folds his hands over them. "I don't want to lose you, Annie," he says. "It would be a shame." His smile is tender; his eyes are smooth and hard as ebony. "If you don't forgive me," he says gently, "it will be very hard on Michael."

The ocean seems to have darkened, the waves grown fiercer. Without me to stand between them, Michael and David . . . A well of fears opens in me. "I don't want to be alone." The words escape before the thought is fully realized.

"You won't be," he says with warm eagerness. "We'll be together. We'll have wonderful times." His eyes have softened, they gaze at me with familiar fondness. "Just like we always had before."

"Before." He was always full of praise for me. Enthusiasm. Small gallantries. When Michael was cold and preoccupied, David was there to put his arms around me, offering kindness and comfort. "Everything's different now."

He shakes his head. "It doesn't have to be. Only if you make it that way. Everything depends on you."

"Why?" I shout.

"Because we love you," he says calmly.

"No! Michael loves me. He's my husband. You're *our* friend. Michael and me are the 'we'!"

"Momm-ee . . ." The wind carries Emily's call. They've moved farther down the beach. She waves, beckoning.

71

"Are we friends again?" His hand stretches toward me.

I close my eyes. Confusion capsizes me.

"Please, Annie. Annushka." He takes my hand and squeezes it. "Say you forgive me."

"Come *on*, Mommy." Emily's cries are insistent. "Daddy's built a castle. . . ."

David leans forward and kisses my cheek. "It will all be fine. You'll see," he whispers. He jumps to his feet. "Okay?"

I nod, my eyes still closed.

"Come on. Let's go inspect the architecture." He pulls me up. "Here comes the expert castle builder," he shouts to the children, and takes off at a trot across the beach.

I follow behind, stumbling in the deep sand.

"Look, David—a moat and everything." Emily tugs at his hand.

"Spectacular."

Michael grins up at him.

Robin thrusts a toy shovel in my hand. "Dig, Mommy," he commands sweetly.

Michael and David build majestic fortresses and tunnels. The children shriek with delight as the ocean reduces their efforts to little mounds of sand.

They swim; Michael teaches Emily to dive under the waves. Clinging to David's neck, Robin thrashes his legs with blissful ferocity.

While the children devour fried chicken, Michael and David and I lean against the juniper tree and drink cans of beer and eat sausage rolls. Warm looks pass between Michael and David, assuring smiles.

On the way home the children sleep sprawled in the backseat. We watch seabirds flying against a livid violet sky. Michael has his arm across my shoulders, his hand on David's back. We talk about our next picnic, farther north this time, maybe an overnight at a campground. David's hand rests lightly on my knee.

"Look." David points to the sky. A seabird, a pelican, hovers over the darkening water. "Watch," David whispers. The bird folds its wings against its body and becomes a small fierce projectile hurling itself downward to pierce the surface of the water. A moment of terrible stillness. The pelican emerges, wings spread in a slow, sure glide, its triumphant beak swollen with its catch.

"Beautiful," Michael murmurs.

My jaw aches with the effort of my smile.

8

THE LOBBY overflows with guests, invited and otherwise, who have come to celebrate the opening of Michael's and David's theater. The crowd is noisy and enthusiastic. The room is sweltering—the air-conditioning contractor must have failed to meet his deadline. The theme from *Limelight* bleats from speakers set into the ceiling. I don't see anyone I know.

"Look at those two." I nudge Michael, who has been uncrating bottles of domestic champagne and arranging them on an improvised bar. "Who are they? They look like parrots."

Two young men pose against the mirrored wall of the lobby. The scrawny one has pink hair standing up in spiky bristles over a partially shaved skull. The other wears a flapping blue silk cloak; his hair, rising in a crest above his forehead, is emerald green. Their mascaraed eyes dart around the lobby assessing the other guests.

Michael, now absorbed in stacking plastic champagne glasses into a shaky pyramid, glances up briefly. "Rock singers," he mutters.

"You actually *know* them?"

A sleek girl in Jean Harlow satin gives me a faint, condescending smile. "Love your place, Mike," she breathes. "Brilliant decor."

"I'm Michael's wife, Annie." I step out from behind the bar. "They did it themselves, isn't it great?"

She offers a limp hand and a practiced smile, and then moves away.

"Who's she?"

"Somebody's secretary." He shrugs. He balances the last glass on top of the pyramid and glances around the lobby admiringly. "It does look good, doesn't it?"

"Oh, yes, wonderful. You did a fantastic job." The heavy Art Nouveau fixtures, the ornate gilt mirrors, the overlush velvet settees and thick, old-rose carpets are meant to look witty and opulent, but I find the overall effect unsettling—as delicately decadent as a Beardsley print.

"Yeah. It's good." Michael smiles with pleasure.

"Almost worth all those nights away from me." I make my voice lightly teasing, but Michael has turned away and is gazing out over the guests.

The crowd has been steadily increasing.

"Who are all those people, Michael? I don't know anyone."

"It's going to be a great party," David calls, hurrying past us with trays of sandwiches. "We're already running out of food."

Michael stands on tiptoes to get a better view of the guests. "Maybe we ought to—oh"—he breaks off—"there's Wally." He plunges through the crowd. I follow behind, murmuring excuse me's.

At the front of the lobby Wally Asher, surrounded by a tight circle of young men, lounges on a settee.

"Lovely party." He beams at Michael. "And Mrs. Michael. Lovely to see you again." He extends a pale, dry hand to me.

"*Annie*," I say.

Michael sits down close to him and they begin to talk in low, earnest tones. Asher rests his pale hand on Michael's knee.

"I'm Michael's wife," I announce to the dark young man nearest me. "Annie."

"How do you do?" he murmurs, not looking at me. He gazes over my shoulder at a blond young man standing behind me. "Good to meet you." The dark young man's eyes are wistful; they follow the blond boy as he moves away toward the bar.

"Nice party, isn't it?" I demand. The dark young man nods and turns to whisper to a bearded man beside him. Above our heads Giulietta Masina grins forlornly from a framed poster of Fellini's *La Strada*.

"Darling," Michael says in my ear, "I've got to talk to some people. Can you circulate for a while?"

I take his arm. "I want to meet your friends."

"Darling, this is business."

"Don't you want to introduce me around?" I try to sound playful. "The woman behind the man?"

Michael disengages his arm. "Don't let anyone steal you while I'm gone." He smiles appealingly. I watch him move through the lobby, smiling and waving at his guests, until he disappears behind the black-lacquered doors leading to the auditorium.

I give Asher an icy nod and begin to edge away. I pause for a moment to give him his chance to call me back. When I turn, the circle of young men has tightened around him. No one's looking at me.

Searching for David, I make a slow circuit of the lobby. He might be tending bar. I join the crush waiting for drinks. In front of me a stout man scribbles in a notebook. When he feels my eyes on him he pockets his notebook and scowls. A man in a Chinese Mandarin jacket and horn-rimmed glasses pushes ahead of me and slides his arm around the stout man's shoulders. He whispers in his ear; the stout man laughs, throwing his head back and opening his mouth wide like a seal barking for fish.

David is not at the bar. I sip the flat, sour champagne and wander the length of the lobby again.

You've put just as much into this theater as David and I have, Michael had said. David agreed. They stood at the kitchen door side by side, the massive bouquet held between them. They looked sweet and earnest, and I was uncomfortably reminded of Robin and Emily presenting me with their first homemade birthday cake. *We wanted to show you how much we appreciate you,* David said. He glanced at Michael, whose eyes seemed moist. *Not just for your support of the theater, but for everything,* David finished, meaningfully. I took the flowers awkwardly, and, laughing, I searched for a vase large enough to accommodate the long-stemmed roses and gladioli while I marveled at the strange swelling of anger in me. This is going to be our night, Michael said, and he and David both kissed my cheek.

I yank open the black-lacquered doors. What "people" did he have to see? The auditorium is dark, cool, empty. The projectionist's booth is empty too.

I search the lobby again. The girl in the ticket booth near the front door hunches over a paperback Rimbaud. She raises her head; the feverish excitement fades from her eyes. "I'm Michael's wife," I say. "Do you know where he is?"

"No."

"David?"

"No." She yawns hugely and returns to her book.

"I'm Michael's *wife*. Do you *think* you know where they are?" Her yawn seemed faked, her eyes were a little too blank. "Have they gone somewhere together?"

"Try the office."

The door marked "Manager's Office, Private" is locked. I tap loudly and twist the handle. Ignoring the curious stare of a tall dark-haired woman watching me, I put my mouth to the door and call Michael's name. He's seen all his "business people" and now he and David have slipped in here to be alone. I begin to pound on the door harder and harder. "Michael, let me in *too!*"

The door bursts open. A balding man thrusts his furious, perspiring face at me. Behind him a figure hides in the shadows of the darkened office. I apologize hastily, and the door closes again with an indignant click.

I find a love seat in the farthest corner of the lobby, near the rest rooms. Two women, arm in arm, emerge from the powder room laughing. Maggie would have kept me laughing like that, with her wonderfully bitchy comments on the guests. Damn her for going out of town with Oliver this weekend. With Maggie around to keep me company, I wouldn't have made such a fool of myself. I wonder how many people heard me yelling at the keyhole. Damn Maggie! Damn *Michael!* I yank open the stiff collar of my navy wool dress and show more flesh. How could I have thought this dress was sophisticated when it's simply dull? I gulp the rest of my champagne. I'll go home. Will Michael be upset?

Will he notice?

"Are you waiting for the ladies' or just hiding out?" David stands over me, grinning.

"Where's Michael?" Despite my relief, I can't keep the stridency out of my voice.

David rolls his eyes comically. "Don't ask." In one hand he holds a bottle of champagne, in the other, a huge tub of popcorn. "Come on," he says, waving the bottle, "we'll have our own party."

"Do you know where he is?"

"He's around. Come on." He leads me up the narrow flight of stairs at the back of the auditorium and into the small projection booth. "I hate crowds, don't you?" he says, settling us on two hard-backed chairs wedged between the projectors and the floor-to-ceiling shelf holding reels of film.

"That's better." He pours champagne into two coffee mugs and raises his in a toast. "To Le Bijou, may it make a lot of money so we can all retire and go live on Mykonos and write screenplays and be famous." He squints at me. "You don't like Greece. All right, the South of France, then."

I smile grimly. "Where did he run off to?"

"You should know by now that your husband loves this kind of thing—dressing up, dashing around, charming the guests, wheeling and dealing. . . ."

"He could have taken me with him. I want to meet some of these people—"

"No, you don't." David shudders comically. "Here . . ." He thrusts the tub of popcorn into my hands. "We should be grateful that he's willing to socialize, it lets us off the hook." He leans back and throws his long legs up on one of the shelves. "We can be cozy here for a while, the movie's not screening till midnight." He gobbles a handful of popcorn. "I hope our guests don't leave in a unified huff. We promised the *Jules and Jim*, but Wally has this thing for Lupe Velez, so they're getting *Tarzan, Lord of the Jungle* instead."

"David . . ." The submerged thought begins to take shape. Chillingly.

"Did Michael send you to find me? To keep me out of the way? Is there a reason he doesn't want anyone to meet me?"

"He's afraid someone will snatch you away."

"*Please . . .*"

"Oh, darling." David waves dismissively. "It's nothing for you to worry about." He refills my cup with champagne. "When it comes to business he gets better results as a solo act. Besides"—he grins—"this way I get to have you all to myself."

"What do you mean, a solo act? What *kind* of business?"

He motions me to lower my voice. "It's nothing, really." He throws his arms up over his head and stretches, arching his back. He glances at his watch. "It's nothing."

"I'm going to find him."

"Annie, listen . . ." David is on his feet, preventing me, gently, from rising. "It's all about the business. We're trying to attract a following. The truth is, we'll stand a better chance if we present a certain image. It doesn't mean anything. The audience we're aiming for likes a sense of belonging. I know you understand what I mean. Don't you?"

"Why can't *you* lure the customers?"

"Michael's cuter," he says, chuckling.

"I don't like it. I won't have it!"

"Honey, if it doesn't bother me, it shouldn't bother you."

Popcorn scatters over the floor as I leap to my feet. David is beside me in a second. He grips my arms. "I'm sorry, I'm sorry," he soothes me. "What a bitchy thing to say. One drink and I have the sensitivity of a rhino." He settles me in the chair again. "Forgive me." He takes my hands and strokes them.

"Don't be upset," he says.

"It's all such a game," he says.

"Here . . ." He squeezes my hand. "This is what you need." He splashes champagne into my cup. "The best remedy for large parties. I hope you noticed, at least, that we broke out the good stuff for you." He holds the bottle up for me to read the label. "French. Expensive." His smile is cajoling. "Don't spoil tonight over this, darling. It's not important enough. Mike'll be back before you know it, and then, after the movie, the three of us will go out and eat Chinese food, and he'll tell us how dazzling he was and how boring they all are." He lifts the cup to my mouth. "Go on," he urges. "Relax, darling. It's all going to be fine."

I drink obediently. With each sip of champagne I feel as if I'm swallowing tears, choking down a potent, addictive sorrow.

"Feel better?"

"My shoes hurt," I mutter.

"Take them off." I do, and he holds one up by its strap. "Very sexy." He takes my feet onto his lap and, putting down his mug on the top of a film can, begins to massage my toes.

"My dress is new too."

"Yes, I thought it was. Let's see. Stand up." He nods his head in approval. "Very elegant. Understated. I like it."

"Thank you," I whisper.

"You're welcome," he says, solemnly.

The sorrow is spreading through my body; my limbs feel heavy with it; I hear it buzzing in my ears.

David refills the chipped coffee mug. I drink silently and he refills it again.

"It's almost time for the screening," he says. "We can watch from right here, would you like that?"

"Yes, thank you." His eyes are gentle. Consoling. "Why

81

aren't you showing *Jules and Jim?*" I mumble. "I love that film. Who cares what Wally Asher likes, anyway?"

David chuckles. "The accountant cares. Deeply." He strokes my hand. "Don't be sad. We'll run it all next week, you can see it as many times as you like. I'll even watch it with you, okay?" He leans over me, his lips brush my cheek.

"Do *you* like *Jules and Jim?*"

"Oh, sure. It's a classic." He pours us some more champagne. "Drink up—better get yourself in shape for the Lord of the Jungle." His smile is so kind. The outlines of his face are blurred with kindness.

"You always make me feel better, David. . . ."

"Good."

"Not so lonely." His shoulders under the soft gray sweater look solidly comforting; his big warm hands lie in his lap.

"You shouldn't feel lonely, you've got a lot of people who care about you."

"You care about me, don't you?"

"You bet." He fishes another bottle of champagne from behind the film shelves and pulls the cork.

"Do you think Jeanne Moreau is desirable?"

He stops pouring and considers. "Yes," he says. "Actually, yes, she's very sexy."

I smile at him and drain the champagne in one long swallow. The small, gray-walled room feels warmer. "They went away to the country together. Remember that part?" My words seem to float out of my mouth.

"Yes, I remember that part."

"Wouldn't you like to live like that? The three of us in a cottage in . . ." David is standing now. He has his hand on my elbow. I realize with surprise that I'm standing, too, staring into his eyes. They're a beautiful, warm brown color. "At the beach, you said you loved me. *Do* you love me, David?" I press closer to him, my eyes on his gentle mouth.

"Of course I do." Deftly he turns me away, guides me back to my seat. "Let's get your shoes on, sweetie, it's almost time for the screening."

I fumble with my shoes; my feet have swollen, the delicate straps cut into my flesh. David kneels and fastens the buckles.

"All set."

"I was going to kiss you," I whisper.

"I'm flattered."

"Am I drunk?" What if I had kissed him? Would he have been outraged? Pitying? "Would you have kissed me back?"

His laugh is faintly brittle. He pats my ankle. "I really should be getting set up here. Maybe you ought to go downstairs and find a seat. You'll be comfier." He takes up the mugs and hangs them on a hook hear the door. He begins checking the projector, turning knobs, flipping switches.

"Don't tell Michael, okay?"

"There's nothing to tell." He glances at his watch.

"It was the champagne, I think."

"Not to worry. No harm done." He smiles conciliatorily, forgiving.

A sudden flame of rage ignites. "Would it have been that horrible? A kiss from me . . . ?"

David gives me a wounded glance. "I'm sure a kiss from you is delightful. But—"

The door flies open. Michael, flushed and happy, bursts into the room. "You won't believe this!" he shouts. "Wally's invited us to go along with him to Paulette's after the show!"

"I'm impressed." David grins. "How'd you swing that?"

"I'm not sure." Michael laughs, delighted. "What I thought we'd do is, after the show, you stay here and tidy up and I'll take Annie home, and we'll meet Wally in front of Paulette's at about two—"

I step closer to Michael. "Why can't I come?"

Michael stares at me as if the thought of my coming along had never occurred to him.

"I'd like to come too."

"It's a little late for the baby-sitter to stay up, don't you think?" He throws an anxious glance at David. David continues his examination of the projector.

"I'll pay the sitter overtime," I say. "She can nap on the sofa till we get home."

"Honey, I don't think . . ." He comes to put his arms around me. "It's not your kind of place. . . . Tell her, David." He gives David a supplicating look.

"Paulette's," David says slowly, "is a very expensive, very trendy after-hours club. For men."

"So what?" I can feel anger stirring; I struggle to keep my voice light. "I'm all dressed up, I want to go out. I missed the party, I stayed up here. Out of your way." I force a light laugh.

"You won't like it, Annie," Michael insists. "It'll upset you."

"I'll be more upset if I can't come." I say this as sweetly as I can, and smooth his shirt coyly, even though all I feel is a coiled anger ready to strike, and it frightens me. "What do you think?" I smile a wide-eyed desperate appeal at David.

"I think she ought to come," he says. "She might learn something."

"See? David thinks I should come."

84

"All right," Michael mutters, disgruntled. "But we've got to clean up first."

"Thank you for putting in a word for me." I smile at David.

"Sure." He winks at me. "Michael, come take a look at this—the gate is sticking."

I watch them bend over the projector, their heads close together. My sense of triumph withers; it's replaced by a new, barely formed fear. "I've got a better idea," I call out. "Instead of going to some crowded, snobby place, let's go somewhere just the three of us. What about our Chinese food? David said we'd go out after the show and you'd tell us all about—"

Michael looks up sharply. "We're going to Paulette's," he said. "It's a great opportunity for the business."

I can feel tears dangerously close. "Can't we just go home, Michael? You and me?" My whisper is barely audible. David is staring at me. His eyes are unreadable.

"If you don't want to go after all," Michael says, sounding hopeful, "I'll drive you home and tuck you in."

David stands still, waiting. What's behind his eyes?

"I want to come," I say.

9

WE PAUSE at the head of the curved carpeted staircase that leads down into the glacial splendor of Paulette's. Moisture prickles the back of my neck as I grip the chrome banister. I glance at Michael. He seems enthralled. David looks careful, remote. When Wally Asher met us at the entrance he'd given me a look of piercing disapproval. Now, at the top of the stairs, he turns to me with a smooth smile. Below us, seated at the damask-draped tables in couples or small groups, well dressed, talking animatedly, intensely absorbed in each other, are the men who frequent Paulette's. "I hope you'll enjoy your evening, Mrs. Morrow," Asher says.

"I'm sure I will. Thank you. This is a lovely place." Perfectly spaced pink marble columns support a domed glass ceiling through which the night sky can be seen. The restaurant is lit by a wavering, aquatic light. I'm reminded of a storybook I once had that told about an underwater castle inhabited by strange and beautiful sea creatures. "A very lovely place," I repeat firmly.

The men observe our descent—some with elegant indifference, others with open interest. My legs are trembling and I wish that Michael would take my arm, but he's looking around in excitement. He seems to be inhaling the atmosphere, as though we were in a greenhouse full of rare fragrant flowers.

"Good evening, Monsieur Asher." A tuxedoed maître d' greets us with well-practiced enthusiasm and leads us down a wide terrazzo aisle to a table in the center of the room.

"Dom Perignon '81," Asher murmurs to the maître d' as we settle ourselves in the velvet chairs. Michael grins. David stares at the heavy gold-plate place settings on the table in front of him.

"Such a lovely surprise to have you join us." Asher lifts his glass in my direction.

"It's lovely to be included. I understand that it's a bit . . ." Asher isn't listening. His eyes have left my face and are circumnavigating the room. He leans forward abruptly and lifts his hand to wave. A startlingly handsome man in dark glasses nods his head in a subdued greeting. "Terrence Hughs," Asher announces.

"You're kidding! Where?" Michael swivels in his seat. David, too, turns to look at the well-known English actor.

"What's he doing here, isn't he married . . . ?" My voice dies away in a spasm of confusion. I hide behind the crystal champagne flute. I want Michael to take me by the hand and run out of here. Back to New York, our old life, we were safe, I knew who Michael was. . . . "He's a wonderful actor," I enthuse. "Did you see *Lights on the Water*? Is he a friend of yours?"

"A very old friend." Asher smiles at Michael.

"I'd love to meet him." Michael returns the smile.

Asher stands, his hand passes lightly over Michael's shoulder. "Come along, I'll introduce you."

David and I watch their progress across the room to the star's table. Terrence Hughs stands when they approach;

the other man with him shifts slightly and makes room for Asher to squeeze between them and Hughs on the banquette. Michael remains standing. Even from here I can see Michael's bedazzled grin.

David moves restlessly in his seat.

"Don't you want to meet him too?"

"Not particularly." David frowns.

"It's a very posh place, isn't it?"

David shrugs. His eyes are on Michael.

"Everyone is so well dressed. . . ." Michael is sitting now, a chair has been drawn up for him. Terrence Hughs is leaning across the table, listening, laughing. His hand covers Michael's for a moment before moving on to complete a sweeping gesture. I touch David's hand with one finger. "He really is a big star, isn't he? He can probably do the movie house some good—publicity or something. . . ."

David stands abruptly. "I'm sick of champagne," he says. "Let's go into the bar. I'll buy you a beer."

I follow him into a dark lounge off the dining room. At leather settees, at bistro tables, and against the polished mahogany bar, men turn their heads to look. They barely glance at me; their eyes follow David. The scent of leather and expensive cologne is mixed with something else, something disturbing that seems to rise off the men's bodies.

"Michael won't know where we are," I say to David.

"He'll find us," David mutters, guiding me over the threshold and up to the bar.

"What would the lady like?" the bartender asks David. He gives a lilt to the word "lady." I fold my arms over my breasts. David orders a brandy for me and a beer for himself. I wish he'd talk to me, but he stands behind me, drinking his beer, his eyes roaming the room. A man at one of the tables smiles at him. David returns a cool nod.

"A friend of yours?" I ask David.

"Not yet." His mouth twists in an unfamiliar smile.

Beside me a middle-aged man in a dinner jacket whispers intently to a beautiful, sullen-faced young man. With trembling fingers the older man traces the finely arched brows and full lips of the younger. His pleading discomfits me. I turn away as the young man jerks his head back.

Someone has started up the ornate, vintage jukebox in the corner; muted jazz begins to play. A man in a silk shirt and suede trousers detaches himself from a group at the bar and begins to walk slowly to the exit. At the doorway he turns around and strikes an insolent pose. He seems to be waiting. Another man leaves the bar and approaches him. The first man smiles languidly and holds out his hand. The two leave together, their arms around each other's waists, their heads close. A small sigh of loss emanates from the group left behind at the bar.

Michael and David don't belong here. They're playful and boisterous together. Like two small boys. Like exuberant teenagers hugging after a triumphant soccer match. This is Wally Asher's place, this place is no part of *our* lives. . . . I feel David's eyes on me. I turn to him with a brilliant smile.

"You wanted to come," he says.

"I'm having a great time!"

The man who smiled at David is approaching us. His smile is less tentative; he lifts his martini glass in greeting.

"Maybe we should go and find Michael now."

"Michael's busy." He turns away from me to offer the smiling man a drink. They begin to talk. Too softly for me to hear.

Around me men are talking, laughing, holding hands. I feel disembodied.

I fasten my eyes on the lounge door, willing Michael to

walk through it and rescue me from this invisibility. He'll put his arms around me and these men will see that I exist, I'm desired, loved. . . .

The door opens. Poised on the threshold, haloed by the blue-green light from the dining room, stands a woman. A bush of brilliant red hair frames her strong, laughing face. Tall and elegant, she carries herself with the languorous grace of a couturier's model.

Two smiling young men escort her, and behind her hover two more. She moves through the room, greeting several of the men rising at their tables. She stations herself at the far end of the long bar; a circle of men surround her. As she speaks to them her hands describe eloquent arcs and spirals in the air. Her mouth is wide and sensual; her animated face, the tilt of her head, the arch of her delicate neck, all evoke wit. The men around her laugh appreciatively at the story she tells. Their eyes are adoring. She runs her hands through her fiery hair and throws up her arms in a gesture of finale. The men rock with laughter. One leans over and solemnly kisses her cheek. Another hands her a drink, which she accepts with regal detachment.

A small flurry of movement behind me pulls my eyes away from her. The man David has been speaking to turns violently and walks away. An urgent hand grips my arm.

"We're going." David's face is a pale, glowering mask. "Come on."

"Who's that woman, David?"

"How should I know? I've had all I can take of this. Let's find Michael and get the hell out."

I follow him to Terrence Hughs's table. Michael introduces the star with elaborate ease, as though they were longtime friends.

"It's time to leave," David says quietly.

90

Michael protests.

"Your wife wants to go," David says, louder.

Wally Asher reclines on the banquette, smiling like a cat. His eyes shift from David to Michael.

Reluctantly Michael prepares to leave. Terrence Hughs grips Michael's hand for what seems a long time. As we pass through the other tables and mount the curving stairs, I keep turning, hoping for another glimpse of the red-haired woman.

In the car, Michael drives in sulky silence. David stares out of the window.

"I wish I could have spoken to her," I murmur. David gives me an indecipherable stare.

"Goddamnit, Annie," Michael bursts out with sudden vehemence, "you said you wanted to come, and then you drag me away just when—I told you you wouldn't like it, I told you—"

"It wasn't her," David interrupts. "It was me."

Michael throws David a venomous look. "Well, what the hell d'you have to be so—"

"I don't want to talk about it," David says. His mouth closes in a grim line.

"Probably I shouldn't have come," I offer. The impulse to make peace is automatic; my mind is engaged with other thoughts. That woman, and how splendid she was. If only I could have asked her some questions . . .

David and Michael make no protestations. They sink into silence until we finally pull up in our driveway.

"Go on into the house," Michael whispers to me. "I need to talk to him."

David nods a frigid good night. I go inside, rouse Heather, the baby-sitter, who is snoring gently on the sofa, pay her double time, and see her to her ancient Chevy convertible. I turn out all the lights but one, undress, and get into bed. For once I'm grateful that Michael isn't here. I close my eyes and melt into the scene in my mind. In the gloom of that lounge, the red-haired woman burned with an unwavering brilliance. How had she insinuated herself so superbly into that world? How had she made those men love her? I see again—her calm assurance, the slender, erect back under the flowing silk shirt, the angle of her head, inclined slightly toward her listeners; the mixture of tenderness, dignity, and wry humor in her face. I should have approached her, spoken to her. . . . I see myself invited into the circle. The men smile at me, they accept me as *her* friend. Afterward she and I go to a quiet all-night cafe. I ask her to take me on as an apprentice, teach me to be like her. We become friends. Together we—

"Jesus!" Michael slams the bedroom door and throws himself onto the bed.

"Shhhh . . . you'll wake the kids." My stomach tightens in anticipation of the dark anger on Michael's' face.

"He can be so damned unreasonable sometimes. The man just wanted to talk to me. He's a star, for Christ's sake. Friendship with him would be great for business." He lights a cigarette, leans against the pillows and smokes, his eyes closed, one arm flung over his forehead.

"Michael, I need to talk to you."

He sighs, impatient.

"About tonight. At the opening. You left me alone all night, you just ignored me, as if I wasn't there—"

"Christ," he groans. "Not you too?" He sits up, his eyes bright with fury. "I'm trying to make this goddamn business work. All you want to do is sabotage me. Both of you." He crushes his cigarette in the ashtray.

"It's not sabotage. It's consideration of me. Of my feelings—"

92

He sweeps his arm in a gesture of exasperation. "Can this wait till morning? Please? I'm exhausted." He yanks off his clothes, turns over on his side, and pulls the blankets over him, ending the conversation.

I search for something, for words to hurl at him, to hurt him and make him listen.

"I made a pass at David tonight."

He looks at me over his shoulder, one eye open. "Are you serious?"

"Yes!"

He opens his mouth wide, shouts with laughter. "Good God. No wonder he was so upset. That explains it!"

"He wasn't upset with me. He was upset with you."

"What did you think you were doing, honey? What did you think would happen?"

I want to slap his grinning mouth. "Nothing. I was drunk."

He rolls over, chuckling, shaking his head. "Unbelievable. Well, I guess everyone's entitled to get a little bombed and make an ass of himself. At least once. God knows I've done it myself. You're okay, though, aren't you?" he asks, abruptly solicitous. "You didn't get sick or anything?"

"No. I didn't get sick." I feel the rage trembling. I sit on the edge of the bed to control it. "And don't worry," I say icily, "I won't do it again."

"I know you won't." He pulls me into a hug from which he breaks away at the moment of contact. "I'm sorry, honey. It was a tough night. I was under a lot of strain. We all were." He pats the pillow beside him. "We need a good night's sleep. Everything will be fine in the morning."

He sleeps heavily, curled at the far side of the bed. I lie staring at the dark square of window, chilled under our blue quilt. *She* would not have been ignored. She would never lose her dignity. *She* would have laughed at Michael. *I flirted shamelessly with David.* Her voice would have been rich with amusement and confidence. *Damned nice of me too.* But her laughter would have been warm, not cruel. Michael would have the same adoring look in his eyes as the men who surrounded her. David would join the circle, his eager eyes mirroring Michael's. My smile embraces him too. They listen to my recounting of an anecdote. I smooth my bright hair. My hands draw pictures in the air. The man around me applaud me with their glances. Michael stands beside me, proud and loving.

10

SLEEVES ROLLED up, Michael is washing the breakfast dishes at the sink. Drinking my coffee at the table, I stare past him out the window and across the street at two workers on a scaffold who are busily replacing the smiling Diet Pepsi girl with the sullenly handsome Marlboro man.

"David's not thrilled, either," Michael says. "But it's got to be done by tomorrow, the printer's waiting." He pours a stream of viscous, white dish-washing soap over the soaking dishes. "It's a damn shame, I know. Em's going to be upset too." He raises his voice to be heard over the running water. "Maybe tomorrow night we'll take the kids to dinner and a movie. *Snow White*'s playing. . . ."

I watch him, marveling at the soft mobility of his features, the tender lift of his mouth, the almost shy smile, the bright benevolence that always suffuses his face whenever he's lying to me. "Bring the stuff home," I say, already knowing his response. "Let David do it alone."

"I wish I could, but there are hundreds of stills that'll have to be sorted through—it'll probably take all night. . . .

Anyway, you'll have a nice day with Maggie. And tomorrow I'll make it up to you—anything you want to do."

If I could have spoken to the red-haired woman last night, even a few words . . .

"Next time we go out, I want to go back to Paulette's."

Michael looks startled. Then he dissolves into laughter. "The kids will love that."

He dries his hands on the dish towel around his waist and comes to the table to kiss me. "The minute the theater's on its feet, we'll do something terrific. Go away for a weekend maybe. Up north. That'll be fun."

He returns to the sink and begins to dry and put away the dishes. "Don't wait dinner for me, sweetheart," he says. "David and I'll grab a sandwich while we're working." There's a carefully suppressed ripple of excitement in his voice.

"Give Maggie my love. Don't you girls buy out the store." He hangs the dish towel on a hook to dry and goes off to change his clothes in the bedroom.

Maggie turns slowly, studying herself in Bonwit's three-way mirror. The red satin mini-dress pulls tight over her flat hips and plunges daringly at the bosom. "I wish I had tits," she sighs.

"It's stunning. It's absolutely you." The fluttering saleswoman emits little cries of ecstasy.

Maggie catches my eye. "What do you think, love? Is it absolutely me?"

"It's a nice dress . . ." I offer uncertainly. The shimmering, hectic red seems to highlight Maggie's pallor, point up the furrows alongside her mouth and the purple smudges of exhaustion under her eyes.

"I think it's cool," she says. She pronounces the words as if they were in a foreign language.

"Dynamite. That's what they say now," the saleswoman corrects. "Dy-no-mite." She drapes Maggie's thin shoulders with a floor-length stole of spangled red tulle. "Isn't that simply dy-no-mite?" She turns Maggie around to face the mirror.

"Shit," Maggie breathes. A muscle at the corner of her mouth twitches. Her eyes brim with pain. She turns away abruptly, moving toward the dressing rooms. "I'll take it," she calls gaily. "And the stole too. . . ."

"Oliver's girls"—Maggies's magenta fingernails tap the arm of her chair—"all of them young, with firm little asses and perky tits. And *terribly* creative, don't you know. The one he's got now writes plays."

The perspiring shoe clerk slips a red satin high-heeled pump onto Maggie's extended foot. "These come in black and beige, too, ma'am." Boxes of shoes, tried and rejected, are stacked on the floor around him.

"Avant-garde plays, no less." She clutches my arm in make-believe intensity, lowers her voice to a gravelly whine. "I am Woman, I am the Spirit of Freedom, I am the Phantom of the Multiple Orgasm. . . ." She hoots derisive laughter.

"Would you like to see something else, ma'am, or have you decided?" The clerk's eyes plead.

"These'll do, I guess." She kicks off the red pumps and fishes in her purse for a cigarette, despite the neat sign politely thanking us for not smoking. "Her name is Cassandra. I've had a peek at her. . . . You wouldn't believe the way she does her self up . . . someone ought to point out to her that the hippie generation is dead."

Her words chase each other, her laughter is tinny and abrasive. I trail after her through the crowded, perfumed department store, encased in loneliness.

"You're not buying anything," Maggie accuses.

"I haven't seen anything I like."

"What do you think of this color?" Maggie waves an emerald-green scarf in front of me. She nudges me with one pink-tipped finger. "Come back."

"I'm sorry," I apologize hastily. "I was thinking about last night. I saw this woman. In a bar—she was terrific looking," I finish lamely, not knowing what to tell her. "She had great red hair."

"Maybe that's what I need," Maggie laughs. "I ought to do my hair red. Not middle-aged auburn, either. I'll go the whole route, be a flaming redhead." She picks up the hand mirror on the counter. "On second thought, maybe not." She chooses some earrings from the display and fits them into her ears. "Did I tell you they're going up to Santa Barbara this weekend? They're going to read their plays to each other and guzzle herb tea and brown rice." She tilts the mirror so the long rhinestone pendants catch the refracted light. "Haven't you got anything with a bit more pizzazz?" She tosses the earrings to the bland-faced woman behind the jewelry counter. "I wouldn't mind so much if he'd just say I'm off to have a bit of slap and tickle with my latest, but he insists it's all to do with getting in touch with one's soul and staring into the eyes of destiny." The saleswoman produces a cluster of enormous red-and-green balls suspended from bright silver chains. Maggie clips them on and shakes her head; her earrings swing, creating a dull, soft clatter. "I think he's going softheaded. God knows his taste has degenerated." She pulls the earrings off and holds them up. "These are dreadful, aren't they?"

"It's the glitter look, madam," the saleswoman explains coldly.

"Oh? Well, why shouldn't I glitter with the best of them? Wrap 'em up."

* * *

"I wish we'd gone somewhere we could've had a drink," Maggie sighs plaintively. A plate of untasted chicken salad congeals on the plate in front of her. She leans back in the white wrought-iron chair and gazes around the tearoom, which is color coordinated to match Bonwit's wrapping paper—violet, green, and white.

"You can't just drink, Maggie. You have to eat."

Her shrug is careless. I drop my napkin over my cleaned plate. "You *have* to eat. You get sick otherwise."

"Oh, look," she says, gesturing with her chin. "Over there."

A woman sits alone at a table for four; the other chairs are piled high with her purchases. Ash-blond hair sweeps the shoulders of her fuzzy pink sweater. She eats with slow, voluptuous enjoyment. Bright bracelets and rings flash with every movement of her hands.

"Whose poor cow of a wife, I wonder, is picking over the polyester at J. C. Penney's so that that bit of fluff can have her Bonwit's charge card and all her pretty things?"

"Why pick on *her?* It could just as easily be either of the two." I point to a pair of brunettes, dressed in quiet good taste, chatting over coffee at a nearby table.

"No, no." Maggie protests vehemently. "I know the look. A certain smugness around the eyes—altogether different from the look of a simple romance. There's something about nabbing another woman's husband that brings out a sort of *glow* of triumph."

"That's nonsense." Have I seen that look in David's eyes? Was that what I mistook for tenderness?

"You'll see," Maggie says ominously. "I know I'm right." One finger taps my wrist. "What about Michael? Is he still seeing his blonde?"

"Blonde . . . ?" Her question has caught me off guard. I fumble for an answer. Nothing comes.

"What is it, love?" She stares at me with alarmed pity. "You've been so distant all day. You look terrible. He's not planning to file for divorce . . . ?"

I shake my head. Michael's face as he stood over the sink this morning, the eagerness in his body, the excitement in his eyes . . . *It'll probably take all night.* . . .

"What?" Her face is furrowed with anxious concern. "Tell me," she urges gently.

"No. I can't." Her eyes are a safe harbor. The pressure behind my own increases; I blink quickly to stop the tears.

"He hasn't gotten her preggers, has he?"

"No."

"What, then?" She strokes my hand in a rare gesture of near-maternal tenderness. "I don't like to see you suffering, love. Whatever it is, you shouldn't have to bear it all alone. Tell me, maybe I can help."

The embankment collapses; tears flood my eyes, course over my face. "It's not a she," I sob.

Maggie recoils.

"Fucking hell," she breathes. Then: "You can't be serious. Michael's a pouf?"

My face burns with shame and guilt and fury. "Of course not," I hiss. What have I done? He'll be furious. He'll leave in a rage . . . never come back. . . . "It was a mistake, it only happened once . . . he was pushed into it. . . ."

"You mean he was forced? Violated?"

"Yes. In a way. The man was desperate . . . suicidal. . . . He's an old friend. Michael was trying to help. . . ." The implausible words stumble over each other, falter to a halt.

100

Maggie leans back, studying me. "Who was it?"

Fresh horror assails me.

"No one you know. Someone from New York."

She nods. "It only happened once?"

"Yes."

"It's over?"

"Yes."

She lights a cigarette without taking her eyes from my face. "I don't think so," she says quietly.

I bury my face in the cambric handkerchief she offers.

"He's trying to find his way back," I plead. "He doesn't want this, Maggie. He loves me. He just doesn't know how to get out of it. . . ."

She shakes her head and exhales with a loud whoosh. "Poor love." Her face darkens. "This won't do. It just won't do."

"You mustn't tell anyone, not Oliver, especially not Oliver! If Michael even suspects that you know . . ."

We stare at each other. She nods; her face has hardened. "So you've been drafted as the guardian of the secret." She snorts. "If it were me, I'd take out an ad in the paper. Let the whole world know my hubby is buggering his pal—"

The room tilts. "Don't. Don't." I grip her hands. "Please promise me, Maggie. Swear on whatever's holy to you, please, please . . . not a word. . . ."

Her mouth twitches with disgust. "Annie—"

"Swear!"

She shakes her hands loose. "All right. I promise."

"And you'll still be his friend?"

She gives a short, harsh laugh. "Sure. After all, you're still civil to *my* old man, aren't you?"

A waitress in a violet-and-green dress appears at my elbow, with a lifted silver coffeepot and a questioning smile.

Maggie shoves her cup forward to be refilled. I turn my head away and dab at my smeared mascara.

"Dessert?" The waitress ducks her head to peer into my face.

"Haven't you got anything alcoholic in this place?" Maggie demands.

"Only brandied cherries, ma'am."

Maggie rolls her eyes. "We'll take two."

"Very good, ma'am."

"Why don't we go somewhere cozy and get you a proper drink?" she says when the waitress has sauntered away.

I shake my head. It feels unsafe to leave without more assurance.

"Maggie . . ."

She stirs her coffee violently. "Don't look at me like that, love. I'll keep his bloody little secret. And I'll be charm itself to him." She tosses her spoon down. "The important question now is, what are *you* going to do?"

"Do?" I echo dully.

"Have you thought about leaving him?"

I shrink away from her probing eyes. "No! I love Michael. We're a family. . . ."

She nods archly. "Ah, yes. For the sake of the children, and all that," she sneers. "You'll stick around and let him decimate you."

"You haven't left Oliver."

For one dangerous moment we look into each other's eyes. Maggie's righteous anger withers. "No, I haven't," she mutters.

Her pain fits so neatly, seamlessly over my own.

"Why not?"

She shrugs. "Because I'm as big a fool as you are." She leans forward, her hands, balled into fists, on the table. "But I'll tell you, I've had my fill. I've had enough!" She shakes her coppery hair away from her pinched face. "This weekend," she announces, "while Oliver's up in Santa Barbara fucking about with his soul, I'll be stretched out on our platform bed doing the same thing, but with the most marvelous man."

"Really? Who?"

She looks away. "I don't know yet. I haven't actually met him." She raises her chin, her mouth is tight. "But I will. I'll get all tarted up in my new dress and my glitter-look earrings, and I'll take myself off to a bar." Her hand slaps the table, the bracelets jump and clank. "I'm going to have some fun for a change. And if you've got a crumb of sense, you'll come with me."

The idea appalls me. "Don't do it, Maggie. I see those women all the time, hanging around in restaurants and cocktail lounges." Usually wearing red dresses and too much makeup. A wave of ugly pity overtakes me. For Maggie. For myself. "Men sneer at them," I plead. "It's degrading. It's horrible. And if you do get someone to come home with you, it won't be anyone you ever want to see again—"

"So fucking what? You can play the understanding wife as long as you like. I want to have a good time. I want to show the bastard that I can give as good as I get." She shakes a long finger under my nose. "And you'd bloody well better go out and do the same thing." Her voice has risen. The blonde at the next table glances at us with mild, benign curiosity.

"Look, Annie," she says, lowering her voice to an intense whisper. "That's just the way it is. If you stay home and play a good little wifey, all forgiving, all understanding, he'll stomp you to pieces. I know."

"Not Michael. Michael's not like Oliver. It's a different situation. Entirely."

103

She stares at me with sullen eyes. "You're daft if you think so, girl. If you think he's going to treat you with any more consideration or that your situation is any safer . . ."

I shake my head vehemently. "I know Michael."

She rolls her eyes. "The hell you do."

"I *know* him. He's involved in something upsetting right now. But I know he loves me. He wants *me*."

Maggie falls silent. She twists the wedding ring on her finger.

"Maggie," I say, placating. "I don't think going to a bar to pick up somebody for a one-night stand is the answer."

"Well, if you have a better one, I'd sure like to hear it, dearie."

The red-haired woman's face flashes in front of my eyes. Strong and calm, full of laughter and good-natured challenge.

"I'm not sure. I just know your solution isn't right for me."

"You're a goddamn milksop. He's got you beat."

"Not yet. I know his 'affair' is almost over. He said so. I believe him."

Maggie lowers her head. Her fingers tap the table. "Good for you," she mutters. Her shoulders sag. Weariness lines her mouth.

I want to put my arms around her. "You look beautiful in your new dress," I offer.

She raises her head. "It's not too much?" She wipes at her eyes covertly.

"No, it's smashing."

"Truly?"

"Absolutely. No one will be able to resist you."

She gives me a crooked smile. "With the possible exception of my husband."

"So fucking what? You'll show him."

"I will, won't I? I bloody well will."

We smile into each other's pain-filled, love-filled eyes.

That evening Emily comes into the kitchen draped in a long white apron. "I'm going to help you cook," she says decisively.

I repress a sigh. Emily's help in the kitchen will cost me hours of clean-up.

"You're glad, aren't you?" She searches my eyes.

"Very glad." I set her to work peeling potatoes.

"I want to help, too, Mommy," Robin pleads.

Emily dispatches her brother with a few emphatically whispered words. Not even daring to cry, he gathers up his toy soldiers and decamps for the living room.

My attempts at conversation fail. Emily answers all my questions with a series of shrugs. I watch her as she works in silent concentration. The thin, aristocratic-looking nose, so much like Michael's; the same seawater green eyes; the same ripe, full mouth, poised between laughter and petulance.

She feels my eyes on her and looks up, frowning. "I can't help it, Mommy, it takes a long time to get the brown spots out."

"I was thinking how pretty you are."

She tosses her head and her fine, baby brown hair sweeps her cheek. "No," she says solemnly, "I'm not pretty." She hurls herself at me, her arms go around my waist, she holds on ferociously. "You're pretty, Mommy!" She buries her head in my waist, her thin arms circle me, tight as piano wires. I put my hands on her thin back to draw her closer. She jerks away. She picks up her paring knife and an unpeeled potato, climbs back on the kitchen stool, and resumes her work, her eyes turned away from me.

105

Later, after dinner and bedtime stories, when I sit alone in the living room, I recreate this moment. Emily and me. Running away! Back to New York . . . mother and daughter . . . closer than sisters . . . a secret world. And then I'm contrite and I have to creep into Robin's room and kiss him on his sleeping eyes to apologize for having abandoned him in my thoughts.

Now, in the kitchen, I give her a brusque compliment on her work, and show her how to slice the potatoes for home fries.

A policeman and a gunman stalk each other soundlessly across the flickering TV screen; on the radio a woman sings a defiant love song. I've let my book slide to the floor. I'm sketching, with Emily's blunt crayon, on the back of her Barbie coloring book, the fountain in front of the Plaza Hotel. At my elbow is a cup of cold coffee. The policeman and his captured prey fade into a toothpaste commercial, and then the overcoiffed anchorman of the eleven o'clock news appears with a smiling, silent recitation of the day's events. The phone rings.

David, who is supposed to be working alongside Michael at the movie house tonight, tells me in an eager voice that he's finally finished with his out-of-town relatives and dropped them at their hotel. He asks me whether the children enjoyed *Snow White*. He says he's discovered a new Italian restaurant. And he asks to speak to Michael.

I tell David that the children hated the movie and they were frightened by the witch, and that Michael's just gone to the store to buy some ice cream for me.

"Well, I need to talk to him—maybe I'll come by for a while," he says.

"Yes," I say. "Do that."

I dial Heather, the baby-sitter.

I go to my bedroom and find the dress—covered in a plastic dry-cleaning bag, shoved to the back of the closet. Red chiffon, low-necked, bare-backed. I last wore it to my cousin's wedding in Brooklyn. I apply makeup, green eye shadow. I arrange my hair in a tousled French knot. Long rhinestone earrings. When I gaze at myself in the full-length mirror, I'm someone else. Full disguise. No one would know me. I'll introduce myself as Anya.

Heather goggles at me through her jam-jar-bottom glasses. "You look *neat*, Mrs. Morrow," she breathes. "Are you meeting Mr. Morrow at a party?"

I try out my enigmatic smile on her. She clasps her hands in wistful adulation. "Well, have a nice time wherever you're going."

The night is unusually damp; fog blurs my windshield. I pull into Maggie's driveway. You were right, I'll tell her. Everything you said is true. Put on your new dress. Let's go.

I ring the bell over and over. There's a light on in the living room, she might be taking a nap. I go around to the back door and pound. I tap on the bedroom window. Maggie's cat scuttles around the house. I look in the empty garage.

Maybe she's on her way home. I settle myself in my car to wait. I'm shivering. Stupid not to have brought a sweater. The clock in my car has been stopped at 7:05 for the past six months. Where was Michael tonight? What new lie . . . ?

Why doesn't she come home? I've been here for hours, I'm certain.

Maybe she's at the bar already. I could meet her there. Where?

Fear, rage, frustration: I feel as if I'm choking. I roll down the car window. The night—dank, chemical-scented, thick with despair—assaults me. My eyes burn. The street

107

is silent, the houses dark. I close my eyes and lean my head against the steering wheel.

The red-haired woman strides across my mind, moving with easy grace, laughing . . . wise. . . .

I rev the engine and pull out into the street. Hoping my instinct is better than my memory, I carefully pick my way back to Paulette's.

11

ONIGHT THE sand-colored building looks forbidden, turned in on itself. My heart lurches: Standing in the shadowed doorway . . . Michael? The man pushes open the heavy oak door. It's not him. I grip the steering wheel.

What will I say to her? She's a stranger. What if she turns away from me?

. . . *I wonder if I could speak to you for a moment?* I push my hand through my hair in a weak imitation of her.

She'll laugh at me, she'll think I'm crazy.

No. She'll look into my eyes and she'll recognize our kinship. She must have had a Michael in her life. Why else would she have entered his territory? And conquered it.

My heart is pounding. My hand on the door handle feels frozen. She *has* to speak to me. I have to make her. She knows things that Maggie doesn't. She can tell me what to do. Be my guide. My friend. Teach me to be like her. . . .

On the other side of the heavy oak door is a small lobby, out of sight of the dining room and the broad staircase. Here the maître d' waits.

"May I help you?" His eyes travel over me with distaste. My red dress glows like neon. He blocks my way, unsmiling, frigidly polite, rubbing his hands together as if they were chilled.

"I'm looking for someone." I sound as if I've been running.

"A party of friends?" He makes a slight, tentative movement.

"Not exactly."

He frowns and throws a protective glance in the direction of the dining room. "Oh?"

"I was here last night. With Mr. Asher." I try to make my voice sound the way I imagine hers would: calm, rich, amused, as though haboring a secret joke at his expense.

"M'sieur Asher." His face lightens briefly. "Unfortunately, he's not visiting us tonight." He raises his empty palms apologetically.

"I'm looking for a woman. I don't know her name. I saw her here last night. She has red hair . . . I'm sure you noticed her. Tall . . . very fair skin, almost translucent . . . elegant . . . and proud. . . .

The man stares at me. Traces of a smirk lift one corner of his well-bred, thin-lipped mouth.

"I'm sorry." His shrug is exaggerated. I wonder if I ought to offer him money. How much do I have with me? Just a few dollars I think. . . . "She's a friend of Mr. Asher's too," I add.

"Yes?"

"He's looking for her. I'm helping him . . ."

"Yes?"

His smile shows signs of strain. I've gone too far.

"I can't help you, madam." He bows slightly and holds open the oak door. His face is businesslike, but as I pass through the door he touches my sleeve delicately, and either out of compassion or the possibility that I might have been telling the truth, he murmurs close to my ear, "You might try Ruby's."

"Ruby's?" I repeat the name as if it were a magic incantation. "Will she be there tonight?"

"I couldn't say, madam." His face is frozen. "It's a popular place amongst her set."

The oak door closes swiftly and silently behind me.

I drive down the dark streets searching for the numbers I've copied out of the telephone book. I stop at a red light. In a graceful old Spanish building on the corner, behind bamboo shades covering the arched, yellow-lit window, two shadows embrace.

A scrawl of red neon splashed across black plate glass announces Ruby's. I scrape the car to a halt against the curb. She'll be here. It's impossible that my daring and persistence should go unrewarded. She'll *be* here.

"Evening." A stocky man in a T-shirt squats on a stool at the doorway. He greets me like an old friend, and collects my two-dollar door fee. "Enjoy your evening," he croaks.

The small entryway opens into a long, narrow room lit crazily by the jangling reds, greens, and oranges of dozens of sets of Christmas lights. Gripping the wall with one hand, I stand gaping.

They fill the booths and tables ringing the small dance floor. They line the long bar set against the artificial brick wall. They lounge in bright clusters at the blaring juke-box. They dance twined around each other, swaying slowly to the music.

All women.

The red-haired woman would never come to a place like this. She doesn't belong here. The maître d' must have known that. He must be laughing at me. I turn to go.

111

"Leaving us already?" The stocky man holds the door for me. I stand in the open doorway. Maybe it *is* possible. Maybe she does come here sometimes. She can be comfortable anywhere.

Besides, I have nowhere else to look.

"I've changed my mind," I whisper. The man shrugs good-naturedly.

The woman tending bar is plump and fortyish, with bland brown hair teased into carefully exuberant curls. She seems kind.

I swivel around on the stool to face the room. Nowhere in the crowd of women do I see a brilliant halo of red hair.

The music blares, the tempo picks up. On the dance floor a beautiful black woman spins, her arms outspread, her sweat-shined face closed on the rapture of her own movements—the women around her start to clap and yell, laughing encouragement—I look away from the mesmerizing sight.

A small, slender girl in trousers, a man's shirt and tie, and a newsboy cap moves from table to table, talking incessantly. Her narrow, grinning face is full of sly humor; she seduces her audience into laughter. Against the wall a pretty brunette in shimmering satin skirts watches her with a proprietary smile.

Wouldn't they rather have a man?

I try to remember what I've read about these women who have no need of men. Sappho. Lesbos. Gertrude Stein peering out of Picasso's canvas, massive, mysterious, Sphinx eyes filled with secret knowledge. And Alice B., who loved her and never left her. All of them seem very brave. Women who need only each other . . .

I can see Maggie's pretty pink mouth formed in a little "Oh" of horror before widening into derisive laughter. *You must be daft, girl. You won't come to a perfectly*

*lovely singles bar, but you take yourself off to some dread-
ful dyke place. . . .* Her eyes suddenly narrowing: *You're
not going to tell me . . .* And then the smile, reassured,
widening again: *No, I didn't think so. Really, love, you
are daft, sometimes. . . .*

There's a flurry among the dancers. An exquisite blond
girl has staggered out onto the floor. With her eyes closed,
her arms sawing the air, she dances alone. In jerky,
convulsive movements she careens in a widening circle,
colliding with the others until they clear for her.

A dark girl, grim-faced, with dark, tormented eyes, half
drags, half carries her from the floor. The blonde droops
in the dark one's arms, her eyes still closed, her mouth
fixed in a dreamy smile of chilling cruelty.

Women who have no need for men . . .

The music shifts again. A female voice, rich and throaty,
sings to a guitar accompaniment. In the shadows against
the wall women press against each other.

I feel off balance, as if I might fall.

A hand touches my shoulder. *Somebody knows me. . . .*

"Would you like to dance?"

The girl standing behind me is tall and graceful. She
wears her light hair swept away from her face, which is
wide-boned and delicate. She looks foreign—a Russian
aristocrat, or a Scandinavian farm girl. Her narrow gray
eyes are solemn. I stare at her in amazement. She
has exactly the kind of face I used to delight in drawing. I would walk the city, for hours sometimes, searching for just that type of knowing-innocent look. Later,
copying from my sketches, I would add these faces to
paintings in progress, often changing a still life into a
portrait.

"Would you like to dance?" she repeats, smiling slightly.

I shake my head, my throat feels frozen. "I don't think

113

so," I whisper. Yet I give her my hand, as though I'm dreaming.

On the dance floor she holds my rigid body gently against her supple form. Her cheek rests on mine. I move in small, halting steps. In high school girls danced together, especially to the slow songs; we tried out our dips and fancy turns and close embraces—just to see how they felt. I try to concentrate only on the music; I try not to breathe in the scent of her perfume, or feel the soft pressure of her breasts against mine.

"You haven't come to Ruby's before, have you?" Her voice is low and clear. I shake my head. "I didn't think so." She smiles.

"Thank you," she says when the music stops. "You're a good dancer." She smiles at me again. Then she's gone.

With shaking hands, I count out the money for my bar check. The man at the front door has disappeared; no one sees my hurried exit.

I ease the car out of the parking space and turn toward home.

Michael's car is parked behind David's in our driveway. I pull up behind and sit looking at our house. The lower windows gleam golden behind sheer white curtains; the upper windows reflect the lavender glow of night-lights in the children's rooms. Geraniums and roses along the pathway echo the darkly purple sky. Smoke climbs from the chimney; two small bicycles lean against the porch steps; seedling basil plants rest in green plastic pots along the porch railing. The house is waiting for me. It seems to croon, to effuse contentment, to reach for me. . . .

The screen door crashes open. Michael appears. Behind him David's silhouette waits in the shadows.

"There you are!" Michael holds the screen door wide. He sounds relieved and cautious, his voice is edged with tension. "Where were you?" His arm heavy on my shoulder, he guides me to the sofa. David stands at the hearth, his hands in his pockets, looking beyond me.

Michael sits opposite me. "I was worried."

The fire has swallowed all the air in the room; parched heat rasps against the back of my throat. "Where were *you*? I thought you were supposed to be working at the theater with David."

The swift look that Michael and David exchanged was not meant for me to see. It's the look of two spies or the mysterious signal of a secret order. Michael sighs. "It wasn't true," he says.

"She knows that." David, sitting in the rocker now, his long legs propped on the coffee table, winks at me.

Michael takes my hand and leans close to me. His eyes are shining. "I didn't want to tell you"—he nods toward David—"either of you, in case the results were zero. The truth is," he announces grandly, "I was with Terrence Hughs tonight." Michael tells us that he sensed last night that Hughs might be interested in the theater, and so he got the idea to meet with him to try to charm him into investing some money into the theater—enough to finance their next project—an adjoining espresso cafe.

"And he didn't want me there to distract the quarry." David gives me a wry smile.

"Not that David isn't a good salesman." Michael laughs. "It's just that I'm better."

David rolls his eyes. He's playing at being annoyed.

"I think Hughs'll go for it, he seems enthusiastic. I'm sorry I lied to you, but it'll be worth it." Michael leans back in triumph.

115

Could he be telling the truth?

His boyish smile dazzles. No. He's lying. "Do you forgive me?" he asks. He looks to David.

"I forgive the lie, but not the insult. I'm just as good a salesman."

"Annie?" The smile grows still wider. "Do *you* forgive me? David does."

How have they done this so quickly? There must have been an argument—David must have confronted, Michael must have confessed. But then—the reconciliation, this complicity . . . Something new has happened between them. What is it? When they look at each other their eyes are scrupulously empty.

"Actually, the reason I didn't tell you"—Michael picks up the fireplace poker and prods at the embers—"I was afraid that if I came back empty-handed, you might think I had other motives for seeing him."

I smile, tilting my head the way she had. Let them have their lie. If it is a lie. "Of course I forgive you. It's wonderful news."

"Good," Michael says, dismissing the subject. "And now you tell us. Where the hell did you go?" He smiles to temper his words.

It's my turn, I have a secret too. . . . "I just got restless, thought I'd go to a movie. . . . Too late by the time I got there, so I drove around, looked at the ocean. . . ." I'm amazed at my ease; the lie rolls out of my mouth like a beautiful silk ribbon. I raise my arms over my head and stretch voluptuously. How wonderful to have a secret. "You weren't worried, were you?"

"I was a little, yeah. Heather didn't know where you went, she said it was so last-minute. Next time leave me a note or something."

He believes me! I glance at David. There's no sign of skepticism in his face, either.

"Oh, I will, darling. Next time I'll let you know. I'm so sorry." I can feel the triumphant magnanimity in my smile. Just as I've seen it so many times in Michael's.

Later, Michael slips into bed beside me and takes me in his arms. "Thank you," he murmurs, "for being so wonderful." His kisses are tender. "I love you. I'm so lucky to have you. You're not like any other woman." His eyes are moist. "I'll never hurt you."

Then stop! I want to shriek. Give up David and stop all this. . . . The red-haired woman's face frowns in the darkness beside me. *That's not the way I do it,* she whispers. *I'm clever and strong.*

Michael winds his arms tight around me. I can feel that he's trembling. "The truth is," he says with effort, "I was very scared when I didn't find you home. Panicky."

"Where did you think I was?"

"I didn't know. . . . I thought maybe . . . You might have been anywhere. Gone. I got very frightened." He buries his face in my hair. "You mustn't leave me. Ever. You still love me. Don't you?"

His trembling hands move over my body. When he touches my breast his hand stiffens, as if the soft skin were dangerous.

I want to scream fury into his face. I want to run out of this house back to New York, or to the ocean. Anywhere.

Instead, I arch my back and close my eyes.

The face of my dancing partner floats like a dream across my mind. What would it be like if she were touching me? Is that what Michael loves about David? Their sameness?

"I want to make you happy," Michael murmurs. His breath is warm between my legs.

When Michael touches David does he seem more beautiful because of their shared maleness? Is making love more exquisite then?

Michael's hands caress my thighs. What does he feel? What I would feel if I caressed her . . . smooth skin, the curling dark hair perfumed with musk . . . perfume rising from her skin . . . silk . . . follow with my own lips and tongue the movement of Michael's. My scent, heavy, musky, tropical, rises out of the darkness. That's her scent too. She moans and arches her body the way I do. She buries her hands in my hair, gasping my name, almost sobbing. . . .

The salty flood fills my mouth, fills Michael's mouth.

I would kneel on the bed over her, tender and triumphant, powerful . . . ask her . . .

"Did I make you happy?"

"Yes, Michael," I whisper.

12

"WHY CAN'T we come, too, Mommy?" Robin sits cross-legged on my bed, peeling the old airline stickers off my brown suitcase.

I smooth out the black lace nightgown and lay it carefully next to the matching robe. "Maggie's going to take you to the zoo and the movies. . . . You'll have a wonderful time, Robbie. You'll see."

"Packing already?" Michael appears at the bedroom door. "We're not leaving till tomorrow afternoon."

"Do you think I'll need these?" I wave a pair of boots. "Maybe so . . it gets chilly up north. . . ."

"Put these in the kitchen for Daddy." Michael hands Robin the bag of groceries he's been holding.

"Chips! Can I have some?"

"Snacks for our trip. Okay, but just take a few."

Pretending to stagger under the weight of the bag, Robin goes toward the kitchen. Michael closes the door behind him.

"What is it?"

He takes a green mohair sweater out of my hands and starts to fold it meticulously. He keeps his eyes hidden.

"You should bring your jacket too," he says. "It can go down to forty at night."

"What's wrong?"

He keeps his head lowered over the open suitcase; he rearranges the piles of folded clothes. "It's David."

My breathing locks.

"It's no big deal, actually." His voice sounds forced. He stoops to retrieve my boots; he begins to wrap them in the piece of tissue paper from their box. "He has to go up to San Francisco too. I told him he could ride up with us." He closes the suitcase lid experimentally. "Have you got much more? You're running out of room."

I clutch the clothes remaining on the bed—dressy black velvet skirt and satin blouse, sexy high-heeled shoes, pink silk teddy. "Ride up with us?"

"Yes. He has friends up there."

"He'll stay with them?"

Michael strokes my arm. "Well, even if he didn't, we'd hardly see him."

"You mean he'll stay with *us*? Come on our trip with *us*?" My voice is rising.

"No, no, no—"

"I won't be needing these, then, will I?" I toss the clothes on the floor of my closet. I try to hoist the suitcase off the bed; Michael takes it from my hands and sets it down gently on the carpet.

"I know it's a change of plans, but—"

I cover my ears to shut out his voice. "You promised!" I shriek at him. He reaches for me, I slap his hands away, race out of the room, out the back door, ignoring the startled looks of Emily and Robin, who are sitting at the kitchen table.

Michael catches up to me at my car. He holds my hands and forces me to look at him.

"Honey, honey, please."

"It's ruined, you've ruined it. This was supposed to be our time together. . . ."

Michael holds me too tight. "Please understand," he begs.

"It won't do. It just won't do." I fling Maggie's words at him.

"Darling," he croons into my ear. "Don't cry."

"I've waited so long. . . ."

Shhh. Don't, murmurs a voice in my ear like the voice of a river.

"Do you want to cancel the trip?" Michael asks desperately. "I don't know what to do. I can't say no to him. You have to understand . . ."

I squeeze my eyes shut. The red-haired woman's face appears, calm and knowing.

"I *don't* understand. I don't want to." I try to pull away from him; he holds me tighter.

If he goes away, the red-haired woman urges in my head, *you'll be left alone.*

"Please come in the house."

He leads me back inside, into the bedroom, closes the door. He kneels beside the bed. "Annie, if you just try . . . we could still have a wonderful time. Nothing has to be ruined. He has friends there. He won't be with us the whole time."

The red-haired woman's voice says, *If you do this for Michael, he'll adore you. If you don't . . .*

My hands fall to my sides. I cry without making any sound.

Michael strokes my hair. "I'll make it up to you. Only let David come this one time. And I promise, we'll have our trip. A second honeymoon. We'll go back to Paris. . . ."

Say yes.

"I was counting on this trip," I whisper.

Go on. I can see her face. She's smiling encouragement. Her eyes are confident, full of wisdom and courage.

I shake my head weakly.

You can make him so happy. Only you can do this for him. Look at his eyes . . . how much he loves you . . . how much he needs you.

"I promise you," Michael pleads.

And I promise you, the woman says. *Or don't you want to be brave and strong? Don't you want to make him love you? Don't you want to be like me . . . ?*

I lower my head. "All right," I whisper.

Michael's eyes widen. "Really? You mean it?"

"Yes."

He throws his arms around me. "This is wonderful. You're fabulous. You're the most fabulous woman in the world. We'll have a great time, you'll see."

The woman in my head smiles. *Yes. You'll see.*

"They've never slept away from home before."

"They'll be fine." Maggie's smile is grimly determined. She crouches beside Robin. "There are some lovely little cakes and things for you in the kitchen!"

He buries his head deeper in the folds of my skirt.

"Baby," Emily bursts out. She pries his arms away from my waist. "You're spoiling everything. Come *on.*"

He follows his sister from the room, his face pale with anguish.

"Maybe I should—"

"He'll be *fine.*"

"I hope so." I stand in her hallway, staring at her white floor.

"What's up? You look like you're off to a burial, not a jolly vacation."

122

"I've never left the kids before."

"Well it's time you did." She gives me a gentle push toward the door. "It's wonderful that Michael's taking you away. You'll get everything sorted out. Come home like newlyweds. It's just what you need. Don't spoil it by worrying about the kiddies."

"Maggie . . ." I throw my arms around her neck and pull her to me in a fierce hug. She feels so far away. She pulls back, laughing, a little embarrassed.

"Go on, you daft thing. Don't keep your old man waiting." She squeezes my arm. "This could be your new start, love. I hope so."

"Thanks."

"Go on."

"Tell Robin I'll bring him a present. Emily too—"

"Go!"

Michael holds the car door open for me. "Maggie's terrific," he says. "The kids'll have a great time." He pulls the car out into the stream of traffic.

"Oh, yes. They'll be fine."

Michael wraps his arm around my shoulders. I give him my hand. As the car leaves our street and enters the wide, winding boulevard, I turn to wave good-bye to Maggie, but there's no one on the front porch.

Michael's hand tightens on the steering wheel as we turn up a hilly, palm-lined street. He lets out his breath slowly.

David lounges against a parked car. He raises his hand in a laconic greeting as we pull up alongside.

"I was just getting ready to give up on you." He lifts his canvas overnight bag into the backseat and climbs in after it.

"Annie had to get the kids settled." Michael watches him in the rearview mirror.

123

You have to start, the red-haired woman whispers. *Go on. "I'm so glad . . ."*

Resolutely I turn around to face David. "I'm so glad you're coming with us," I tell him.

He leans into the backseat. His mirrored sunglasses capture my face in miniature. He smiles slowly. "I was going to say the same thing to you."

"Do you have the map?" Michael asks quickly.

"One-oh-one to Big Sur, then One into Frisco." David tosses a red-penciled road map into the front seat.

"San Francisco." I smooth my skirt over my knees.

"That's what I said."

"No." I smile brightly. "Only tourists call it Frisco."

"Heaven forbid anyone should mistake us for tourists."

"I thought we'd stop in San Luis Obispo later on for a bite," Michael interrupts. "What do you think?"

"I think it's not a wonderful idea to leave at the height of rush hour." David takes off his sunglasses and rubs his eyes.

"We'll be out of this in no time." Michael switches on the radio. A beautifully modulated voice delivers a recital of local and worldwide miseries.

David's long fingers drum his knees.

"We ought to bring the kids a present," Michael says.

David rolls down the window.

"Maybe something from Chinatown." Michael turns the car off the wide street and eases onto the freeway, where we pick up speed. "A dragon kite, maybe—"

"Oh, God! Did I pack Robin's blanket? He won't go to sleep without it."

"He'll be fine. It's time he gave it up anyway."

"He won't *sleep.*" Did I kiss Emily good-bye?

"They'll be fine," Michael says.

I want him to turn the car around, I want to go back; my eyes burn with sudden tears.

Don't think about them now, her voice reassures and commands.

"Pass up some of those chips, Davey. And a Coke." Michael twists the dial on the radio till he finds the jazz station. He sings along with the music.

The air in the car is thick; it weighs on my eyes. The sun is still high. Sun glare, bouncing off chrome . . . like long fingers piercing my eyes. My mind drifts over dark pools of sleep. . . .

"What?" I'm jerked out of a doze.

"My arm's numb."

"Sorry." I lift my head from Michael's shoulder and sit up. The sun has disappeared behind a pink mountain. The road climbs and dips between bare brown hills. A hot wind blows through the open window, the desert twilight covers us, huge trucks rush past us, headlights sweep Michael's face, I can see the muscles working his jawline. Smoke from David's cigarette burns my eyes.

We stop for a rest at an all-night roadside coffee shop. We sprawl in the horseshoe-shaped orange-vinyl booth. David stares out the darkened window at the empty parking lot. The cake and coffee Michael ordered for him rest untouched on the table. I spoon up peach pie and ice cream, keeping my eyes trained on the historical landmark map of Northern California printed on my paper place mat.

Michael sips black coffee watching, first David, then me. "Isn't this amazing?" he says in a hushed voice. "The three of us going away like this?" He reaches for our hands; David withdraws his, I allow mine to be tightly gripped. "I think we're really special."

"What the hell are you talking about?" David stabs his cigarette out on his cake plate. "Jesus." He slumps lower on the plastic cushions.

Michael looks crushed. His eyes entreat. "You know what I mean, Annie."

Let them reach each other through you.

Hesitantly I put my hand on David's. "It's true, you know." I slip my other hand into Michael's. "Who else do you know who's this open to experience? This willing?" I squeeze their hands. "We're going to have a wonderful trip."

David gives me a grudging smile. "You're pretty amazing," he says.

Michael's eyes shine with gratitude. A current is passing from Michael to David through me.

Yes. That's the way. The woman smiles.

I feel the giddy lift of elation.

Sometime after midnight we pull into the driveway of a lodge buried in pine woods. There are no lights burning. The wind moves in the trees; far below us we can hear the muffled murmurings of the ocean.

"This place looks like it's been closed down for years," David mutters.

We follow Michael into the deserted lobby. He switches on an overhead lamp. Old farm implements on the walls cast odd shadows; braided rugs are large, soft islands on distressed oak floors. "Wait here." Michael disappears down a dark passageway.

David jangles coins in his pocket. I stand at the window. Velvety black roses crawl over a trellis covering the glass.

"You folks must have got a late start." A sleepy-eyed man in overalls precedes Michael into the room.

"My wife and my wife's brother . . ." Michael is saying.

"No problem," the overall'ed man yawns, sorting through keys.

David slides his arm around me. "See, I told you there'd be no problem." His fingers bruise my waist. "*Sis.*" He gives Michael a malignant smile.

Michael's hand slices the air in an irritated gesture. Frowning, he turns to sign the register.

The rooms are small cabins set back in the pines. Michael, holding a flashlight, leads the way; I follow, my high heels wobbling on the gravel path. David trails behind.

Michael opens the cabin door and fumbles with the light switch.

Facing us across the cedar-paneled room are three single beds. A grin of relief lights Michael's face. "Well, we can always pretend we're back in Scout camp," he jokes.

The three beds, each made up with a patchwork quilt, wait in an orderly row against the wall. Three identical nightstands and three old lamps occupy the spaces between each bed.

"Dibs on this one, kids." David sets his bag on the middle bed.

Michael turns away quickly. "We need a fire." He begins to stack logs on the hearth.

"I suppose there's no hope of getting any ice." David extracts a bottle of vodka from his bag. He circles the room in a vain search for glasses. "Very rustic. I hope you're fond of tepid vodka." He takes a sip and offers me the bottle.

"That's too strong for her." Michael crams newspapers under the logs.

David proffers the bottle again. "It'll keep you warm. Our Eagle Scout doesn't seem to be having much luck with the fire."

"Do you want to try? The wood's damp."

"The whole place is damp." David presses the bottle into my hands. The vodka sears my throat and leaves me

127

gasping. I sink into a rickety-looking rocker. A tiny flame appears in the hearth, shudders, dies.

"Lovely roaring blaze you've got there. Makes me proud to be your brother-in-law."

"Give it a rest, David." Michael stabs at the fire. "We need kindling."

"That's not all we need." David tilts the bottle to his mouth again.

Michael takes it from him and sips gingerly. "Hey," he says with forced humor, "Annie's going to get sick of you before we even get to Frisco."

"San. San Francisco." He retrieves the vodka, takes another long wallow. "Isn't that right, Sis?"

"Oh, come on," Michael cajoles. "What else could I say to him? You saw him—we're way out in the country now."

"See? That's what's so good about all this free-spirit stuff." David beams at me. "You can take it all back whenever you think it might get unpleasant. Isn't that true, Michael?" His smile is venomous.

"Don't start all that again," Michael says sharply. "You're going to ruin our weekend." He gets to his knees with an old copy of *National Geographic* he's found and tries desperately to fan life into the faltering fire.

"Am I? Ruining your weekend? Am I, Sis?" David leans across the rocker and rest his hands heavily on my shoulders.

"No, David."

"You see?" He yodels in triumph. "I'm not ruining our weekend, you're ruining our weekend, Michael." He lurches forward to kiss my cheek, loses his balance, and flops at my feet.

"Jesus Christ." Michael snatches up his sweater and the flashlight. "I'm going to look for kindling. Try to pull yourself together while I'm gone." The cabin door bangs shut; we listen to the sound of Michael's feet on the gravel until we can hear only the calling of crickets.

"Goddamn." David lets his breath out sharply. "Do you mind?" He leans his head back until it rests on my knees.

"Are you drunk, David?"

"No."

"Is he all right out there? It looked very dark."

"Don't worry about him. Never worry about him." He tilts the bottle to his mouth.

"If you're not drunk now, you're going to be," I say. He settles against my legs; I feel as if I'm being held captive.

David sighs and closes his eyes. He seems to fall into sleep. I move my legs slightly. He stirs and sits up, smiling. "Another sip?" He offers the almost empty bottle.

"No, thanks."

He nestles his head against my legs again. "Annie," he says slowly, "what do you think would have happened if there'd been a double bed and one twin instead of three singles?"

"I hadn't thought about it. I would have slept with Michael, I suppose, and you—"

"What if I insisted that I sleep with him?"

"But I'm his wife—"

"And I'm his lover. What if *he* insisted?"

"He *wouldn't*. I'm the mother of—"

"Nope. Foul. You left that behind in L.A. You're in neutral territory now. This weekend it's just Michael, David, and Annie." He holds up the bottle. "Sure you don't want a little?"

I take a sip. The bottle jerks against my mouth—my hands are trembling. "What is it, David? Why are you talking this way?"

He rests a hand on my bare feet. "Freezing." He peels off his sweatshirt and wraps it around my feet. "I was

129

wondering . . ." He rolls the empty bottle into the cheer-less fireplace. "Where did you really go that night?"

My breath catches in my throat. "Which night?"

"You know . . . when the baby-sitter was there, and no one knew where you went . . . ?"

"I told you . . ." A mixture of panic and excitement turns in my chest. "I went to look at the ocean, and I—"

He holds up a hand. "You don't have to tell me. I don't care if you've got a fella tucked away somewhere."

My legs jerk involuntarily. David sits up. "Oh, sorry. I didn't mean to crush you." He moves to the bed and sits on the edge, staring intently into my face. The darkness of the pine woods at night floods the room.

"You think you have all the pain." His voice is strong, his slurred speech is gone, he no longer seems drunk. "You think it's only about you." He leans forward, his long-fingered hands laced on his knees. "I love him, too, Annie," he says steadily. "Whatever you're doing in your free time, he can't know about it."

"I'm not doing any—"

"Michael is terrified you'll leave him."

"I'm not going to—"

"And I'm afraid too." David's dark eyes are naked; I see the tenderness I remember, and the longing. But now I know they're not for me.

"When you're with him, Michael feels safe."

"I feel safe with him too—"

"Safe to love *me*."

His eyes are horrible. Unguarded, and cruel. "I don't want to talk anymore, David."

He lays a hand on my arm. "As long as Michael has a wife—has you, I mean—he feels free. Safe. If you take yourself away from him, he'll panic. I'll never see him again."

Do you hear what he's saying? He needs you.

"You need me."

He looks at me levelly. "Yes. I do. Without you to pretend with, he'd have to admit that he could be happy just with me. He'd have to admit that he's—"

"He isn't homosexual." The word tastes like metal in my mouth."

David's jaw tightens. "Annie, listen—"

Don't talk anymore now.

"I'm going to bed. You're drunk and I'm tired."

"Do you think you can make him happy?" David lays a restraining hand on my shoulder.

"Yes."

"You can't. He'd be miserable without me. Or someone like me. He'd blame you."

"No."

"Just the way he'd blame me if you left him. You've got to be what you've always been to him. You agreed to this, to all of it, when you decided not to leave him."

I shrug off his hand and stand up.

"It's essential, Annie."

Ah! Her triumphant smile warms me.

I make him repeat it. "What do you mean, essential?"

"I mean we need you, to be happy."

He said it!

I told you.

"You want him to be happy, Annie, don't you?"

No!

Yes.

"Yes, of course."

The doorknob rattles in a small explosion of sound.

Michael stands in the room hugging a bundle of twigs and dried leaves.

"What's going on?" His worried eyes move from my face to David's.

"Nothing. Talking." David takes the kindling out of his arms and begins to remake the fire. "Sorry I was so charming before. Demon rum." The fire catches immediately and roars up the stone chimney. "I'm going to sleep it off. I'll leave you two to enjoy the blaze." He stoops to retrieve his sweatshirt. "Night, Sis."

Michael and I lie on the thin, shaggy rug in front of the fireplace. He looks over at David's sleeping form. "Did he get drunk?"

"Not really. We were talking. He told me I mustn't ever leave you."

He slides his arms around me. "Were you thinking of leaving me?"

"No."

"You mustn't. Ever. I love you."

"I love you too."

I wake up cold. The fire has long since gone out. I can sense them in the dark, Michael and David. The rustling of bedclothes. Or is it the wind? Two clinging forms on the narrow bed. The cabin is in darkness, but still I can see their joined shadows moving on the walls. Slowly at first, then faster. I hear the ocean. Faster. Their whispers. Sorry . . . forgive . . . love you. And then: Annie . . . she . . . Annie. Soft laughter.

Let them play, we don't mind.

Without us, they'd have nothing.

Yes.

Yes. I smile into the dark.

132

13

"Y OU'RE GOING to love Donald," Michael says. "Isn't she?" He gives my waist a squeeze. "And he's going to be crazy about you."

Michael and David and I are climbing the narrow, hilly streets of the Castro. David carries a loaf of French bread, Michael holds purple jonquils wrapped in green paper. I walk between them, searching the crowded streets for the presence of women. There are none. There are only men. Mostly young, mostly handsome, dressed in a uniform of blue jeans and plain shirts, they amble or walk briskly, smiling, sure of the flow of the powerful currents of this city inside a city. They all seem to know each other, they all seem to have similar destinations.

"I told you all about him. I'm sure I did, honey," Michael insists. "I met him at UCLA, in the screenwriting class. He writes music. . . ."

He might have told me. I might have forgotten. . . . The afternoon is beautiful. The San Francisco Bay blue air has a ripe apple crispness; the pure sunlight renders everything flat and bright, like a child's painting.

And Michael is holding my hand with a special tenderness. . . .

"Oh, yes. Donald. I remember now." I twine my fingers tighter around his.

The fragrance of good French coffee pours from the open doorway of the Castro Street Coffee Bean.

"Let's take him some coffee," I suggest.

Michael beams at me. "Great idea."

The shop is tiny and aromatic. Crowded with men. They browse among exotically labeled sacks and barrels.

"May I help you, sugar?" The old man behind the counter smiles a small, pursed smile. His skin is as taut as stretched rubber. His hair is the color of egg yolk. He winks at David as he hands me the wrapped package. "You're in for a treat," he says.

I return a wide smile, hoping he hasn't seen the sudden, violent revulsion he's aroused in me.

Outside again, we pass an ornate movie house plastered with oversized posters of Bette Davis, Greta Garbo, Ida Lupino, Joan Crawford—alluringly posed. "This Week: Hepburn Retrospective," the marquee announces.

Next door, the plate-glass windows of a gymnasium display glistening, muscular young men and sleek, complex machines.

The flower stands on almost every corner are shimmering points of color in the crystal light—pink, lavender, purple.

Michael stops to peer into the window of a shop filled with cashmere sweaters. "Italian!" We follow him inside.

I lean against the counter and watch first Michael then David try on their choices.

"What do you think?" They turn slowly for me.

"Very nice."

"And they wash beautifully," the salesman tells me. "A little mild soap and cold water . . ." He writes up the sales slip and hands it to me.

134

They wear their new sweaters draped around their shoulders, sleeves loosely tied at their throats.

"Annie needs a present too," Michael says, outside.

"We'll find her one later," David says. "We're almost at Donald's. It's just down the street."

The building we enter is high, cool, white. David points skyward. "Fifth floor. Walk-up."

The broad staricase is thickly carpeted, maroon roses swirling on a scarlet background. A wave of claustrophobia seizes me. I long to bolt down the stairs and out into the clear sunlight.

"Just a little farther," Michael says. "You'll *love* him," he adds in a whisper.

I fasten my eyes on the swirling roses. I feel numbed. On each landing is a neat square of sunlight. The roses inside each square are a pallid pink, as if they've been drained of life. I avoid stepping on the squares. As we ascend the secret smell of the place reveals itself. Disinfectant . . . cabbage . . . incense . . . What else . . . ? The warm, polished wood of the banister feels like flesh under my cold hands.

"Hello! Up here!" In his open doorway stands Donald—tall and skinny, in his late thirties. His feathery hair is the same color as his gray tweed jacket; his small, well-shaped head perches on an absurdly long neck. He has a sharp and inquisitive nose; behind gold-rimmed glasses, his close-set eyes are watchful.

"You made it. I'm so glad!" He throws his arms around David as we arrive at the top of the stairs; then he hugs Michael.

"This is Annie." Michael urges me forward.

"At last. You're adorable." He takes my hand in both of his. "Lovely to meet you." His hands are warm, but dry and thin as twigs.

135

"Come in, come in . . . Oh, what have you got there?" he exclaims over the offerings of flowers and bread.

"We brought coffee too," I whisper.

He holds the package under his long nose and rolls his eyes. "Blue Mountain. Heaven!" He leads us into his living room and bustles off to the kitchen.

I sit on the frayed corduroy cushions that line the window seat. David and Michael flop onto huge pillows ranged around the floor. There is very little furniture in this bright, high-ceilinged room; most of the living space has been taken over by plants. An enormous tree in a straw basket presides over one corner. Its leaves brush the ceiling, cast lacy shadows across the striped Indian rug. Ivy climbs the walls, encouraged here and there with bits of string. Pots hung from the ceiling spill an opulence of ferns. In a large aquarium against the wall, silver and blue fish perform smooth arabesques. Opposite this a beautiful, lovingly polished Steinway gleams in solemn splendor.

"Here we are." Donald brings the wine in odd, tiny ceramic goblets. "I made them myself. Aren't they wonderful?" He sets a plate of diminutive petit fours next to me on the window seat.

Everything so little and perfect . . . "Like a doll's tea party . . ." My voice startles me. I flush with embarrassment.

"Better get out the pretzels and beer, Donald." David arches an eyebrow. His mouth is cold.

"I only meant . . . everything is so pretty . . . your place is so nice. . . ." A frantic fluttering of my hand sends the plate of pastries sailing onto the floor.

"I'm so sorry. . . ." My face burning, I stoop to retrieve them.

"That's all right." Donald smiles kindly—an indulgent uncle. "Don't worry about it. Would you like to see the rest of the apartment?"

David is watching me with unreadable eyes.

"Yes, please." I move toward Donald. "I'd like to see your place."

I follow him down a long, dim hallway into another bright, nearly bare room.

"The master suite."

A small mountain of pillows rises from a throw-covered mattress on the floor. Crammed bookshelves line one wall; the other is hung with framed photographs.

"These are beautiful." A snowstorm at the beach. Pigeons on a deserted city street at dawn. A little boy feeding an ice-cream cone to a policeman's horse. "Did you take them?"

"No. James did." He points to a photo of a plump, smiling older woman; she has one arm around Donald, the other around a handsome, dark-haired man.

"James?"

He nods.

"And your mother?"

"The very same."

"James is your brother, then?"

He chuckles delightedly. "My *lover*."

My eyes widen. "Your lover," I repeat foolishly. The scene presents: Michael standing over his fierce, frail mother. Mother, this is David. My lover. Her face unmoving; only her eyes move, seeking refuge among her antiques while her small hands, like paws, remain clasped over her breast. Later, in front of her statue of the Virgin, she damns Michael's soul to hell for all eternity. . . .

"Your mother accepts you, then," I blurt. "Accepts your . . ." Appalled at myself, I shut my lips over the rest of my words and move stiffly to the bookcase. "My, what a lot of books you have. . . ."

"Yes," he says, the kind uncle once again. "She does

137

accept me. She loves James too. She's a marvelous lady. I'm very lucky." He smiles fondly at me. "I think Michael's very lucky too. I've heard all about how great you've been, how understanding. I've known quite a few married men whose wives couldn't handle their being gay."

"Oh, Michael's not gay."

He stares at me, his eyes amused behind their thick lenses. With his head cocked, he looks like a quizzical stork. The image makes me smile. Donald smiles back and it seems as if we share some mutual joke. I like Donald, I decide.

"Okay." He shrugs. "Whatever. Come and see the study."

We pass through a small room holding only a desk and stacks of musical scores, then through the tiny kitchen and back out into the living room.

Michael and David lounge next to each other on the window seat.

"It's a lovely apartment," I say, waiting for them to shift and make room for me to sit between them.

David stands abruptly and moves to a pillow on the floor. Michael pats my knee. "How's James?" he asks Donald.

Donald goes to the stereo, selects a record. "Well, you know, it's the same old thing. . . ."

I lean back into the cushions and sip wine from the absurd little cup. Donald talks about his lover. The golden notes of a flute merge with the late-afternoon sunshine; everything is touched with warmth and color.

". . . and I said I adore you but there must be commitment . . ."

"You're going to make him feel . . ."

". . . yes, trapped, but also . . ."

". . . of course, but still . . ."

138

The conversation ripples like the music; glides and darts like the fish in the aquarium.

"What do you think, Annie?" Donald raps my ankle with his long finger.

I sit up, startled. "About . . . ?"

"James. Yes."

I glance at Michael. He's leaning forward expectantly, eager for my answer.

"I think . . ." Donald's mother with her arms around both of them . . . How does she truly feel? Is she really happy for her son? "I think you should be very loving. And very patient. That's all."

"She's right, of course," Donald says with a sigh. "She's very wise, your wife."

Michael beams.

You're learning.

"I just wish I could be more like she is." Donald smiles at me. On the pillows, David reaches for the wine bottle; he uncorks it with a small, violent sound.

Walking to the restaurant where Donald works as a cocktail pianist, he and I lag behind Michael and David. Donald holds my elbow and asks me about the children.

"Robin and Emily . . ." He says their names as if they were exotic plants. "I wish I had kids, I'd be a great father. I love to take care of people."

The restaurant is softly lit, intimate. Murals of the Manhattan skyline cover the walls. A white baby-grand piano dominates a corner of the bar.

Donald taps an irritated tattoo on the table. "Where the hell is James?"

"Don't get upset," David says. "He probably got held up at work."

139

"It's *late*," Donald hisses.

Most of the tables are already occupied. By men. In couples, in groups. Eating, chatting, drinking. They appear happily relaxed.

"This looks like a nice place," I tell Donald.

He snorts. "A dump. And look at *him*. . . ."

My eyes follow his to a brawny, thick-featured man in a linen suit leaning against the service bar. "Our proprietor," Donald sneers. "He devotes his waking hours to impressing all us poor pansies with his raging heterosexuality. How many women he had before breakfast." He snorts again. "Meanwhile, he can't stop twitching when he sees some of the men who walk in here. But he'd rather be dismembered than come out. Fucking coward," he mutters. Then he raises his voice. "What's he doing owning a place like this, I'd like to know . . . ?"

A waiter approaches Donald, leans, and speaks into his ear.

"Time for the first set," Donald says, standing. "Never mind. As soon as I'm done we'll go somewhere decent."

He crosses the dance floor and seats himself at the piano. "Good evening. Welcome to the Skyline Cafe. I'm Donald Neilson, but"—he points to a blond young man at a table nearby—"*you* can call me Donny. Anytime." There's a low murmur of congenial laughter. "I'd like to begin by introducing our host, Mr. Tony Pastori"—a scattering of cool applause—"and I'd like to dedicate the opening song to him."

Donald launches into "All the Sad Young Men," singing in a whispery tenor. Pastori leaves the service bar and moves heavily toward Donald. Donald breaks into an upbeat version of "I Left My Heart in San Francisco." Several men in the audience applaud in appreciation.

"Sorry I'm late." The dark-haired man from the photograph is sliding into Donald's empty chair.

"Good to see you, James." Introductions are whispered. He grips my hand with cool fingers. He has strong, well-defined features. When he smiles fine lines appear around his eyes and crease his tanned cheeks. He looks like a model or a movie star.

"I'd like to dedicate this next song to a close friend," Donald announces. He glowers in our direction. He sings from the score of *Kiss Me Kate:*

"But I'm always true to you, darlin', in my fashion, Yes, I'm always true to you, darlin', in my way."

"He's pissed, eh?" James chuckles. He applauds loudly. Donald inclines his head with mock dignity and segues into a medley of Gershwin tunes.

Only a few diners remain, lingering over coffee, when Donald finally rejoins us. He squeezes James's shoulder and sits down next to him.

"You were wonderful, Donald," I tell him.

His long nose wrinkles in distaste. "Ugh. Later on I'll play you some of *my* music. This is just half a step up from washing dishes for a living."

"Donald is a superb musician," James says warmly.

"You!" Donald whirls on him. "Where the hell were you?"

James smiles, shakes his head. "Donald . . ." he says. His voice is tender, but the warning is clear.

"Let's get out of here if we're going," David says quickly.

"Ramparts?" Donald asks.

"Fine." James nods, standing.

"Wait . . ." Michael throws me a doubtful look. "I don't know . . . Ramparts is a little . . ."

David tilts his head back impatiently. "Ramparts is fine. She'll be all right." He thrusts his face close to Michael.

141

"We all want to go there, Michael. If there's a problem, we can see you and Annie later. . . ."

I stand up. "No, we want to come too. Don't we?"

Michael gets slowly to his feet. "Maybe Annie would rather wait for us back at—" The look on my face stops him. "I guess it will be okay."

Donald laughs. "You'll adore it."

"Well, I like the name."

Donald puts his hand on my shoulder and guides me to the door.

14

WAREHOUSES THROW jagged shadow. across cracked pavement. A dog growls quietly at us from behind a twisted fence. Overhead the freeway bridge shudders and moans. We walk without speaking. Uneasiness flutters in my stomach. I wish that Michael would talk to me. Or even walk beside me. The red-haired woman has abandoned me. I move closer to Donald.

"Here," Donald says.

The man guarding the door frowns. "She can't come in here."

"She's with me." Donald smiles seductively.

"She can't come in." He points to my feet. "Insurance regulations. No open shoes."

Donald lays two fingers on the man's chest. He leans close and whispers to him. The man's face turns hungry. He slides away from the door. "She can't go on the dance floor, though."

"What did you say to him?" I whisper.

Donald winks at James. "A word or two." James rolls his eyes in amused exasperation.

The heavy metal door is opened. Sounds rush out at us: shouts, laughter, music. Acid-yellow light burns my eyes.

In a high, narrow packing crate of a room, men press against each other. Jammed in tight, they crowd the bar, shove in the aisles, spill into the dining area. Music shrieks. As we press through the crowd hips push against mine, a hand brushes my breast but with no intent, no reaction. The smell of beer and sweat. Leather. Too-sweet cologne. Near my ear a burst of shrill laughter:

"Darling . . ."

"Bitch!"

"This way." Donald shepherds us to a tiny table at the very back, close to the dance floor.

"Drinks on me," he shouts above the racket.

"What can I get y'all?"

David stares at the muscular, bare-chested waiter.

"Vodka, tonic," Michael says deliberately. "All around."

"I'd rather have wine. . . ."

Donald orders a carafe of white wine for me. "Chardonnay, right?" He's staring into the crowd at the edges of the dance floor.

A thin figure glides in and out of the crowd. A glimpse of blond hair . . . My breath catches. Is it *him*? Stalking us . . . his pale eyes behind the rimless glasses fixed on Michael. . . .

". . . North Coast Chardonnay . . ." Donald is holding a glass toward me. "Hello, Annie, hello . . . ?"

"What is it?" David asks. "You look upset."

Michael swivels in his chair to look at me. "What's wrong?"

"She saw someone. Didn't you, Annie?"

"Did you, sweetheart? Who?" Michael looks puzzled. Real or pretend?

"You're so cagey, Michael. So innocent." David takes a long pull on his vodka.

"What the hell is he talking about?" Michael appeals to me.

"Who was it you saw, Annie? Someone you know? A friend of the family?" David's mouth is ugly.

"I didn't see anyone. . . ." Did I? Was it him?

The music is so loud, it's hard to think. . . .

"What's the game, Michael? Who did you tell to meet you here?"

"Don't be absurd."

"Or is it someone who lives up here . . . ?"

"You're paranoid. I—"

"Children, children . . ." Donald thrusts a fresh drink at Michael.

"An old college pal? You have so many old college friends. . . ." David's voice is rising. Several amused faces turn in our direction.

"Donald, tell him—" Michael pleads.

"I don't have to take—"

"David, you're being—"

"Who was it? I bet I know—"

"Would you like to dance?" James stands above me; his movie-star smile flashes like neon.

Donald waves airily. "Don't give it a thought. You angels just go ahead and cut a rug or get down or whatever the youth of America is doing these days. I'll straighten things out between Hedda and Louella." He moves his chair between David and Michael. "Now, you two . . ."

James leads me to the dance floor. He's the only man in the place wearing a suit and tie. His dark hair is combed in the neat style of a 1950s leading man. The music slows to a syrupy ballad. He puts his arm around me; I rest my hand on his broad shoulder. His cheek rests against mine; he smells of sandalwood. His hand at my waist is gentle and firm; he leads me in a set of smooth, old-fashioned dance moves. My mother and father gliding alone on the dance floor, guests of honor at the Yacht Club's Admiral's Ball. . . .

"Who did you see, actually? Was it one of Michael's ex-lovers?" I miss a step, lurch against him. "Of course not! Michael doesn't have—people like that in his life."

James's smile flashes on and off. "Of course not." He leads me into a slow spin. "You're a good dancer," he says. "You and Michael must go dancing a lot."

"Michael doesn't dance. I learned from my father."

He laughs mysteriously at this. "How long are you planning to stay? We ought to show you around a little bit. . . ." James makes cordial small talk, tells me about his public relations job, his recent trip to Vermont. Around us the men are moving slowly to the music. They have their arms around each other. Some of them have taken their shirts off. A heavy scent rises off their gleaming bodies. They hold each other and move together to the music.

"James . . . ? That boy I saw—I thought I saw—he has absolutely nothing to do with Michael."

"It doesn't matter."

"It matters to me."

"Whatever you say, Annie." He flashes his neon smile.

Near us a young man laughs. He runs his hands over his partner's bare back. They sway to the music, eyes closed. . . .

"Everyone is looking at me, James," I whisper. "I can feel them."

"No one's looking at you," he says.

Beside us two men are kissing; their mouths are pressed hungrily together. "It's very close in here, James." My

146

heart hammers. The air is too thick to breathe. "Can we go outside for a little while?"

In the alley he pulls an empty crate up against the wall. "Sit down. Are you cold?" He drapes his jacket over my shoulders. "You're shivering."

"I'm fine." I wish he would stop smiling so solicitously. I wish he would stop stroking my shoulder.

"You know, Annie . . ." He takes a pipe from his pocket and begins to fill it. His face is set in an expression of tender confidentiality. ". . . I think it's very moving, the way you want to protect Michael."

"I'm not—"

"I don't just mean your loyalty," he says hastily. "I think you're a terrific lady."

"I've heard that a lot this weekend."

He looks startled. "Well, it's true. Michael's a very lucky man."

I shrug his jacket off my shoulders and hand it to him. "I don't need this."

He takes his jacket from my hands. "I wish my wife could meet you."

"You're married?" I look at him with new interest. "Where is she? Why didn't you bring her with you tonight?"

"I mean I *was* married. We've been divorced awhile."

"Oh." Of course. Bastard. "You left her?"

"She left me."

"I see." Yes. She pleaded with him to give Donald up. Over and over again. I'll do anything if you just give him up. And then finally: If you don't give him up, I'm going to leave. . . . "I'll bet Donald was happy about that."

"Actually, she left before I knew Donald. Before I even

147

knew I wanted a Donald." He strikes a match and touches it to his pipe. "She fell in love with somebody else . . . and took off. I thought I would go crazy, I loved her so much."

At the far end of the alley a door opens and shuts; music blares and fades.

James runs his hands through his hair. "Ready to go back inside?"

"If you loved her so much, why didn't you find another woman? Instead of Donald."

He looks at me for a moment, then sinks down beside me on the crate. "I don't know. I'm not sure how it happened. I was lonely. . . . But it wasn't only that." He shrugs. "Maybe it would have happened anyway."

In the coarse light of the streetlamp I notice for the first time the slight sagging of his jawline, the furrows in his cheeks. "Does she know about Donald?"

His eyes narrow in a sudden spasm of pain. "Yes. She does. She won't let me see my son."

"You have a child! How old?"

"Nine."

Same age as Emily. "I'm sorry. I didn't know. . . . I'm sorry if I said anything rude. . . ."

The neon has faded; his smile is sad and shy. "His name is Jamie. James, Jr. I'm fighting her, of course. I've got a lawyer. . . ."

"That's terrible. I'd never keep Michael away from his kids."

"That's why you're such a special person."

"James . . . when you finally get to see your son, are you going to tell him about Donald?"

He says nothing.

"Are you?"

He stands up and holds his hand out to me. "We really should go back inside. Your husband's going to think I eloped with you."

"*Are* you?"

"Are you going to tell yours about Michael?"

A gust of wind rattles the metal trash cans against the wall. A door slams on someone's hoarse, indecipherable shouts at the far end of the alley.

"Let's go back inside," he says.

I move away from him. "You go ahead. I'll be there in a little while."

He nods.

I sit down on the crate, watching him move down the alley and knock to be let back into the building.

I should have said, Of course I'll tell Emily and Robin. They'll understand. They already love David. . . .

Will I? *How* would I tell them? Which words?

But it doesn't mean anything. Not really.

What will I say? *Your daddy* . . .

Your daddy *what*?

Will they hate him?

Will they forgive him?

Will they grow up to be like him . . . ?

A black-and-white cat scuttles across the alley like a piece of blown newspaper.

Michael's not like the other men here. . . .

My father in his low-comedy, lisping falsetto: "Oh, my dear, you look divine." His hoarse laughter. His outrage. *Look at those pansies, Belle. What makes a kid turn out like that?*

Brutal fathers, dear—poor things, my mother says with relish.

What will I tell them?

149

I wish the red-haired woman would come back. I close my eyes tight, try to summon her voice. Silence.

I slide off the crate and hurry to the front door. Michael will help me. He'll put his arm around me. Maybe we won't ever have to tell anyone. . . .

"Sorry, miss, I can't let you in." The doorman looms in front of me. "No open shoes."

"We've been through this already." I take an impatient step closer to the door; the doorman moves in front of me.

"I came with friends just a while ago. Donald said something to you, and you let me in."

"No open shoes."

"This is ridiculous." I move forward. He moves forward. "Don't you remember?"

He gazes over my head, his mouth set.

"Why don't you let me go in and get my friends? Then we can straighten this out. . . ."

He folds his arms. "Sorry." Is that a smile at the corners of his mouth?

"One of them is my husband!" I burst out.

He stares at the streetlamps.

"This is crazy."

I climb onto the crate again and lean back against the wall. I can feel the rough brick through my silk blouse. A sea-scented wind has come up from the bay. I wish I'd kept James's jacket. From where I sit I can see the doorman pacing back and forth, looking pleased, occasionally sipping soda from a can. I send him a poisonous look. I settle down to wait. Michael will come looking for me.

I'm shivering by the time they emerge from Ramparts, looking around in alarm. Michael rushes to me, taking off his sweater and wrapping it around me. He keeps his arm over my shoulder. James walks on my other side, apologizing for "deserting" me.

"You poor angel!" Donald bustles. "We'll take you right home and you can get all nice and warm."

David walks a little behind us. His face is impassive.

I feel soothed and cared for, and I leave my anger behind in the alley. At Michael's suggestion, we take a taxi back to Donald's apartment.

15

CANDLES BURN in the windows. Harpsichord music shimmers and dances. Donald brews coffee, pours brandy. James and Michael chat over their cups. David dozes, stretched out on the rug. The silver and blue fish glide in their aquarium.

I'm not fooled by any of this.

Michael's smile is as fragile as the Limoges cup in his hands. Behind his closed eyes, David seethes. The sound of the harpsichord is like breaking glass.

Donald and James. David and Michael. I can feel their impatience.

"Well," Donald says. He smiles helplessly.

"That record's very scratched. You'll ruin your needle." James's finger traces over and over the flower pattern on the cushion.

"Well." Donald corks the brandy bottle. He glances covertly at me. He uncorks the bottle, pours.

David's hands are clenched on the Indian rug. Michael's cup trembles in its saucer.

Donald's eyes meet James's. "Well," Donald says. "It's getting late. Maybe we ought to—"

"I'd like to hear some of your music." My voice quavers, too loud. "Wouldn't you, Michael?" We have to leave, Michael. *Now.*

"Sure. Great. You bet." He refuses to look at me.

Donald hesitates, watching James. He taps his lips with a long, thin index finger. "Maybe one of the shorter pieces . . ."

His music is full of anger. When he's finished he sits at the keyboard for a moment, his head lowered, as if he's trying to regain his usual self.

"I loved that," I lie. His music made me feel as if I were being pulled inside him, forced to share his pain. "Donald, your music is *exquisite.*"

"Do you think so?" He's pleased; he comes to sit near me. Do *you* play?" I shake my head. "You have good hands for for it."

I ask him about his musical training. He tells me about his father, who made him practice five hours a day every day, slapping his hands when Donald struck the wrong keys. I ask him to tell me more about his childhood.

David sighs. He flings his arm over his eyes and turns his face to the wall. James stands abruptly. "I'm going to clean up the kitchen. Want to give me a hand, Michael?" They go into the kitchen together.

Donald doesn't seem to notice. He talks on about his father's brilliance and cruelty; his own eyes shine with cruelty and brilliance. ". . . But then he died and I could play my own stuff. I started to fall in love with the sounds I was making. . . ."

"Michael and I have come up with a solution." James stands over us.

"To what?" I stand to face James.

"To the lodgings problem," he says easily.

"There is no 'lodgings problem.' We're staying here.

153

Donald invited us." When I turn to him for support Donald gives me a vague smile and turns away to tidy the pillows on the window seat.

"Where's Michael? I want to talk to him. . . . You *did* invite us, Donald, didn't you?"

"Yes . . ." He looks forlornly at James.

"There's no problem," James says heartily. "Donald, you and I will stay at Roger's. Michael and David can have my place. And Annie can sleep here." He smiles, triumphant.

"Where's Michael?" My voice is strident; my hands and my legs are shaking.

"In the bathroom." James stares at me. "Is anything wrong? Did I say something . . . I thought . . ." He turns to Donald. "Michael told me—I mean . . ."

Donald moves toward the bedroom. "I'll need to put clean sheets on the bed."

I yank open the bathroom door. He's leaning heavily on the sink, staring into the oak-framed mirror.

"What's going on, Michael?"

He keeps his head down and mumbles. "I'm going to James's with David. You'll stay here."

"You're not really going to do this?"

He turns to face me. He looks dazed and frightened. "Yes," he whispers. "David said . . ." he straightens his shoulders "and he's right—no more games. No more lies. You understand, now. You know I love you. You have to accept. Everything's going to be open from now on." He lowers his eyes. "I owe David something, too, you know—"

"No!"

"Don't be this way, don't spoil—"

"Let me come with you."

"You're crazy."

"What's going on here?" James's worried face appears in the doorway.

"Annie's upset."

"What is it? Isn't she feeling well?" Donald joins James. "She looks a bit faint."

David stands aloof in the hallway, holding Michael's coat.

"Maybe she should lie down for a few minutes." Donald takes my arm.

"I'm not sick, leave me alone!" Where is the red-haired woman? "Don't leave me here, Michael. . . ."

David is at my side, his face close to mine. The others have retreated behind the closed bathroom door. He speaks slowly and deliberately. "You have to let him do this, Annie," he says. His eyes are like the old David's. "No more pretending. You know that Michael sleeps with me. I know he sleeps with you. I've had to learn to accept. Now you have to. If we tell each other the truth, maybe we can all be friends again. Let him know it's okay, Annie. You have no choice. . . ."

And if you do . . . Her voice, rich and sensuous, embraces me. *If you let Michael do this, he'll love you for it. And David will love you too. Neither of them will ever leave you again.*

You've come. Why did you stay away so long?

She smiles and brushes away my tears. *Send him off with your blessings. It will be worth it, I promise.* I can smell her perfume—pine forests, ocean, earth. . . .

"Tell him," David says. Michael stands in front of me, pale with misery. "Tell him it's okay," David hisses in my ear.

Go on.

"Michael, I'll be fine here."

Michael nods wordlessly. He turns and walks to the front door.

"In the morning, we'll have breakfast together." There's no hint of triumph in David's small smile. "Good night, Annie." His lips brush my cheek.

James and Donald wave their good nights. I hear the front door close, hear their footsteps down the stairs.

In the bedroom there is one lamp burning. I lie down with my clothes on and pull the blankets over me.

The bed is a pale island in the shadowed room.

You're certain he'll love me for this?

Shhh. Yes. Sleep now.

"Hon-ee!" A shriek of laughter like a scream of pain. I sit up in bed.

"Dickie!"

"Fuck you, darlin'!"

Men are calling to each other in the street. Music flares. A motorcycle revs.

"Come on down here, bitch."

I turn on my side, away from the window. On the floor beside the bed are a candle, a book of matches, and a squat bottle labeled Almond Love Oil.

I open the bottle and pour a little on my fingers. Cool and slippery. Do Donald and James use it? The sheets smell faintly of almonds. Slick with oil, Donald and James . . .

"I'm waiting for you, baby."

Outside, under this window, men are hunting each other.

In this bed, Donald and James . . .

"Come on, baby."

The blankets are suffocating me. I tear them off.

"Come *on*, baby."

David and Michael?

"*No!*" My voice tears a ragged hole in the silence.

Seeping from the walls, the emptiness fills the room, black, obliterating. I struggle for breath, I can hear myself panting as though I'm being pursued.

I find my shoes and coat. When the front door locks behind me, I remember that I have no key.

The night is stunningly clear. From the top of Castro I look down the street. The shops and restaurants are closed. The movie house is dark.

But the street is alive.

Men wait in doorways. Lean against walls. Pose on street corners.

The ones they wait for walk the street in slow deliberation. Up and down. Making choices. Being chosen?

I walk, too, shivering in my coat. Why have I come here?

Eyes watch me—an intruder in the jungle. . . .

A man dressed in black leather stares at me from an open first-floor window. His eyes rake my body.

A car slows at the curb alongside me, then speeds away.

Rustle of silk, high heels tap on the pavement . . .

Sniggering laughter, conspiratorial whispers . . .

"You're on the wrong street, honey."

I have a right to be here! I have a right to *see*. . . .

Halfway down the street, between a closed restaurant and an unoccupied store—a young man turns down an alley.

I *have* to see.

I slip into the shelter of a doorway. Keep myself hidden. I can hear my own ragged breathing. In the deep shadows of the alley, figures are moving, coming together, parting, coming together again, dissolving into the dark.

Whispers . . .

I press myself into the doorway.

In the corner . . . one figure crouches, his arms around the waist of another. His open mouth . . .

157

There . . . against the wall, lit by the faint glow of a nightlight in the window above. Men moving together, moving faster, moving inside tight, muscled bodies . . .

Michael, David . . .

At the bottom of the hill, a blur of neon—the Station. All-Night Coffee Shop.

Only when I hurl myself, gasping, at the glass front door do I realize I've been running. I slide into a red vinyl booth. Yellow plastic roses stare up at me from a knobby white-glass vase. The mirrored cases hold coconut-custard and cherry pies, green Jell-O and halved cantaloupes.

The sleepy-looking waiter wears a badge that says "Stanley."

My heartbeat slows to normal, my shaking hands grow still. I order coffee. The green ceramic cat with the clock in its middle says three-fifteen.

The coffee shop is almost empty. Two men share a corner booth. Busy over their food, they barely speak. In another booth a rumpled gray-haired man reads a book. A policeman eats doughnuts at the counter. Not far from me sits a woman. She is writing in a notebook, drinking coffee, smoking a cigarette and nibbling at a muffin all at once. Comforted by the presence of another woman, I shrug out of my heavy coat. Someone has left a newspaper behind. In an unexpected agony of self-consciousness I stand—I glance at the customers; no one is watching me—and retrieve the paper. *Nightlife: An Entertainment Guide*.

As I finish the last of my coffee I feel eyes on me. I look up from the movie ads, cabaret bills. . . . The woman is watching me with a quizzical half-smile, trying to catch my eye. As soon as I surrender a glance, she breaks into a bold grin and nods her head in greeting. Embarrassed, I return a faint nod and retreat behind my paper. *Beach Blanket Boys* . . .

"Sorry to disturb you . . ." The voice is husky, rushed, full of energy and curiosity. "My name is Claire Kelly, by the way." She's petite but she seems to vibrate with life and power. She stands over me, one hand extended.

"Hello." I take her small, hard hand.

"Do you mind if I sit down?" she asks, clearing a place for herself. She has dark hair that flows over her shoulders like a girl's; she's probably thirty-five. Her eyes are bright gray, rebellious. A lighted cigarette dangles from her huge mouth. She's dressed in a blue ski parka, black tights, and an enormous red sweater. Her hands punch the air when she speaks. "Go on eating, don't let me stop you." She nods toward the heaped tangle of camera, flashes, light meters on her table. "I'm a photojournalist. Free-lance at the moment, but never mind, the swine will regret it. I specialize in photo essays—you know, character stories. I'm doing a book. I love to come here late at night, I can always pick up on some kind of angle. Stanley . . . !"

She orders coffee refills for both of us. "Now you know about me"—she pours cream into my cup and hands it to me—"I want to know about you." She grins. "I can't figure you out. Look at you." She shakes her head. "Obvious suburban housewife, shirtwaist dress, spectator sandals, alone at three A.M. in this place." She calls across the restaurant to the short-order cook emerging from the kitchen. "Carlos!" He waves happily. "*Come sta?* We need pie. How old is the banana cream you're hiding in there?" He laughs. "Two, then, *Va bene?*" She turns to me. "You want ice cream? Yeah. Two," she calls, "with two sides of cioccolata."

She leans forward, her elbows on the table, her chin in

159

her hands. "What did you say your name was?" Her gray eyes seem to be scrutinizing and recording every detail of my face.

"Annie," I murmur. "Morrow."

"So, Annie Morrow, what are you doing at the Station?"

"Is this an interview for your book?"

She grins at me. "Nope. Just curiosity." Her hands are beautifully shaped, very brown, freckled. She wears a heavy gold ring on the middle finger of her left hand. "So . . . ?"

The waiter sets dishes of pie and ice cream in front of us. To my amazement I begin to eat.

"I got locked out," I say through mouthfuls of pie.

She raises her eyebrows.

"I'm here with my husband and a friend. We were visiting some people and I went out to get something from the store and got locked out."

"You were there alone? Where was your husband?" She pushes her dessert toward me.

"You haven't touched it."

"I changed my mind. Go ahead. So, what were you doing alone in these people's apartment?"

"It was a business thing. They had to go out to a business dinner." I finish my pie and start on hers. I eat with my head lowered, looking only at the food.

"Late, for a business dinner."

"They're in the movie business. I mean, they own a theater. They're always out late. . . ."

She leans back in her seat. "I see." She watches me until I've finished. "Do you have children, Annie?"

I look up, startled. "Two. Why?"

"I thought you might. Where are they?"

"With a friend, back in Los Angeles. For the weekend."

She stares at me a long time without saying anything.

"You're really pretty pushy." I falter. The indignation won't come. Instead I bow my head under her scrutinizing smile. My fingers shred the paper napkin in my lap.

"What are you going to do for the rest of the night?" she asks finally.

"Stay here, I guess."

She sighs and shakes her head. "Jesus," she breathes. Then: "Would you like to come back to my studio? It's very near."

A lifetime of admonitions against trusting strangers races through my mind. "Yes," I say. "I'd like that."

I help her gather her equipment. She insists on paying our check. "You're an out-of-towner—you get treated."

Outside, the streets are empty. They sky is lightening. Claire zips up her parka and points toward a hill climbing steeply ahead of us. Under a pastel-pink and gray dawn sky, I follow her.

A trolley car clatters distantly in the street below. Claire leads me past a row of old-fashioned homes until she comes to the foot of a flight of steps leading up to a tall wooden house painted primrose yellow and blue. She looks up at the house, then turns to me and smiles. Beside her a tiny garden blooms.

16

CLAIRE'S STUDIO is a narrow high-ceilinged room on the top floor. Thick black shades cover the beautifully ornate bay windows. Cameras and floodlights stand against a wall hung with photographer's background paper. On the other side of the room a white cat sleeps curled on a sagging white sofa. Paper-white narcissi bloom in a white ceramic pot. The walls are bare except for a large black-and-white photograph of a nude.

"Make yourself comfortable." She hangs our coats on a brass hat rack and disappears through a swinging door.

I sit on the sofa. Immediately the cat wakes, stretches, and moves into my lap, where she settles down to resume her nap.

"Her name is Mitsou." Claire reappears carrying two bottles of wine and two glasses.

"*Salud*." She sits cross-legged on the floor; her eyes are fixed on my face. She's watching me.

I wish she would raise the shades, open the windows. The bottom of the wineglass is wet, I dry it on my skirt. "That's a very nice photograph." What if Michael is looking for me?

"Did you take it?"

"Umm-hmm."

"It's very nice." Michael has no idea where I am. No one knows where I am. "I like your place."

"Thank you."

"I love these old Victorians." Did I hear her lock the door behind us when we came in?

"You haven't touched your wine."

"Oh." I raise the glass to my lips. There have been cases . . . I've read about them. A woman lures an unsuspecting woman to her home where her psychotic boyfriend waits . . . "I'm sorry, what did you say?"

"I asked if you wanted anything to eat."

"No. Do you have a telephone?"

"You've never done anything like this before, have you? Gone home with anyone before you were properly introduced."

"Why do you assume that?" I can feel my face burning. "You can't say that—you don't know anything about me."

"I know you're very nervous."

"Well, a little. I don't know anything about you. . . ."

"We're even." She kneels Japanese fashion on the floor beside the sofa. "Let's find out. I'll begin."

The cat sighs and curls deeper into my lap. Claire's gray eyes travel over my face.

"Why do you call yourself Annie?"

"It's my name."

"Isn't it Anne, or Anna?"

Again I flush with indignation and humiliation. "My name's Annie. That's what everybody calls me."

"What do you call yourself?"

"Annie!"

She makes a face. "*I'm* going to call you Anne. Okay, Anne. Your turn."

"What?"

"To ask a question."

I watch her pour herself a glass of wine. I try to think of a question that will reduce *her* to shame. She watches me watching her. Her smile is unabashed, unafraid. "Well?"

"I can't think of anything," I mutter. "Are you married?"

"No. My turn. Where's your husband tonight?"

"I already told you. At a business meeting. My turn. Why aren't you married?"

"No one ever asked me."

"Really?"

"No questions out of turn. I go. Is the friend with you and your husband a woman?"

"No. Why didn't anyone ever ask you? You're very pretty."

She throws her head back and laughs. I stiffen. "No one ever asked me because I'm stubborn and mean." She laughs again, and I find myself returning a small smile.

"I'm sure that's not true," I say, primly polite.

"Yeah. It's true. My turn. Why did you get married?"

"Because I—"

"No, don't say because you loved him. Lots of people love lots of other people and don't get married. Why did you?"

"Because—" I break off and meet her eyes. Her stare is unwavering. I lower my gaze and try to remember. Michael was handsome. He was bright and talented. I thought I'd have a good life with him. . . . "I knew he would take good care of me."

"Ah." She drains her wineglass. "And does he?"

"That's two in a row. It's my turn."

"Sorry." For the first time, her smile includes me. "You learn fast. Okay, go on."

"Do you wish you had children?"

"Sometimes. What makes you happy?"

"Painting. And my children, of course."

"Of course. Your turn."

"What makes *you* happy?"

"Waking up alone. Next?"

"Claire . . ." Why do I want to ask this? I feel like a fool. . . . "What do you think of me?"

Her smile disappears, her eyes soften. "I think you're sweet."

"Is that all?" It's a cry of anguish, and it shocks me. "Sorry, sorry. That was out of turn. Go on."

"Why is it important to you what I think?"

"Because . . ." Because you seem brave and smart and free, and I want you to like me. . . . "*Is* that all you think of me? Sweet?"

She shakes her head. When she speaks her voice is gentle. "No. I think you're sad and frightened and trying very hard to be brave. I think you could be a fabulous woman—strong, full of passion. Also, I think you're beautiful."

Sudden violent sobs shake me. I can't stop. I can hear the sounds I'm making, feel my chest heaving, but I can't find my mind. I can't think.

At the end of it, when I finally force the sobbing to subside into trembling sighs, I realize that Claire is beside me holding my hand.

"Better?"

"Yes. I'm so sorry."

"You're going to be all right," she says. "I can tell."

"Do you really think so?"

"Yes." She smiles. "I really think so." Concern has changed the look of her face. She seems younger, more vulnerable.

Shakily, I return her smile. "I don't think you're so mean and stubborn. I think you're sweet."

165

Her gray eyes appraise me. "Do you?"

"Yes."

"How sweet?"

"What?"

"*How* sweet do you think I am?" Her smile is a challenge.

I pull away from her. "I don't know—"

"All right, all right. Questions, then. My turn." She slips off the sofa onto the floor. She opens the second bottle of wine. I watch with fascination the way her small strong hands deftly uncork the bottle. She finishes what's left in her glass and pours out another. "Your husband's gay, isn't he?"

"No, of course he's not!" She *is* mean and stubborn. I push the cat off my lap. My navy skirt is covered with a layer of white hair. "God, don't you ever brush your cat?"

"Yes. My turn again. Does your husband leave you alone a lot?"

"Yes. No, I mean. Sometimes . . . just what's normal in a marriage." I feel as if she's used up all the air in the room. My eyes burn. . . . "Can we open a window?"

"Yes. My turn again."

"Really, this is *not* fair—"

"My house, my rules." She smiles, and her face looks like the white cat's, who is posed sphinx-like, in front of the door. "This man, this friend who's with your husband now, does your husband sleep with him?" She crosses the room, raises the shade, and throws open the window. Chilly, harbor-scented air fills the high, white room. The light is grainy; the streetlamps are growing dimmer against the lightening sky.

"I don't have to answer your questions."

"That's true," she says placidly. "You don't have to answer *my* questions."

"They're very rude."

She holds up a hand to silence me. "You pass then. My turn again. Is your husband gay?"

"No! Are you?"

Her wineglass is arrested in midair. She sets it down carefully on the floor. "You're braver than I thought."

"I'm sorry. I don't know why I said that." My heart races, I can feel it lurch against my chest. "You don't have to answer."

She shifts so she can look at me. "Yes," she says. "Sometimes I make love to women."

I have to turn away from her clear, calm gaze.

"My turn," she says. "Does that upset you?"

The white cat, stalking imaginary prey, leaps at her feet.

"No." I swallow.

"Go on," she prompts. "Your turn."

"Why?"

"Why women, you mean?"

I nod.

"Because women are more interesting."

"Is that all?"

"No," she laughs. "They're prettier too." She stands slowly. "My turn." She moves to the sofa and leans over me. She smells of wine and patchouli. She brings her face close to mine. "Would you like to know what it's like to make love to a woman?"

I shrink back against the cushions, sudden panic fluttering in my chest. "No."

"Aren't you curious?"

"No." My eyes are locked on her hand, which is moving slowly toward my leg.

"I think you are."

"No." I leap to my feet. "I'd better leave. My husband—"

"We're not talking about your husband, we're talking about *you*." She looks up at me with a playful, languorous smile.

"No. I don't want to. No."

"Jesus." She laughs. "All right." She shakes her head. "All right." She pats the daybed. "Sit down. You're scared to death. Come on, I'm not going to jump you."

I perch rigidly on the edge of the bed.

She puts her hand over mine. "May I?" she asks archly.

"I'm not . . . I'm sorry if you thought . . . I shouldn't have come here. . . ."

"Shhh. It's all right. Really." She strokes my hand, her smile is amused and kind. "I would have sworn . . . But never mind." She leans over me, her long hair falls over my face. "You're so sweet. A sweet baby." Her soft mouth presses against my cheek. She slides her arm around my shoulders. "Get some sleep," she says. "Everything will be better in the morning."

"I can't sleep here." The weight of her arm on my shoulder fills me with a jangled trepidation.

"Of course you can. There's nothing to worry about. Lie down. I'll rub your back." She pushes me gently down on the daybed. "Close your eyes," she commands. Her small, strong hands knead my shoulders. "Your husband must be crazy," she murmurs. "You're beautiful." Her hands stroke my back.

Unbelievably, I feel my body loosening, my mind sliding into sleep. I close my eyes.

"Don't worry about a thing," Claire croons.

17

WHEN I open my eyes I see Claire in a white terry-cloth robe, standing at the sun-filled windows, gazing out at the city, stroking the cat, who grooms herself on the sill.

Before I can clear away the sleep-mist enough to appreciate the picture they make, panic slices through me.

"Good morning." Claire turns, smiling, to me. "Coffee? Hot chocolate?"

"What time is it?" My voice is harsh. "I've got to call my husband."

The cat bounds onto the bed and begins to knead my pillow.

"I have to call—he doesn't know where I am."

Claire sits beside me on the sofa bed. "Hi." She leans toward me.

I jerk away from her. "What time is it?"

She looks at me for a long moment. She stands and tightens the cord on her bathrobe. "Nine-thirty, the telephone's on the floor over there—there's coffee in the kitchen. I'm going to take a shower." She walks briskly into the bathroom.

What will I tell Michael? What will he think when he finds me gone?

I can hear the shower running in the bathroom, Claire's muffled singing.

Still wrapped in the blanket, I kneel on the floor beside the phone. It won't matter what I say to him. Somehow, he'll know. I spent the night sleeping in a woman's arms. I dial with trembling fingers.

I long to shout for Claire to come back. If she's beside me when I call, I'll say the right things. . . .

When I've counted twenty rings I replace the receiver on its hook.

"Are you all right?" Claire stands above me. She smells of Ivory Soap, her hair is wrapped in a blue bath towel.

"He's not there," I whisper.

Claire looks as if she's going to laugh, then changes her mind. "Well, good," she says carefully. "Then you don't have to rush away. You can have some breakfast. How do you like your eggs?"

I don't understand. He should be there. Maybe he's been calling Donald's apartment. . . .

"Bacon or Portuguese sausage? Or both?" Claire bustles in her tiny kitchen.

If he's called over there, he knows I'm not there. He might be frantic.

Claire breaks eggs into a bowl. Bacon and sausage hiss in a pan. "Why don't you go have a shower? This'll be ready soon."

"What will I tell him?" How will I explain . . . ?

Claire pulls the frying pan off the stove. I see her force annoyance into equanimity. "Look," she says. "You don't need to be so worried about him. Obviously he's not all that worried about you."

"Don't say that. You don't know Michael, you don't

170

know what he feels." Where is he? Why isn't he there? The fury I thought was under control starts to seethe. I pace the studio, my blanket trailing behind me, stirring up motes of dust that dance in the sunlight pouring through the raised windows.

Claire takes me by the shoulders and sits me down on the only chair at a small white table by the window. She sets a plate of food in front of me. She eats standing, lounging against the windowsill.

"I didn't say that to upset you," she says. "I think it's an excellent thing when husbands and wives can give each other some breathing room. You're not eating. It's getting cold." She gives me a little prod with her bare foot. As she leans forward her robe falls slightly open. Her breast is small and very round, paler on the bottom where her bathing suit has hidden it from the sun. She sees me looking at her and smiles.

I feel myself flush with humiliation. The whisper in my head rustles like dead leaves . . . *sick.* . . .

Claire pours herself more coffee and butters a blueberry muffin. She feeds crumbs of it to the cat.

"You know, Anne," she says quietly. "Being curious about loving a woman doesn't make you a lesbian."

The word clatters like a knife dropped on a stone floor. I feel myself recoil. What would the red-haired woman say?

"You were lonely," she goes on. "Maybe wanting to experiment a little bit. Or maybe"—she shifts so she can look into my eyes—"wanting to punish your husband?"

"I *wasn't* curious. I didn't come here to—"

She puts her hand on my shoulder to silence my protest. "It doesn't matter. It's okay. Don't waste too much time over it. Do whatever it is you've always wanted to do." She grins impishly. "And if you ever decide to have a real go at this . . ."

I feel myself blushing furiously again. "You make it all sound so easy. It's not like that. It's not that simple."

"Sure it is. It's as easy as you make it."

"For you, maybe. Not for me."

Claire leans against the windowsill with her arms folded, studying me, her head tilted to one side, her black hair, free of its towel, spilling onto her shoulders. Behind her San Francisco is golden in the clear, crisp morning. The white cat sprawls in Claire's arms, its eyes the same blue as the sky over the city.

"I'd like to paint you just like that," I murmur before I have time to think myself silent.

Claire's face lights up. "I didn't know you were an artist."

I fumble with my cup. "I mentioned it last night. . . . I mean, I'm not really. I used to. Before . . ." I bury my face in my coffee cup.

"That's wonderful." She looks genuinely excited. In spite of myself, I'm moved. "I *knew* there was something about you." She goes to the table, begins to clear away the dishes. "You know what let's do today? Let's go over to Golden Gate Park. I'll bring my camera and we'll get you a sketch pad, and we'll wander and find fabulous things—"

"I'd love to do that!" Again the words burst out before I can hold them back. I draw a deep breath and set my jaw. "But I can't," I say firmly.

"Why not?" Claire challenges.

"What will I tell Michael?"

She slides the dishes into the sink with an exasperated shrug. "Why tell him anything? Just do what you want."

I stare at the patches of sunlight on the wooden floors. What do I want? The question makes me feel invaded.

"After the park we can go to a cafe, sit and watch the people, or read to each other. . . ." Claire's smile shines.

"But Michael . . ."

"Call him now. Tell him you got hungry last night and went out to get a bite. You ran into me. I can be an old college friend. You stayed overnight to reminisce."

I looked at her in amazement. "It is simple. At least when you do it, it's simple." I grin back at her. Claire's spirit is contagious—for the first time in a long while, I feel happy.

She hands me the telephone.

"I can't do it," I mumble.

"Of course you can." She puts the receiver in my hand.

I dial. What about Michael? Suppose he wants to spend the day with me? Suppose he's been looking forward to it?

But I want to be with Claire.

But I shouldn't lie to Michael. When he finds out he'll never trust me again. . . .

"Hello?" Donald's voice sounds far away and faintly startled. "Sweetie—where are you?"

"I'm with a friend, Donald. Is Michael there?" My voice trembles. Claire crouches on the floor beside me and begins to load film cans into her camera bag. She smiles at me and winks.

"Annie—"

"Hi, Michael . . ."

I'm astonished at how effortlessly I lie, how eagerly Michael believes me. Is he sure it's all right? He's sure. He sounds relieved that I have something to do. So I won't intrude on his day with David. . . . Anger flares. I can't let it devour my day. . . .

"Thank you for being so understanding, Michael."

"That's all right, honey. Go ahead, have a good time with your pal. We'll manage."

When I hang up I feel exhausted. Claire slaps my knee good-humoredly. "You're a trooper," she says.

I can't tell whether she's teasing me or not.

"Hurry up, get dressed. The light is wonderful today."

Golden Gate Park is stippled with light and color: green and yellow, red, pink, violet.

"Like a Seurat," I say.

Claire beams, as if the park were her personal accomplishment.

"Look . . . !" Claire points. The narrow, hedged path we've been following opens into a bright, grassy meadow. A group of young street performers dressed in imitation motley has assembled to rehearse. Singing bits of songs, calling out wisecracks to each other and to the small crowd gathered to watch, they juggle Indian clubs, turn cartwheels, balance on each other's shoulders to form a wavering human pyramid.

"Isn't it great?" She kneels on the grass focusing her camera. She darts here and there, snapping pictures, calling out directives to the performers, who laugh good-naturedly.

"I'm impressed," I tell her. "You seem like a professional."

"I am."

Then she sits beside me under a Spanish oak and watches me making quick action sketches of the troupe.

"You're very good."

"Not really." But I like these sketches. They have some of the liveliness of my old New York drawings. . . .

"Yes you are," Claire insists. "You're *very* good."

"Thank you." I flush with pleasure at her praise. "It's good to be drawing again."

"Come on." She pulls me to my feet.

We saunter along a gravel path lined with rose bushes. As we walk our hands brush from time to time. This secretive touching seems more intimate than if we openly held hands.

An elderly couple, he in a Panama hat, she in a lavender dress, approach us, moving in slow appreciation of the sunshine and the flower beds. They nod to us as we pass; the old woman gives us a sweet motherly smile.

Claire shows me the Japanese garden, with half-moon bridges spanning ponds on which lotus blossoms and water lilies bloom. We sip green tea in the little teahouse.

In the fragile-looking glass Victorian conservatory, I stare at rare orchids. Flesh-tinted petals.

"It's so steamy in here, Claire. I can hardly breathe."

"One more picture."

We eat ice cream by the side of a duck pond. Ducks and swans, even a forlorn-looking goose, clamoring for our leftovers.

Claire snaps pictures; I make lightning sketches, trying somehow to distill and capture the joy and relief of this afternoon.

The park is growing crowded: bicycle riders and skateboarders; ball players and couples pushing baby strollers, groups of tourists and a busload of children in uniform are all converging on the grassy lawn.

"Let's go," Claire says abruptly.

I rise obediently from the sketch I'd been making of a sparrow perched on a drinking fountain and follow Claire happily out of the park.

On the terrace of the cafe, under a flapping blue-and-white awning, Claire orders espresso for us.

I take out my pad and begin to draw the man at the next table. He's bearded and shabby, his hair is long and unkempt, and a magenta scarf billows around his neck. "Aging flower child," Claire says.

"But a great face. Lots of crags."

"Burnt out."

"But *interesting* burnt out."

Claire bursts into laughter. "You're really funny," she says. Her eyes soften. *"And* sweet." Her lips brush my cheek just as her hand passes over my hair.

At that moment I'm aware of the couple. In their mid-thirties, both of them tanned and attractive, dressed in expensive tennis outfits, they sit opposite us. The man has his arm protectively around the woman; she leans against him with the ease of familiarity. A diamond wedding band twinkles on her finger. They have been watching us. Now they bring their heads close together and whisper.

I stiffen. "Don't do that. They're *looking* at us," I hiss. Claire follows my gaze.

"Good," Claire says loudly. "Let's give them something to see." She grabs for my hand; I jerk it away.

"Don't, Claire—please—"

She looks annoyed. "They're yokels. Who cares?"

"I care." The back of my neck prickles. I can feel myself reddening. "I'm sorry, Claire," I whisper.

"It's nothing. You don't like to be looked at. Lots of folks feel the same. Don't worry about it." She sips her espresso. She smiles reassuringly. But the golden afternoon is flawed.

Claire begins to talk to me about moving to San Francisco.

"You seem to belong here," she tells me. "You could set yourself up a studio. . . ." She outlines the kind of life I could live, what the practical needs would be, how happy she thinks I'd become. I nod and arrange my face in a listening attitude. But my mind is captured by the couple.

What are they thinking? How must we look to them? Me in my "suburban housewife" dress, Claire in her blue jeans and baggy sweatshirt. I restrain a longing to rush to them and explain that I'm not that way, I'm a wife and mother.

"But I can't move up here, Claire," I almost shout. "I have a husband and children." I turn my head slightly to see how my words have registered with them.

Their table is empty. They've gone away without knowing the truth. *There were these two dykes in the cafe,* they'll tell their friends. . . .

"What is it?" Claire's concern penetrates my misery.

"I don't know." I can't meet her eyes.

"You make yourself a prisoner," she says. "A lot of women do that. You think you can't have a life because you have children." She opens a pack of cigarettes and offers me one. I start to refuse, then accept and let her light it for me. I stopped smoking years ago; this cigarette tastes acrid, burns my throat horribly. Looking at her, I draw deeply.

"I saw this woman once," I say cautiously. "At a bar. I thought she was so wonderful. . . ." Careful, careful . . . The sense of danger makes me dizzy. I can feel her presence, hiding in the shadows. "She had red hair, very beautiful." Not knowing what the woman would think of all this is making me rigid with tension. "I wanted to be like her."

You still do. The voice is calm. And absolutely unyielding.

Yes. I still do. I run my hands over my eyes in confusion.

"Are you okay? Do you have a headache?" Claire's voice sounds far away.

"No. I'm fine."

"And?"

"And . . . ?"

"What about this woman you were telling me about?"

"Oh. I think . . ." The woman's face is partly revealed now. Her eyes are cold. "I think you're . . . terrific too," I

177

finish weakly. What had I been going to say to Claire? I can't remember.

"Well, thanks." Claire orders two Cinzanos from the hovering waiter. "So, how about it? Will you think about moving up here?"

"I'll think about it," I mumble.

"No, really think about it." Claire squeezes my hand. This time I don't pull away. "Boy, if I were the kind of person who worried, I think I'd be doing a *lot* of it about you."

We smile at each other, and for a tiny moment the afternoon is wonderful again.

"Thank you," I say. I reach for my pad and charcoal. "Hold still."

When I've finished the drawing she studies it critically. "You made me too pretty," she says.

"No. You *are* pretty."

"I'm going to hang it over the sofa."

"No." I reach for the pad. "I need to keep it."

Her eyebrows raise at the passion in my voice. I try to laugh. "A souvenir. Of San Francisco."

"Here's another one." She fishes in her wallet and extracts a card, which she hands me. "When you're ready to get on with your life, you call me. I can put you up while you're looking for a place." She pats my hand playfully. "I can even accommodate your brats. If I have to."

We drink our aperitifs. Soon it will be time for me to meet Michael and David, time to start for home.

I feel my life sinking with the sun. The darkness slowly enveloping the sky wraps me too.

"I will move up here," I say sadly. "You'll see."

The red-haired woman sighs.

Claire looks beyond me into the distance.

18

I PUSH OPEN the smudged glass doors of The Station Coffee Shop—the place I chose to meet Michael and David. They sit at the counter, shoulders touching; Michael talking, David listening; a couple.

Suppose I turned around and left, walked back to Claire's studio. *I'm never going back home, Claire. . . .*

Would Michael even care?

"There you are." They turn, smile, make room for me to sit beside Michael. They offer me sandwiches, coffee. They show me the picnic Donald has packed for our trip home. They talk about the route we'll take; we'll drive inland, the fast route.

Michael seems flushed with suppressed excitement. David looks voluptuously self-satisfied.

They both go out of their way to be warm to me.

No one asks about Claire.

"I think we're ready to go, honey." Michael squeezes my shoulder. He stands.

The car races over the Bay Bridge, rushing toward Interstate 580. San Francisco is disappearing behind us; ahead of us red taillights stretch in an unbroken chain.

Michael and David sit in intimate silence in the front seat; David's arm is thrown, casually possessive, over Michael's shoulders.

Lying down in the back, I close my eyes. I'll lean forward over the front seat, burst through their coziness. Listen, I'll say. About Claire. She's not an old college roommate. I just met her. Claires loves women. Not like you. Or David. She thinks I'm smart and beautiful. And as soon as we get back to L.A., Michael, I'm going to gather up my things and the kids and get on the next plane back to San Francisco.

Tears will fill Michael's eyes.

But David will comfort him.

. . . David hangs his gray sweater and baggy tweeds in my closet. He lays his silver-handled brushes and his after-shave cologne on my glass vanity tray. He sleeps on my side of the bed. . . .

The breeze coming in the open window has lost its ocean scent; the landscape has flattened into a desert of billboards and weeds.

We pull into a gas station and park behind a half-empty Greyhound bus. David goes to get us some coffee.

"I'll call Maggie," I say.

The phone booth is littered with the pale husks of dead insects. Carefully I take Claire's card from my purse. Claire, it's Anne. I've made up my mind. I'm moving up there. I rehearse silently as I count the rings. On the fifth I hear her voice.

"Hello? Yes? Hello . . . ?"

My heart hammers. My breath roars in my ears.

"Hello?"

Gently, I replace the receiver.

"How are the kids?" Michael holds the car door open for me.

180

"Maggie wasn't home."

"It's late for them. . . . Where do you think . . . ?"

"A movie, probably. She said something about *Sleeping Beauty*."

David dozes, his head lolls on Michael's shoulder.

"Annie?" Michael whispers from the front seat. I pretend to be asleep. Michael switches on the radio. From time to time he glances down into David's sleeping face.

We drive straight through to Los Angeles. It's nearly dawn when we enter the city; the morning is already tainted, the air is hot, thick, and parched, exactly as it was when we left.

We drop David at his apartment. His good-bye to Michael is hasty and whispered. He blows me a quick kiss.

Our house smells abandoned. Michael unloads our suitcases, then moves around opening windows and drapes. It feels as though we've been gone a year.

"Coming to bed?" Michael yawns. "I'm beat."

"No. You go ahead. I'll unpack first."

I curl up on the sofa. In three hours it will be nine o'clock. I'll call her then. Then I'll be braver. I close my eyes.

. . . Emily drinks cocoa out of Claire's blue-and-white French cups; the white cat laps milk out of a saucer Robin holds. Claire spreads honey on toast and hands it to me; under the breakfast table our bare feet almost touch. . . .

The doorbell jolts me out of sleep. Maggie is standing at the back door, Robin and Emily in tow. "Here are your darlings, they couldn't wait to see their mummy."

I hold my arms out to them. Suddenly shy, they come to me and allow themselves to be embraced. They smell of Maggie's perfume.

"What, no coffee made?" Maggie heads for the kitchen.

I sit at the Formica breakfast table. Robin kneels on a

181

chair beside me. He keeps his hand on my shoulder while he tells me about their trip to the zoo. Emily leans against the kitchen counter, her eyes fixed on me, her taut little body tensed for flight.

"Where's Daddy?" she asks.

"Sleeping." I pat the chair beside me. "Sit down. I want to tell you about San Francisco. . . ." I choose my details carefully. The white cat, the Japanese garden, the swans in the lake.

"We saw an ostrich," Robin says.

Emily wanders from the kitchen.

"He eats popcorn." His eyes seem to plead.

"Yeah, Dad's sleeping all right," Emily announces, re-appearing at the kitchen door.

I increase my efforts: Alcatraz Island, sailboats in the bay, sidewalk cafes with blue awnings.

"Can I take my bike out, Mommy?"

"In a minute, Em."

She sighs. "I really missed my bike. . . ."

I relent. "Go on."

"Great," she whoops. "Call me when Daddy wakes up." The screen door bangs behind her.

"What about you, Rob?" I ask hopelessly. "Do you think you'd like San Francisco?"

He considers, his small face serious. "Yes. I like swans. Mommy"—he tugs on my sleeve, his eyes eagerly expectant—"can I have it now?"

"What?" Misgivings instantly awaken.

"My present." He beams. "I was good. Ask Auntie Maggie. . . ."

"Mind your coffee, love." Maggie pats my shoulder as she swabs my spilled coffee off the table.

"Robin . . ."

He stares at me. "You forgot." Appalling realization. Accusation. His face crumples into despair.

"No, no, I didn't forget. San Francisco had the worst toys—I looked in every shop. We'll go out today and pick out something wonderful. . . ." I can hear myself babbling. Robin is not fooled. He climbs from his chair and moves to the door.

"Where are you going?"

"I want to see my trucks," he says in a voice of terrible sorrow. The door clicks softly behind him.

"Oh hell, Maggie . . ."

"Never mind, love." She is instantly consoling. "You'll make it up to him. You must have been having a grand weekend, eh?"

"Yes," I whisper. An involuntary shudder hunches my shoulders.

"That's what you were supposed to be doing. Having a marvelous time. Don't look so guilt-stricken."

She moves her chair closer to mine. For the first time I'm aware of her constrained excitement. "The most fabulous thing's happened. I've been dying to tell you."

"How could I have forgotten his present?"

"He'll be fine," she insists. "Listen. I've met someone, at a bar. The night before you left. I was bursting to tell you. Isn't it dreadful of me?" She giggles, completely absorbed in her experience. "He's got blond hair and a lovely body." She smirks. "Absolutely smashing in bed. And"—she pauses for effect—"he's only twenty-two." She leans back, triumphant.

I didn't even phone them. The whole time I was away, I barely even thought about them. . . . "Sounds terrific. What's his name?"

"Chip! Isn't that absurd?"

"Yes. Congratulations." I forgot them. I forgot about my children! "What does he do?"

"We didn't really discuss careers. He paid for the drinks if that's what you're getting at." Her voice is edged.

"Good . . . good . . ." Robin was crying for me. Comforting himself with the thought of the gifts I was going to bring. . . .

"I thought you'd at least pretend to be interested." Maggie looks genuinely hurt.

"I am, Maggie." I try to focus on her; I lean toward her and clasp my hands on the table. "Where did you meet him?"

She rolls her eyes. "Christ. I told you. In a—"

"Bar. Yes. Does Oliver know?"

She laughs. "You bet he knows. He's pretending to be delighted, but he's furious. . . ." Her voice chirps on, pouring out the details of her affair.

She stops and looks into my face, then abruptly turns and glares out of the window.

"I know what you're thinking," she says. "He's ridiculously young, I'm being a top-grade ass." She shakes her head. "I know. But you can't imagine how good it felt." She turns back to me. There's a new frankness, a kind of raw pleading in her eyes that I've never seen before. "Just being wanted, someone thinking you're sensational—it hardly even matters who it is. Can't you understand that?"

"Yes," I whisper.

"I've been lonely for such a long time," she bursts out. "It's all right for you—you've got your husband back now. You've had your lovely weekend away. But fucking Oliver—" I can see her struggling for control.

She rummages in her purse until she finds a small tortoise-shell hairbrush and a compact. "Well, it was fun with Chip. That's all. Even if he doesn't ever call me, it was fun." Her jaw juts defiance. She stalks into the bathroom clutching her cosmetics bag.

I sit motionless at the table. I can hear Robin shouting orders to an invisible road crew in the garden. I can hear Emily's panicky bicycle bell as she wobbles over the lawn and across the driveway.

If Maggie sees Michael and David together . . . she'll know immediately.

She returns to the kitchen to pour herself some more coffee before she sits beside me again.

"I didn't mean to be such a bitch," she says, contrite. "Forgive?"

"There's nothing to forgive."

"I suppose I'm a bit jealous." She smiles ruefully. "It's wonderful that you've made things up with Michael. A miracle . . ."

"Yes."

She lights a cigarette. I hold out my hand for the pack. "Since when?"

"Since yesterday."

"*You're* falling into sin, aren't you!"

"I guess . . ." The thought lays hold of my mind, envelops me: as long as Maggie thinks a miracle has happened, it will certainly occur. Michael will leave David and come back to me. . . .

"There were so many of them at that bar," she says. She runs nervous hands through her auburn hair. "Standing around, watching the women . . . judging . . ." She drags deeply on her cigarette.

"Anyway, you're well out of it, aren't you?" Her smile is grim. "But I'm going back again next weekend. Maybe Chip'll be there."

"You don't have to do that!"

"No, *you* don't have to do that." She glares at me.

185

"You don't either! We make such prisoners of ourselves, Maggie, we lose ourselves." Claire is so free. . . .

"That's utter rot. I'm talking about having a good time. With a man."

"You don't need a man."

"Sure. A vibrator's effective. But it's not much on conversation."

"No. You don't have to be so desperate. You can be happy without having to go through all this. . . ."

"I'm not desperate, for Christ's sake. I'm just sick to death of spending nights alone."

"Look," I say, the words tumbling out in a rush, "I met a woman in San Francisco. She was so terrific, so strong, her life was so free. All because she doesn't give a damn about men."

"No woman doesn't give a damn about men. She's lying. Or she's a bloody dyke."

Maggie sees me stiffen. She pulls back and looks at me, her eyes alert. "*Was* she?"

"Was she what?" I draw a hasty, protective curtain around my memory of Claire.

"Was she a dyke?"

"I don't know what you mean."

"For heaven's sake, love." She waves her hands in exasperation. "A dyke. A sapphist. A lesbian."

"I don't know. What's the difference?"

Maggie hoots derisive laughter. "Quite a lot, I should think. Where did you meet her? Is she a friend of Michael's?"

"No!"

"Where did you meet?"

"It doesn't matter."

"Did she try to pick you up? Come on, tell. Why would she go for you? Where was Michael?" She leans forward hungrily. Mixed with the curiosity in her eyes is a trace of laughter. "This is wonderful."

An astonishing wave of hatred buffets me; I want to slap her.

"I met her in a coffee shop," I say coldly. "Michael was shopping. No, she didn't try to pick me up. We simply got into a conversation."

"I see." Maggie's mouth is pursed in a withheld smile.

"And she said a lot of very wise things. She's not afraid of anything, or anyone."

"Good for her. She probably has a black belt in karate."

"It's because you're scared to death, Maggie," I shout abruptly. "You're terrified. That's why you suffer."

"How the hell would you know?" she hisses. "*You're* not suffering. *You're* not left alone night after night. You've got your husband back, so don't come around yelling about your bloody bull-dyke friend. I'm on my own, just trying to cope, trying to get something more out of my life."

"I know, I know." I sink into my chair, my anger spent. This is not the conversation I imagined we'd have.

"Look, Maggie, what I wanted to say . . . you have no kids, you have your own money. You could leave. Go away. You don't have to stay here. Move to San Francisco. It's beautiful there. The air is like New England."

"I don't want to go away."

I brush her words aside. "Everything is clean and clear. They have little gardens, no palm trees. . . . I lean toward her, my excitement mounting. "We could go together. That way we won't be lonely. Claire said I could stay at her place till I got settled. She could put you up too. Oh, Maggie, it would be so wonderful. . . . She has a studio, photography, all white, and a lovely white cat. . . . She'll let the kids stay there too. . . ." I've gripped her hands

187

hard; she struggles to pull away, but I hold on. "You'll love her, she's so warm. . . . She could teach us to be strong. . . . We'll go to the park every day, I'll sketch. . . . We'll sit in cafes and read. . . . We'll have each other. . . . A new life . . . !"

She yanks her hands away. "What the bloody hell are you going on about?" She rubs her wrists where my fingers have left red marks. "Are you daft? You've just gotten back together with your husband and now you want to go off to San Francisco and be roommates with a dyke?" Her eyes widen. "Fuck," she breathes. "You aren't trying to tell me something, are you? First Michael, and now you?" She stands, keeping the table and chair between us.

I freeze. My face burns. "No! No, it's nothing like that. It's only . . . don't you see? She's so"—I search for the right word—"intact."

Maggie shakes her head. "I don't understand you. I don't know what more you want. You have a husband who wants to be faithful to you. Who wants children." Her eyes brim. "I'm just trying to get by. And you come home from your glorious weekend spouting all this rot about freedom and stupid white cats and new life. . . ."

"Maggie . . ." My head throbs. A dark curtain falls between us. "I didn't mean to upset you. You seem unhappy . . . I wanted to help. . . ."

"Come with me, then," she says, challenging. "Come to the bar with me. It's a nightmare to go alone. Besides, now that Michael's on the straight and narrow again, don't you want to pay him back, even a tiny bit?"

The packed warehouse bar, the hungry-eyed men. Maggie in her red dress. A wave of nausea grips me. I pass my hands over my eyes. "I can't, Maggie. I don't want to."

188

"Of course not. Why would you?" Her eyes are glacial. She purses her mouth in hurt anger.

"Maggie, please don't . . ."

"I'm not mad at you," she says icily. "It's your choice. But I've got to look after myself, now, don't I? You're all taken care of."

"But we're still friends, aren't we?" I can hear the childish quaver in my voice.

"Of course." Her eyes are like broken crystal. "Well, I'm off," she says, not looking at me.

"Stay a little longer."

"I'm sure you've got things to do. And so have I." She gathers her purse and cigarette case. "Tell Michael I said hello."

"I will," I whisper.

She slips through the door.

19

THE CHILDREN storm the kitchen demanding food. Michael wakes, wanders in with an armful of clothes to be washed. He eats, dresses, leaves the house on a business errand. The children leave for school. The day confronts me—smug, flat, voracious.

I cook meals, wash dishes, launder clothes. My body moves through the small rituals of my day. Now and again appears: a lotus flower in the Japanese garden; Claire's cheeks and hands and feet, so pink after her shower . . . pink as ripe peaches . . . Maggie's cold eyes, her withdrawn angry face. . . .

The children return. Michael returns. He seems tense and preoccupied. The sun sets with dull, orange efficiency.

The children are fed, bathed, bedded. I seek out Michael.

"Maggie and I had a falling-out."

"Yes?" He's buried in his accounts record book. He chews his pencil. "Over what?"

"It wasn't exactly a fight. I just think she doesn't want to be my friend anymore."

"Nonsense." He hunches lower over his books.

"Michael! I feel afraid."

"Nothing to be afraid of. You two will make up again in no time."

"No. Not that. Other things. Can't you help me? Can't you fix this?"

"Honey . . ." He succumbs to the interruption, sits up straight, closes his ledger. "What is it? What's wrong?" His eyes are restless.

I move closer to him, hoping he'll touch me. I stand in front of him, my hands at my sides. "You and David . . . what you said in San Francisco . . . about being honest now, no more lying . . ."

"Yes?" His face grows guarded.

"Does that mean I can talk about you and David? Tell Maggie and Oliver? My family? The kids?"

"You're not serious?" His bland tone is contradicted by the panic in his eyes. "First of all, it's not really any of their business, is it?" He makes me lift my head and look at him. "Is it?"

"No."

"Secondly, they wouldn't know how to deal with information like that. It would be very destructive. Very selfish of you to put that kind of burden on them."

"Yes. So does that mean I have to keep lying?"

"It's not lying, it's protection—because you love them."

"And protection of you too."

"Well . . ." He smiles reluctantly. "That not such an unexpected thing for a husband to want from his wife."

"What about me? Don't I get protection?"

"From what?"

"This feeling—"

He hugs me; his hands on my back feel unwilling.

"I love you, Michael." This must be true. . . . It's always been true.

"I love you, too, sweetheart." He kisses me. But in-

191

stead of taking me to bed, he releases me and sits down again to his books.

Soon, as I've been expecting, he stands, yawns, rubs his hands through his hair, and says:

"This is a mess. I'm going to have to take these over to David's and clear up some of this—"

"I thought you were going to be open with me from now on. Why don't you just say what you're going over there for?"

Michael's face reddens. He turns away and begins to pack things in his briefcase. "Don't be silly. We've got to get these accounts figured out. That's all. I'll be home as soon as I can."

I take the telephone into the bedroom and close the door—against what, I'm not sure. My heart beats painfully.

"Hello?" Her voice is hoarse. Was she asleep?

"Hi."

"Hi." She sounds startled to hear my voice. "How are you?"

"It's Annie. I mean, Anne."

"Yes, I know. How was the trip home?"

I twine the phone cord around my trembling fingers. "Long. Dull. Claire . . . ?"

"Yes?"

"I don't want to stay here anymore. You were right about Michael. I'm leaving him. I'm moving up there. I'm coming to be with you." The words pour out in a garbled rush. She asks me to repeat. "San Francisco," I say slowly. "I'm moving up there."

"Oh. Great. Good for you."

There's a faint buzzing in the phone. I can hear music playing on Claire's end.

"Great," she repeats. Then: "Just a second . . ." Sound

is muffled. I press the phone hard against my ear. Sweat trickles down my back. "Hi, again," she says. "It's terrific that you're coming up. Give me a buzz when you get settled. I've got some great shots of you in the park." I can hear her exhale; see her flick her ash into the square crystal ashtray. "It was good talking to you, Annie. I'm really sorry, I've got to run. Don't forgot to call me when you're moved in—we'll get together. Good luck. Bye-bye."

"Bye," I say to the buzzing dial tone.

The bedroom is completely dark. After some time I stand up and turn the lamps on. I switch on the TV, picture only. I tune in the radio to a talk show. The uncovered bedroom window stares like a sightless eye. I draw the blinds and the drapes.

A picnic by the duck pond . . . Robin and Emily, Claire and me . . .

A foolish, sick notion . . .

I undress, get into bed, pull the covers tight over me. I should be grateful. She's saved me from a hideous mistake. Dyke. Lesbo.

I could still go. Just me and the children. I'll take care of them, I'll protect them. Just the three of us. In the Victorian conservatory . . . laughing at the street jugglers . . . Emily riding a cable car to school. . . . We'll have our own apartment, our own cat. . . .

What if Robin cries for his father at night?

What if Emily hates me for taking her away?

I squeeze my eyes shut, drive myself toward the dark comfort of sleep. When it finally arrives, damp and dreamless, it's the embrace of a reluctant savior. In the morning Michael is asleep beside me, one arm flung protectively across my shoulders.

In the next few days I launder clothes, cook meals, wash dishes. With grim determination I sew new, bright curtains for the kitchen. I replant the herb garden. I wax the living-room floor.

Tonight he's dressing to go out. The bedroom is filled with the scent of his cologne. Familiar desperation rises in me.

"The kids are going to forget who you are.'

"I don't think so." His smile is teasing. He chooses a sweater from his drawer, pulls it over his head.

"Did I tell you that Emily's teacher said she's failing math, that we have to—"

"Yes. You told me. We'll get her a tutor."

"This could affect her whole school career."

"We'll get her a tutor. She'll be fine. I was no math whiz myself."

"It's not that simple. The other day I found her playing with matches. You have to talk to her."

He nods, rolling the sleeves of his sweater.

"And Robin's gone back to sucking his thumb. The dentist said—"

"Yes, you told me. Braces. I'm not surprised."

He slips on his tweed jacket.

"The lock on the back door is jammed again. It doesn't close, you know, anyone could just walk in here while you're gone, the kids and I are all alone—"

"I'll take care of it when I come back."

"David doesn't need you all the time. I need you. Em and Rob need you. They're going to wind up hating you."

"I doubt it."

"The dishwasher's broken, everything is falling apart."

"Honey, you're just going to have to handle it. This is a very crucial time for the business, the plans for the cafe are—"

"Who gives a damn about the goddamn business? Anyway, it's not the business, it's David. Every single night—"

194

"And every single day you come up with a new problem. Why can't you handle these things? It would be such a help to me."

He passes the hairbrush over his hair. "You know how much I love you, but lately it's almost a relief to get out of here and go to work. Every ten minutes there's something else to worry about. David's getting fed up—"

"David!"

"You keep phoning me at the theater with some problem you can't handle."

"Things happen . . . I need you here."

He gathers his wallet and car keys. "We'll have to talk about this tomorrow. I'm late." The front door clicks shut.

I stare into the mirror at the empty bedroom behind me.

The door reopens. Michael is beside me, his arms around my waist. "I'm sorry," he says. "I really am. I'll come home early tonight and fix the lock. I promise. And everything else." He kisses me lightly, and gives me his beautiful boyish smile. "Let's try to help *each other*, honey. Okay?"

"Yes."

He hugs me, not hearing the bleakness in my voice.

Through the screen door I can see Michael sitting cross-legged on the floor in front of the dishwasher, an open manual on his lap. He rises to take the bags of groceries from my arms.

"I thought you'd have it fixed by now."

"Maybe you'd like to try . . . ?"

"I'm only teasing," I soothe, stacking cans of soup in the pantry.

He flops onto the floor again. "You need a goddamn degree just to read the manual. What the hell is a rotor?" He opens the dishwasher door, thrusts his head inside.

"By the way," his voice emerges, a dim echo, "your mother called. They're coming out."

My hand, lifting a box of cereal onto the shelf, freezes. "Here? My parents?"

"Yeah. Can you find me the flashlight, honey?"

Sunday dinners with my parents in New York, Michael laughing, joking easily with Ethan, kissing Belle, flattering her, making her blush and laugh . . . "Your fella is a real ladies' man, Annie."

"When?" My excitement rises. My father, strong and solid, hearty, generous; my mother sweet and gentle—they'll bring with them the cozy serenity of the past. In their presence Michael will be restored to his real self, we'll be a family again. . . .

"Do they have their tickets yet?" I hand him the flashlight.

"I think I see the problem—there's something dangling here."

"How long are they staying?"

Michael's head emerges; he rummages in his toolbox. "She didn't say. Things sound kind of rough. She said your dad's been under a lot of stress lately, things haven't been going too well with the business. She said he hasn't been feeling well."

My heart lurches. "What's wrong?"

"Nothing serious. Sounds like his frame of mind, he's been a little depressed, she said." He squints at the wrench in his hand. "I wonder if this is too big. . . ." He tests the weight of it. "She sounded pretty upset herself, poor thing. She cried a little."

"Oh."

"She thinks a trip out here might pull him out of his depression. Seeing the kids, spending time with us . . . She said our marriage, our 'beautiful little family,' is the one thing in the world he's got to be happy about." His head plunges back into the dishwasher.

I sink into a kitchen chair. "They can't come."

"Why not?" He sits up on his heels. "Why can't they come?" He sounds genuinely bewildered.

"Oh, Michael." Midway between a reproach and a wail. "You know why. All this mess . . ."

Michael frowns. "That has nothing to do with them. We don't have to tell them anything."

"Don't pretend to be dense, they'll *feel* something's wrong. They'll know it."

"What d'you mean? There is nothing wrong. Or there needn't be, anyway. That's up to you."

"For God's sake, Michael," I burst out. "I can't do that, I can't play-act in front of my parents around the clock like that. Even if *you* can," I hurl at him. "They can't come. You have to call them back, make some excuse!"

"What do you want me to say?"

"I don't know. . . . We have plans already . . . a business trip . . . *anything.*"

Michael sighs, shakes his head, reaches for the telephone.

I listen to his voice, warm with concern, distraught with apology and disappointment, unfolding the lie effortlessly, soothing, making promises and protestations of love. . . .

His skill is astonishing. This is the expertise that kept me blind and deaf so long.

"She wants to talk to you," he hisses, proffering the receiver.

"Hello, Mother."

She speaks, I speak. The words bounce across the immeasurable distance between us. I hear my own voice, coming from far away, hear my own bright assurances, my promises and pacifications.

In the end, stalwart, she tells me not to worry about Daddy. He'll be just fine.

Later, in bed, despite Michael's arm around me, I feel as alone as if I were dying. While he strokes my hair and murmurs tender apologies, I close my eyes and plead for the red-haired woman.

I'm going away, I tell her when she arrives at last. I can't stand any more.

Where are you going?

I don't know. San Francisco. New England. Somewhere.

The red-haired woman laughs.

If my parents could have come . . .

Nonsense. You and Michael's being happy together had nothing to do with your parents. Don't you remember? Before?

Before. New York. Our warm, book-filled, cluttered apartment. The view of the river through the floor-to-ceiling windows. Emily, a baby, playing on a blanket in front of the fire while I sketched. Michael at his writing desk, interrupting his work to cross the room to kiss me. We were happy, we held hands in the street, we laughed at the same jokes, people envied our dreams.

If we'd stayed in New York, I could have protected Michael, kept him safe from his longings. He would never have known he had them. . . . We need to move back to New York. Is that it?

Think. The red-haired woman exhorts me. *It wasn't the city that kept him with you. Think. You wore a floor-length velvet robe, your hair was long and loose. . . .*

I stood against a backdrop of snow falling against city-bright windows. Emily, pink and sleepy, nodded on my shoulder. Michael was beside me. His hand caressed the tight globe of my stomach.

You're going to have a little brother or sister, baby Em.

Do you know that? Michael had whispered into Emily's ear. His eyes were full of awe and adoration. He told me I was more beautiful that I had ever been. He called me "little Mommy." I put out my hand to touch his hair, blond like Emily's. He kissed my palm. . . . I possessed him utterly.

Do you understand? Her voice has never seemed so certain, so warmly seductive, so full of promise. *Now do you know what you need to bring him back?*

"Yes," I breathe, my excitement rising. "I understand. Yes!"

In the morning I wake hopeful and happy. I clean the house with extra care. I fill a vase with daisies and marigolds from the garden. I find the loaf pans at the back of the cupboard and bake two loaves of banana bread. I simmer meat and vegetables for soup.

Michael watches me.

"You're in a good mood today."

I smile without answering and go out to the garage to search for scrap wood to use in the fireplace.

"I'm going to wait up for you tonight," I tell him as he's getting ready to leave. "Can you come home a little earlier? We'll have a midnight supper—something special. . . ."

"I'll try. What's going on?" His smile looks nervous. It makes me laugh.

"Nothing. I just want to do something nice for you. Will you try to get away early?

"I'll try."

"Try hard."

"I will," he promises.

Waving good-bye to their school friends, Robin and Emily climb into the car.

199

"I thought we'd go to the park today." I smile brightly over my shoulder at them, sprawled in the backseat.

"I've got Campfire Girls, Mom, did you forget?" Emily's voice is edged with alarm.

"I did forget. Sorry. I'll drop you at Melanie's. How about you, Robbie, want to go to the park with Mommy?"

"Do we have to?"

"Yes!" I soften my voice. "Come on, it'll be fun."

He tugs at his lower lip, his eyes fastened on the window. "Mommy," he says hesitantly. "Could you call me Rob? Robbie's a baby name."

"Rob. Okay. I'll try to remember."

At the playground he ambles toward the high slide near the basketball court.

"No, let's go in here, sweetheart," I call. "It's much nicer. Look, you can run your trucks in the sand pit, and climb to the top of the little jungle gym, it's just the right height." In the kiddie park several toddlers are digging in the sand. A group of four-year-olds pedal their tricycles around and around the small enclosure.

Robin makes a face. "That's the *baby* park, Mom." He tugs at my hand. "Let's go to the *real* part."

"But all the stuff, the equipment, is so tall. . . ."

"So? I'm tall too." His gap-toothed smile is proud. "Dad says I'm tall. He says he's getting me my own two-wheeler and everything. He's going to teach me."

"So he told me." I pull him to me in a sudden hug. He squirms gently away.

"Dad says I'm not a baby anymore, I have to get a real bike. And boxing gloves and a BB gun and a motorcycle and a—"

"Did Daddy really say all that?"

"Well, he said about the bicycle." He dances beside me. "Watch me go to the top of the twisty slide, Mom."

200

He wheels and races away, his sneakered feet kicking up small puffs of gravel.

The park is filled with older children, but across from the fountain I spot what I'm looking for.

She sits on an isolated bench, singing softly to her infant, who suckles her contentedly.

She returns my smile as I settle beside her.

"How old is she?" I stroke the tiny hand.

"Two months." She adjusts the pink blanket over the baby's head.

"She's beautiful." The diminutive fist closes over my finger. "What's her name?"

"Sarah," she says reverently.

"I'll bet your husband's crazy about her."

"He sure is." She shifts the baby tenderly to her other breast.

"And crazy about you too."

She laughs, embarrassed. Her face is radiant.

"Are you watching, Mom?" Robin waves from the top of the monkey bars. "Watch!" He hooks his knees around a bar, releases his hands and swings, triumphant, upside down.

The young mother follows my gaze. "Your son?"

I nod. "It goes very fast. Before you know it your little girl will be right up there beside him."

She hugs her baby in a silent protest. Sated, the baby releases the nipple and smiles dreamily up at her mother.

"They're wonderful, aren't they?"

"Yes," she murmurs. "Are you going to have any more?"

I smile at her. It's always so much easier to confide in a stranger.

That evening, like an answered prayer, a cold wind blows in from the desert, and the evening turns chilly enough to light a fire in the fireplace. After the children are in bed I make my preparations. I place the card table in front of the fire. I set out the lace tablecloth, our best china, the antique crystal wineglasses. A lighted candle illuminates a bottle of Côtes du Rhône. Finally I find and put on my long velvet robe.

Michael arrives home shortly after midnight. His face is tense. When he sees the table he looks startled.

"What's going on?"

"I told you. I want tonight to be special."

Frowning, he sinks into the sofa. "Jesus. I don't know if I can rise to the occasion." He runs his hands over his hair.

I'll have to revise my strategy, be less direct.

"Did you have a hard night?" I pour wine and hand it to him.

"Yes, I had a hard night." His voice is combative. "David and I had a fight. Can you guess over what?"

"I'm afraid I can." I sit on the floor in front of him.

"I told you David was getting fed up. . . . He got furious with me because all I could think about was some jerk strolling in here because you won't call a locksmith."

"I'm sorry, Michael."

"When I'm not spending time with you I'm worrying about you. David feels he doesn't even get a shred of my attention."

"I'm sorry."

"And I'm not getting any work done either."

"It's all going to change. Tonight is the beginning. From now on, everything will be different."

"I hope so. Otherwise, I don't know what I'm going to do."

"It will. You'll see. Drink your wine. . . ." I tell him that I'll become a model of efficiency, that he won't have to worry about a thing. And neither will David. "Come and sit down. It's all ready. Come on," I coax.

I ladle soup into his plate. "Remember this? We used to have it on wintry nights. . . ."

"Pistou. I haven't tasted this since we've been out here."

"Is it good?"

"Yeah," he admits. "It's delicious."

"Let me tell you about Robin in the park today. He was adorable. . . ." I weave an amusing anecdote. ". . . and he's expecting a motorcycle and an air rifle and boxing gloves." I laugh. "He's entering his thug phase."

Michael chuckles. "What happened to his fireman ambitions?"

"Oh, that was *last* week. This week he said he wanted to be a Chinese waiter when he grows up."

Slowly Michael relaxes, his face softens. He begins to tell me about the progress of the cafe that will adjoin the movie theater. I offer menu ideas. The conversation slips into the old, easy flow. We talk about movies. And books. The places we've traveled to, places we'd like to see. Whenever I sense that David's name is about to come up, I steer the talk in a different direction.

"Did you like the veal?"

"Excellent." He holds out his wineglass to be refilled. "This is really nice," he says. "But I still don't know what the occasion is."

"We're celebrating. Do you remember this robe?"

He laughs. "Where did you dig that up? I haven't seen it since pre-Robin days. As I recall, you said you were going to burn it as soon as the baby was born."

"I hung on to it. For sentimental reasons."

"It's pretty," he says. He sips his wine. "So what exactly is it we're celebrating?"

"Us."

A faint shadow crosses his face.

"The three of us," I amend quickly. "And our children." I lean forward to kiss him. I cross my fingers for luck. "At least *there* I have the edge over David."

My tone is exactly right. He chuckles appreciatively. "Yes, I suppose you do." He returns my kiss. "This is the way I love you," he says. "This is the old you."

When he's gotten into bed I prop up the pillows behind him. I set the tray carefully on the bed between us.

"What's this?"

"Dessert."

"Where did you find raspberries? And what's this?"

"Framboise. Taste it."

"This is nice. This whole evening was nice."

"It's going to be nice from now on." I set the tray on the floor, dim the lamps, slide under the covers. "I'm going to make you happy, Michael darling. You're going to be so happy." My mouth covers his; my hands move on his body. "Remember, we used to make love in front of the fire and watch the snow afterward?" I whisper. My hands grow more insistent.

Michael closes his eyes; his breathing grows more rapid, a soft moan escapes him. I slide beneath him.

This baby will be more beautiful than Emily or Robin; this baby will look like an angel.

20

"MICHAEL, I want you to see these." I cross the lawn to him.

He looks up from where he crouches, surrounded by pieces of Robin's brand-new bicycle. "What's that . . . ? Oh." He turns back to his toolbox. "We just looked at pictures. Last night."

I hug the leather-bound photo album closer to me. "Not these."

He searches the toolbox. "Where the hell is that wrench?"

"Look . . ." I crouch beside him and open the album. "I'd just bought that dress, but then I got pregnant and couldn't even button it. Remember?"

"Yeah." He attacks the bolt with his hammer. "Damn . . ."

"And this. Easter Sunday at your mother's—the egg hunt—remember? Emily was just learning to walk. . . ."

He isn't looking. The magic won't work if he doesn't *see* the pictures. "Look, Michael, Christmas. Robin's little wooden railroad . . ." I hold the album in front of him.

"Annie . . ." He pushes my hand away. "Can't this wait? I'm right in the middle—"

"No!" I stop myself, gain control of my voice, and smile at him. "No. It can't wait. I want you to see them now."

"Honey, I told Robin I'd have this ready to ride by the time he gets home from school." He licks his dry lips and wipes the sweat off his forehead with the back of his arm.

"I know, I know," I soothe him. "But just for a minute."

He sighs, sits back on his heels, shakes his head. I turn the pages for him. Birthday parties, Christmas Eves, first day of school . . .

"Oh, jeez . . ." Robin, under a huge bowler and wearing a painted-on mustache, grins out of a photograph. "What was that about?"

"Halloween. His first trick-or-treat . . ."

He chuckles and turns the page. "Look at those curls on Emily. . . ."

I move closer to him and put one arm around his shoulder. "Oh, where was that?"

"Montauk. I took Emily fishing off the pier. She actually caught something. A porgy, I think. . . ."

I lean back, satisfied.

"You're right, they're great pictures," he says, closing the album and handing it to me. "Too bad about the old Polaroids, though, they're really fading."

"Maybe we can have them restored."

He turns back to the bicycle and taps the fenders with his hammer. "Afraid not. They're goners."

"It doesn't matter. There'll be others." He's going to be so happy . . . "What do you think of the name Sarah?"

"Kick that wrench over here, will you?"

I hand it to him. "Do you like Sarah?"

"Sarah who?"

"No—the name. Don't you think it's a pretty name?"

"Sure." He tightens the wrench over a nut.

"For a baby."

"Whose baby?" He positions the front wheel.

"Sarah Morrow. Wouldn't that be nice?"

"*What* are you saying?" The wrench slides off the nut. "Oh, you're teasing."

"That's what you said last time!"

"You're not serious."

"Don't you think a baby would be nice?"

"You said you wanted to go back to art school."

"School can wait."

"A baby! Forget it!" He puts on a stern face. "We're just starting to get out of debt." He turns back to work on the wheel hubs. "Anyway, we always said a boy and a girl . . ."

Men are like this. They're always afraid at first. They always find reasons to say no.

"You'll see, Michael. You're going to love this baby."

He turns around. "What the hell are you talking about?" His eyes flash panic. "You're not pregnant. You can't be." I see his mind racing; then I see his face go slack with relief. "It's not possible."

I smile.

I don't need to say any more right now. The idea will grow in him. The way the baby will grow in me. By the time she arrives, Michael will be happy. For now I'll be kind and clever and say nothing. I shrug elaborately. "You're probably right. I'm probably not."

"Of course you're not." He frowns and begins to gather up the bicycle parts; he stacks them in a spiny heap. "A baby. Jesus," he mutters. He nudges the pile with the toe of his sneaker. "I don't know, Annie. Maybe you need to be married to somebody else. Someone less complicated. Someone who could give you as many babies as you wanted and the kind of life you need."

My heart beats spasms of alarm. Who has taught him to think like this? He used to plead with me . . . if only I promised to stay with him.

He begins to load the bicycle parts into the car. He keeps his face turned away from me.

"I don't want anyone else, Michael."

"I hope not. I love you. I want us to stay together. But I'm never going to be—to change. If you can't live with that . . ."

"I can." The baby will change him. The baby will change everything. "Where are you going?" I catch at his arm.

He removes my hand gently. "Just to the bike shop." He stares down at Robin's dismembered bicycle. "I can't put this damn thing together," he says sadly.

Michael returns long after dark. The bicycle, whole and ready to ride, is in the backseat. David is in the front.

"Where were you? Robin went to bed in tears."

"I stopped in at the theater and saw David." Michael starts for the kitchen. "He had a tough day. I told him we'd fix him something nice for dinner."

"There's nothing in the house." I stay as far away from David as possible. We avoid each other's eyes.

"I thought you were going to make beef Bourguignon."

"I forgot to take the meat out of the freezer." I had planned a light supper for Michael and myself, a picnic in bed.

"Well, how about a salad, or an omelet?"

"I didn't go shopping."

"That's all right," David mutters, "I'll go get a burger."

"No!" Michael's voice is insistent. "Stay right there. We'll order out."

He glances distastefully around the room as he pages through the phone book. "What were you doing all day? You weren't cleaning."

Robin's toy cars are scattered on the rug; the books he'd pulled from the shelves to construct roadways lie where he left them. The remains of Emily's lunch stand on the coffee table; her socks and sweater are wadded in a corner of the sofa.

"Kids' clutter." I shrug. "I was reading."

"You got to the bank, though, didn't you? To deposit that check I gave you . . . ?"

"Sorry. It slipped my mind." After I'd finished reading through my old copy of *Pregnancy and Birth*, I'd lain on the bed, imagining myself telling Robin and Emily about the new baby; imagining Michael's tenderness, his reawakened attentiveness. I must have drifted into sleep. When I looked at the clock it was too late for the bank. "I'm really sorry. First thing tomorrow—"

"Tomorrow is too late. What happened to all those promises to take care of everything around here? You can't run this house *now*, how do you think you'd manage with a baby? Can you believe all this?" He turns to David. "You think I have a problem getting away *now*? Imagine what our lives would be like if Annie had a new baby to take care of. . . ."

My face burns. I know this tirade is only for David's benefit. Still, I have to swallow hard before I can speak. "It would be your baby too."

"Damn right." Michael paces the room. "I remember when these kids were babies, I was on duty round the clock—"

"I was *nursing* them."

"Yeah, and I was doing everything else."

"You loved it."

"That was then, this is now. Things are different." He glances at David for confirmation. "What do you think, David? Isn't she being unreasonable?"

"Why ask him?" I burst out. "It has nothing to do with him!"

"Oh yes, it has. It has everything to do with him. He's part of my life—"

"Not *this* part. You said so yourself. The other night. I can do what David can't do, I can give you a child."

"I don't want a child!"

"Yes, you do. You said the same thing last time. You were too afraid, I had to talk you into it. But you love those kids, you would have been miserable with—"

"Annie, listen," David says. "You can't force anyone into something he doesn't want. I think we'd all be happier if you could calm down a little, stop pressuring him—"

"Am I pressuring you? Does wanting to have your child come under the heading of 'pressuring'?"

"I've already told you, Annie." Michael's voice is cold. "I don't want another baby. Not now. Not ever."

I run to the hall closet, grab my coat and purse, slam the front door behind me. As I drive I whisper to myself, It doesn't matter, he was the same way before, he'll see, he'll be happy, we'll be happy. I head the car toward the beach.

The chilly blue lights of the deserted parking lot cast weird shadows on the heaped sand. Seabirds huddle around the empty metal waste cans. The sound of the ocean seems to be coming from inside me. I walk as fast as I can; the sand under my stockinged feet is cold and damp.

Suppose it hasn't happened? Suppose I'm not pregnant? Michael will never again be as unguarded as he was the other night. . . .

But I feel something. It's too soon, I know. But there is, unmistakably, something. I felt it with Emily too. Right away. A warm, soft, inhabited feeling.

Far out in the ocean, waves are crashing against a dark, protruding shape. A stranded swimmer? A sea animal? Or a jutting rock? I strain my eyes to see. The ocean is pale silver, reflecting the light of an almost-full moon. As I watch, the shape disappears beneath the waves.

Exhausted, I sink onto the sand. I lie, listening to the waves. All I can do is beg the red-haired woman to help me. Please, I whisper. A baby. I stare at the moon with eyes half closed. I remember a fairy story about a princess who longed to swallow the moon. I open my mouth wide; it fills with the cold salt taste of longing. . . .

When I wake up the horizon is lightening to a pale pinky-gray. I feel very tranquil, very still, as if a decision has been made for me.

I creep into the house. The children sleep peacefully; Michael snores gently in our bed, one arm resting on my pillow. I put my wet, sandy shoes on the back porch. In the kitchen I brew coffee, glance at the newspaper. I warm my hands on my cup. I take a sip. With my heart racing, I take another sip, and one more, just to confirm what I feel. Yes. My stomach recoils. I want to shout with happiness. This was always the first unmistakable sign. It *is* true, then. I clasp my hands over my stomach. The nausea abates. I take another swallow of coffee, and the queasiness reasserts itself. I hug myself with delight.

I fix Michael's breakfast, take it to him on a tray. He looks up at me through sleepy eyes.

"I brought your breakfast," I say, forcing the excitement out of my voice. I sit on the edge of the bed while he eats.

"I'm sorry about last night," he says. "It was an overreaction, I guess. We should have talked about it calmly. I know how much you want a baby. But you need to understand, this is the worst possible time. Maybe someday, but not now."

"Michael," I whisper. "This morning my coffee made me sick."

He stares at me. "No," he says. "No. You're coming down with flu. You look feverish." He feels my forehead, touches my hands. "Your hands are freezing. There's a bug going around. You've caught it."

A wave of fear grips me.

"You should take some aspirin, get into bed."

I rest my hand lightly on my stomach. No. I'm certain. I know the difference. . . . This is not a virus. But . . . "You're probably right," I say. This is not the moment to tell him.

"Does your throat hurt?"

"Yes," I lie.

"See? It's flu. You ought to rest today."

Later, in the shower, I thoroughly soap my breasts. Are they tender? I stand naked in front of the mirror. Isn't my waist beginning to thicken? And my ankles? A bit swollen?

Although it isn't necessary yet, I put on my largest, loosest dress. How long will it be before I outgrow it and have to move on to maternity clothes? I smile to myself, remembering the outrageous ruffles and ribbons of my old maternity wardrobe. Maybe I'll go shopping today . . . browse in the mother-to-be shops, see what the new styles are. . . .

David and Michael arrive home at dinnertime. David hands me a bouquet of daisies. His eyes are sullen. "Sorry about last night," he says.

"You're feeling better, sweetheart?" Michael touches my forehead. "You look better." He takes the flowers, begins to arrange them in a vase. "The fastest pregnancy on record," he teases, patting my stomach. "Cured by two aspirins." He winks at David.

212

I fold my arms, and braced against the sink, smiling at both of them, I say, "The aspirins didn't work."

I can't restrain a laugh at Michael's stunned face. "I wasn't going to announce it yet. But it's true." I shrug with elaborate helplessness. "I'm sorry, Michael, I know this isn't what you want, but it's happened."

"You can't possibly be certain," he says stiffly. "It's too soon."

I take the kitchen calendar off the wall and hold it in front of him. "This is when we had our midnight supper. And this is when I should have started my period. . . ."

He shakes his head. "You're just a few days late."

"Almost a week."

"I can't believe this." He sinks into a chair. His appalled eyes beseech David.

David, pale, stands against the window.

"Abortion is legal," he offers.

"Never!" I smile at David; in his eyes I see my triumph.

The three of us stand silent and frozen.

"Congratulations." David hurls the word like a knife. "Well done, Michael." His voice breaks. He strides across the kitchen, yanks open the screen door, and is gone.

I soothe Michael, reassure him that David will get used to the idea, just as he will. I tell him that babies bring good fortune and forgiveness. "You'll see"—I stroke his hand—"David will be crazy about this baby, he'll be the first one here with presents."

In bed, I hold him, promise him that we'll all be closer than ever. "This baby will become so special to him, Michael," I whisper, "as if she were his own child."

"Annie, Annie!" Michael is shaking me awake. Sunlight pierces the room. Michael's face is suspended over me.

"Wake up. Look . . ." He has drawn back the covers. "Look."

The red is brilliant against the white sheet.

"I knew you weren't, I knew it," Michael crows, jubilant with relief.

I reach for the bookshelf. In chapter two of *Pregnancy and Birth* I find what I'm looking for. " 'Occasional light bleeding in the early months,' " I read to him.

Michael shakes his head. "That's not light." He lifts the stained sheet again to show me.

"I'm sorry to disappoint you," I say frigidly. "I know that I'm pregnant."

Michael refuses to relinquish his relief. "There's only one way to be sure." He goes to the telephone and dials.

In the bathroom, I wipe a thin trickle of red from my inner thigh. I look at myself in the full-length mirror; I touch my belly. Nothing's changed since yesterday.

"All right," Michael says when I emerge, "Dr. Feinstein will see you at three."

The doctor sits at her wide, cluttered desk. On the wall behind her is a large, rainbow-colored chart detailing the growth of the fetus in the womb. The doctor's smile is benevolent. "I don't know if you want to be congratulated or consoled," she tells us cheerfully, "but I don't find any evidence of pregnancy."

"I'm pregnant," I tell her.

"You're welcome to get another opinion."

"Michael, I've been pregnant twice before. I know what it feels like. Whether you like this or not, we're going to have a new baby."

Michael takes a deep breath. "All right," he says. He rubs his hands over his face. "Maybe you've had a miscar-

214

riage. Maybe that's nature's way of taking care of false
starts. Maybe next time there'll be a baby. . . ."

"I know you're humoring me," I say gently. "You don't
have to. But you're right. I hadn't thought about it before.
Miscarriage is always a danger. They're very fragile at this
stage. I'm going to need rest." This life feels more fragile
than the others. Maybe because this baby is so precious,
so needed.

"I don't understand why you won't see another doctor,
won't get—"

"I don't want to discuss this anymore." Miscarriage.
"Stress is no good for the baby." We mustn't argue anymore. Michael's doubts could damage the baby. "I can't
listen to you. I need to rest." I need all my strength, all
my concentration, all my energy to make this baby grow.

"Are you getting up today?"

At first he sat on the edge of my bed stroking my hair.
Now he flings words and exasperated sighs at me from the
bedroom doorway. "Are you getting up?"

The children fidget beside the bed. "When will you be
better, Mommy?"

"Mommy's not sick," he says, his face grim. When they
leave he paces the room. "I don't understand why you're
doing this. I don't know what you hope to gain. A week
you've been lying there. You know you're not pregnant.
And you're not sick, there's nothing wrong with you. This
is sheer manipulation. I don't know what you want."

"I need to rest." To store up strength for the baby. I
can feel her growing bigger every day. I stroke my belly.
Soon I'll be feeling her move.

I lie against the pillows and watch the two windows
opposite change color—gray dawn turns to purple, purple
to pink, pink to washed, bone white. In the evening the

215

dark comes with no warning. I lie here and dream about our new daughter. I can see her face, the shape of her hands and feet. I can feel the soft fuzz of her hair and her little mouth tugging at my breasts. I can see Michael, his face shining with love for us, bending over the bed, watching me nurse her.

I can feel him leaving David. Loving us forever.

Michael brings me dinners on a tray. He's worried. I can see it in the way he glances at me when he thinks I'm not watching; in the way he straightens the bedclothes. I long to put my arms around him and tell him that everything is going to be wonderful. The way it was before.

David pulls up a chair beside my bed. "How are you feeling?"

He looks drawn, thinner.

"I feel fine. How are you?" There's no need to be angry at David anymore. In fact, his sad, weary face moves me to sympathy. "You look tired."

"Well, I've been working very hard. And you have us all pretty concerned. Actually, Michael has been just about nonfunctional since . . ." He waves his hand over the bed in a vague gesture. He moves his chair closer. "Annie, you've been here for two weeks. You don't have to do this. Whatever it is. Michael loves you. And"—he lowers his head—"in . . . spite of all the anger and jealousy and the tangles, I care about you too. A lot." His voice trembles. "I don't want you hurting, I don't want you to do this to yourself." He raises his eyes; they're full of pain.

I hold out my hand to him. "Let's make up," I say.

He grips my hand.

"You see"—I smile—"I was right. Babies bring fortune and forgiveness."

"Annie," he says carefully, watching my face, "I've spoken to Michael, he's spoken to your doctor. There is no baby."

I drop his hand. "Did Michael ask you to come here and say that?"

"No. But you have to give up this, whatever it is, this game. Michael is frantic with worry."

"This is no game, David." I try to be as gentle as possible, try not to lose patience. "I'm having a baby. Michael has a very strong denial system, but you'll see— very soon he'll begin to accept her."

"Annie, listen to me. This isn't going to work. This isn't going to win him away from me. You're only going to do damage. To all of us. In the end you'll regret it. . . ."

I close my eyes. I can't listen to David's words, they're dangerous for the baby. I concentrate until all I can hear is the sound of the ocean. When I open my eyes David is gone.

"Chockies, darling." Maggie holds out a huge box of chocolates. She flops down on the bed beside me. "What's all this, then? You lying up here like a great, bloody fool. Get your arse out of bed, you silly cow."

Her gaiety seems forced, her words well rehearsed.

Even so, I'm happy to see her.

"You look so pretty."

"Well, you don't." I can hear the annoyance behind her teasing. "Why don't you chuck all this nonsense and get up?" She tugs playfully on my arm. "Come on, ladybug. Your house is on fire, your children will burn."

I grin up at her. "It's good to see you, Maggie. I've missed you."

Discomfort flickers across her face. "Well, I'm just down the road," she says. "If you miss me, all you need to do is get out of bed and come and see me."

I shake my head. "I can't." I fold my hands over my stomach. "I need to rest."

"You've rested enough, I think, don't you?" She stands. "Come on, girl, get up. We'll go shopping, have a marvelous lunch—there's a new place opened, Italian"—she drops her voice—"smashing waiters. And I hear the food's quite decent. Come on, what do you say?"

"I'd love to. But I need to rest, Maggie. Really. For the baby."

She stands looking down at me. She shakes her head, throws up her hands. "I've done me best," she mutters.

Through my half-opened bedroom door I can hear her in whispered conversation with Michael. There is a sudden pause; a hand closes my door quietly.

When I wake from a nap I see Emily standing by the door. Robin hides behind her.

"Hi, darlings. Come and sit next to me." I hold out my hand to them.

Emily shakes her head.

"How about a kiss for your mom, then?"

They stand unmoving.

"Don't you want to come on the bed with me?" I cajole. "I'll tell you about something wonderful."

"Dad says to tell you you have to get up," Emily whispers in a rush. Holding hands, they bolt from the room.

Tears trickle over my temples and dampen my hair. I sit up and reach for the box of tissues. When I brought Robin home from the hospital, Emily stood at the doorway, looking at me with the same expression of fear and outrage. But in a very short time she was hugging him, bringing him her favorite dolls to play with. I wipe my eyes. I mustn't get upset, there's nothing to worry about. The baby will fix everything.

"When are you getting up? When are you going to stop this game?" Michael's litany. Every day. He sets the food tray on the bed, looking grim and martyred. "There is no baby. When are you going to stop?" Over and over. I no longer answer him. I just sigh, "I'm sorry, love," and turn my face to the windows until he leaves. I feel bad about burdening him, but this will all be worth it.

Since conversation is so painful, so dangerous for the baby, it's clear that silence is the wisest course. I've made the determination not to speak until the baby arrives safe and sound.

The red-haired woman visited me last night. *What does Michael know?* She smiles contemptuously. *He's a man.* She strokes my face. *Rest. Be still. Don't think. I'll take care of you.*

This morning I feel much calmer. Utterly peaceful. As if a soft, thick gray curtain has been drawn around the baby and me; warm, sweet, soft silence.

Michael's voice is insistent, sharp enough to pierce the gray curtain.

". . . an appointment for you to see another doctor, Annie. You have to come with me."

I shake my head dreamily.

He glances around the room as if he's searching for help. "All right," he says. "Okay. Listen, I think for the sake of the baby, you need to see this doctor."

I raise my head to look at him; his face is genuinely concerned. He's accepted her! The pleasure that I feel seems oddly detached, as if it's happening outside my

219

body. I smile up at him, trying to tell him with my eyes how happy I am.

"Look," he says, "you should be feeling movement by now, shouldn't you?" He slides his hand under the covers, rests it gently on my stomach. "Nothing," he says. His hand feels like ice against my skin. "The baby's not kicking. Is it?"

"No," I whisper. My voice is hoarse, my mouth feels rigid.

"Something might be wrong," Michael says.

I shake my head. I know nothing's wrong.

"It's not wise to take chances. You might need vitamins or something. Please, Annie," he begs. "You've got to come with me."

His anxiety for her moves me. "All right," I murmur. For his sake.

He helps me to my feet; my body seems unwilling to obey. With trembling fingers, he helps me dress. I keep one hand protectively over my stomach. He supports me gently out to the car. The daylight is shattering. I long to be back in the warm safety of my bed. But Michael is so eager. And now I want to please him any way I can.

This doctor's office is nothing like Dr. Feinstein's. No charts decorate the walls, no clutter of books, papers, framed photographs on the desk. I am not asked to undress, I'm not examined. Instead the doctor, silent, behind thick glasses, listens to Michael talk. He asks me questions. I give the shortest possible answers. My heart races, I want to run from here. But I keep myself calm. For the baby. I'm asked to wait in the outer office. A gray-haired woman behind a glass window points to magazines in a rack on the wall. I take one, hold it tight against my chest. In my mind I sing to the baby to soothe her in case she can feel my fear. Or my rage. Michael lied. Again. I force these thoughts into silence. I'm readmitted to the room where Michael and the doctor wear the sly faces of conspirators.

The doctor begins to talk to me. His words drone like flies. At the end he leans toward me. *I'm recommending hospitalization.* Michael keeps his eyes hidden. *A place to rest,* the doctor says. *Rest and recover.*

I pull the gray curtain around me. I will not listen. Nothing will harm my baby.

21

M Y NEW room is small and pale green; it smells ugly. Three pale plants droop on the windowsill; one of them is growing out of a grinning blue ceramic dog. Behind the window, thick mesh screens separate daylight into gritty, gray-brown particles.

When I was first brought here I became furious. I was about to scream accusations at Michael. But then she quieted me. The red-haired woman convinced me that this might be a good place to rest while I'm waiting for the baby.

But don't tell! she whispers. *If they know about the baby, you'll lose her. The people in charge are heartless. They have certain rules. Say nothing.*

So I stay submerged, floating with my child in an amniotic sac of silence.

Every day they come and sit by my bed. "Talk to us, tell us your story." Like a mob of horrible children beating the surface of a pond, trying to capture turtles sleeping on the bottom. "Talk to us." Not just nurses and aides, but patients too. They say my name over and over.

Don't answer them, the red-haired woman warns.

A smiling young man with wary eyes holds my elbow and leads me down a fluorescent-lit corridor to a polished wooden door.

"Go right in." He nods. "Dr. McShay is expecting you."

"Hello, Annie. Have a seat." The doctor's dark hair curls over his forehead and ears; black-rimmed glasses cover his eyes. A thick beard crawls over the rest of his face. From under his mustache a carved ivory pipe smolders.

"I hope you're going to talk to me today, Annie."

He shuffles index cards on his desk. Shuffles and re-shuffles. His clever hands make elaborate passes over the deck. But I catch him pulling a card from his sleeve . . . "Maybe we can help you to decide."

Be careful, warns the red-haired woman, *he has no face.*

They give me pills. Every day a fat-faced woman pushes her cart into my room. "For you, honey." Her voice is sweet and sticky; the pills are candy-colored.

Jenny, the girl from the next room, stands outside my door and watches. She has eyes like silver buttons. She smirks. "Now they've got you."

My child and I are where no one can find us. The spring night climbs onto my windowsill, claws at the bars, puts its wet sweet mouth against the iron mesh screen. The night drinks us—breathes us into itself, draws us right through the window, through the mesh, into lilacs, hyacinth, narcissus. My child cradles me. We sing to-gether—as loud as we want to. They won't find us.

Dr. McShay's long, crooked fingers form a little tent on his desk. His voice floats above us, mingling with the stale pipe smoke and the stench of all the secrets that have been revealed in this office.

My hands and feet weigh hundreds and hundreds of pounds. My head—monstrously heavy—lolls on my neck. Words cling to my thick tongue.

"I . . . feel like . . . a ghost."

His well-oiled voice says, "You'll begin to adjust to your medication soon. . . ."

"Since this is your very first visitor, you'll be allowed only a few minutes alone with your husband." The nurse smiles and rustles away.

Michael holds a bunch of yellow daisies. His eyes are frightened.

How are you feeling?

We keep the room between us.

These are for you.

He lays the daisies on the foot of the bed.

I sit beside the flowers.

The kids send their love.

Momentary stirring of pain, then the blanketing fog rolls in.

How's it going with the doctor? Michael wipes his hand across his forehead. *He seems pretty competent.* He perches on the edge of the white metal chair. *What have you told him? About us, I mean.* He folds his arms across his chest. His hands are trembling. *Did you tell him about David?*

I shake my head.

Good, because doctors have a funny way of seeing things. He might not understand. A muscle twitches in his jaw. *I want you to get better. I want you to come home. You want to come home, don't you? To me? And the kids?*

I nod.

We know what we want, don't we?

Sunlight through the mesh screen makes square patterns on the linoleum. It reminds me of something, but the memory is hidden behind the fog.

Doctors can be very rigid in their ideas of what's normal. Our marriage wouldn't exactly qualify. He laughs with the sound of a key scratching on iron. *He might try to talk you out of coming home.* He rubs his hands over his knees. *I just don't want him to talk you out of what you've already accepted. Goad you into hysterics all over again . . . then you'd never get to the real problem . . . the stuff about the baby. . . .*

I stare hard at the squares of sunlight.

I wouldn't even mention anything about me and David. You're not yourself. The things you say might not be the real truth. His blue-green eyes shine dark and hidden like water at the bottom of a well. *Do you understand?*

I bow my head.

His face seems to have changed its size, seems to be nearly filling the room. I have to look away, concentrate on the yellow daisies. When I look back at him, his face is normal, but pale and sweating.

I love you so much, he says. *And there's something else.* He shifts in the chair, his eyes search the room, finally return to me. *David is thinking about moving up north.*

A sound like the distant drumming of the ocean fills my head.

The nurse's starched voice crackles. "I'm afraid that's all for today. Dr. McShay will speak to you now, Mr. Morrow."

Michael stands and presses my hand to his lips. *I just want us to be happy. Like before.*

Before?

He's already gone, following the stiff white back of the nurse.

Under the desk, the doctor's feet are crossed. He brings his toes together, keeping time with his words. *Your husband mentioned that you were feeling very isolated. Is that true?*

I stare at my clasped hands.

Why don't you tell me about your marriage? What was it like?

Careful. He has ways of making us speak. Don't let him trick you into saying anything. . . . I concentrate on his socks. Pumpkin-colored. A thin band of black around the ankles. Halloween socks.

Did you and your husband communicate?

I nod. I'll have to buy trick-or-treat candy for the neighborhood kids.

You feel you had a satisfying relationship?

I nod. We'll have to dress up. Robin and Emily can be ghosts. I'll wear Michael's clothes, he can wear mine. . . .

How about your marital relations? Could you tell me a little about your sex life?

"Your socks are very nice. Seasonal."

He taps his stack of index cards; his face is stern. *I can't help you if you play games with me.*

Jenny, the girl in the next room, gets flowers from her parents every week. Baskets of roses and baby chrysanthemums, like centerpieces for a wedding or an elegant dinner party. They die almost immediately. Something about the air in here.

At night the faces of my mother and father float above my head, almost lost in the gray fog. They have not written or called. Is this a punishment? Or has Dr. McShay torn up their letters, turned away their phone calls? The fog presses on me, locks me in silence and stupor. But something, a dulled, chronic ache, lives just below the surface of my mind, freezes my thoughts, crushes my questions.

Maggie brings me a box of chocolates, foil-wrapped, shaped like little animals, a gift for a child.

When I start toward her, she stiffens; when I kiss her cheek, I hear the sharp intake of breath, as if she's afraid of contagion.

I take her hand and lead her to the vinyl-covered settee. Next to it a woman sits in a chair, facing the wall, rocking her body rhythmically from side to side.

Do we have to stay here? Maggie whispers. Can't we go in your room?

We're not supposed to, I tell her.

Come on, she says.

I wait till the head nurse has turned away to care for an old man in pajamas who has lost his way and lead Maggie down the corridor to my room.

How are you feeling? she asks when she's settled herself in the straight-backed chair near the window. What have you done to your hair?

Someone came and fixed it. A volunteer of some sort. I run my hands through my stiffly curled hair.

Not to worry, she says. It'll grow out again. She's wearing a dress of carnation-pink silk; her long, shining hair flows over her shoulders. On her feet she wears pink high-heeled sandals. Her skin is the color of ripe peaches, her topaz eyes sparkle. She looks like a goddess.

You're feeling better, then?

Her eyes travel over my shapeless housedress, my bare feet in their terry-cloth scuffs. She studies my face, the lipstick and rouge pulsing with neon garishness against my yellowish skin. I shrink under her gaze.

You look well, she says. The lie makes her purse her mouth into a tight little smile.

Thank you. I fold my trembling hands in my lap.

She extracts a gold cigarette case.

We're not supposed to smoke in our rooms.

I won't tell if you won't. She lights two cigarettes and hands me one.

Well, I'm glad you're feeling better, she says. She stares at the window with its thick mesh screen. Bloody hell, she whispers. When do you get out of here?

I don't know.

You've got to hurry and get well. Your kids are really missing you. Michael too. She shakes her head with wonder.

But he's being bloody marvelous. I don't know how he does it. Keeping the theater running, taking care of the house, making sure the kids are okay. . . .

She pats my hand.

So, you mustn't worry, love. Your family's being looked after. Everyone pitches in with the chores. Even Robin does a bit of dusting and washing up. Emily does the shopping—she's being so grown up. I've been doing most of the cooking, even though I'm not much of a chef, as you well know—although David's been showing me a few new dishes that aren't too hard. Anyway, I've been trying to keep their spirits up, taking them out to the movies and so on . . . get their minds off things. . . .

His name slices through the fog. David.

So, you see, we're all rallying round, and . . . Oh."

She squeezes my hand.

Love, don't look like that. You mustn't fret about your

babies. They'll be fine. All you need to think about is
getting well and out of here, coming home. . . .

Maggie, Michael, David, Emily, Robin, their hands linked,
are dancing. Their faces are bright, smooth, luminous
with love and contentment. They sit down together to
laugh and eat. In my house there is no trace of me. At
night Maggie sleeps with a child on either side, their
heads on her breast; while in our room, under the blue
quilt my grandmother made, Michael and David move
together, moaning, clinging, breathing each other's names.
  My baby and I stand on a black cliff, looking down into
an arid, empty ravine where jagged rocks and parched
earth are slowly enshrouded by a thick, poisoned gray fog.

Three times a day a nurse hands me a glass of water and
a doll-sized paper cup holding candy-colored pills. I put
the pills in my mouth and sip the water. The nurse gives
her automated smile and says, Good girl. I go to my
room, spit the pills into a piece of Kleenex, and tuck them
inside a sock in my bureau drawer.

Rain is pounding against the mesh screen, bending the
palm trees, flattening the hibiscus bushes.
  Michael and I, safe and warm, sip tea laced with brandy
in front of our fireplace and watch the rain dimpling the
surface of the Hudson. The baby sleeps in his bassinet by
the fire; Emily stands on tiptoe in front of the window,
crowing with delight at the beautiful silvery droplets. We
smile. Michael's eyes are luminous with love and perfect
contentment. When the rain stops we go out, wheeling
the baby in his pram, Emily toddling beside us, jumping
in the puddles. Michael's arm around me, the sky, the

river, the city, sweet and refreshed, everything shining, Michael's face shining. . . .

I press my hands against the mesh screen. The thick, heavy sky empties itself with a steamy, tropical violence. The air is dense with futility and loss; it suffocates.

In the sibilance of the rain I hear the red-haired woman's whisper:

It's over. You failed.

You couldn't learn to be like me. I'll teach you something else.

There's no place for you, she says. *Or for your baby.*

You need to rest, she says.

She's put my hoarded treasure into my hand. The capsules glitter, jewel-like, in my palm.

Go on. Don't be afraid. I'll stay with you.

I see her in the shadows by the window, the burning halo of her hair, her easy grace, her calm, sure smile.

Michael will find you, wake you with a kiss . . . happily ever after. . . .

Go on. Don't be frightened. You only need to rest for a while. She brings me to the mirror. *Watch. It's beautiful.*

Together we follow the iridescent rainbow path of each capsule as it moves down my throat and bursts inside my body, filling me with color and light.

She helps me to my bed, she arranges the pillow behind me.

Only think how much he'll love you now.

I'm afraid.

Shhh. She lies down beside me and holds me. In her arms I feel weightless. She lays her hand over my eyes. She sings a lullaby in a language I've forgotten. Wherever her body touches mine I feel warm languor.

Hush . . . sleep . . . I'll help you.

She rolls on top of me.

She grows heavier, heavier, monstrous, she's crushing me . . . my chest is collapsing under her, I can't breathe . . . I tear her hands from my eyes. She is smiling. Where her eyes were are shafts of darkness.

I struggle to throw her off me. I hear her laughter, the sound of earthquakes, hurricanes.

Someone is weeping. My mother stands beside the bed. My father and my children stand a little apart. Their faces are sorrowful and recriminatory. They turn away.

The red-haired woman fills the room. Her mouth is a tunnel. Flames burst from her, orange-yellow bloodred. Black forms slither from her mouth, her nose, her eyes. Men shapes. Dancing. Shrieking silent laughter. Men coupling with men. The red-haired woman, her charred skin hanging in tatters from her body like bloodied scarves, joins hands with the men. They dance together. *Look, look*, she calls to me in the shrill, triumphant voice of betrayal. The men lift her. *Look. Michael belongs to us now. Your life is over. But we'll live forever. . . .*

The scream begins at the moment of my conception, it travels through my birth, my infancy, my childhood, through my marriage, the births of my own children, through accumulated griefs, through rage, through pure blackness until it explodes from my torn, gaping mouth: *No!*

The force of the explosion obliterates the men shapes; it rips through the red-haired woman, slams her against the wall. She lies, pulped, lifeless, a sodden mass flung into the darkest corner of the room.

My baby is torn from my body, spins away in a cloud of dust and chaos.

Don't die, don't die!

A monstrous wave picks me up high, higher. I hold my breath: beneath me I see the white house, white curtains

231

blowing at the open windows, daisies and marsh grasses, the wooden walkway winding down to the water's edge. . . . I stretch out my arms reaching for safety. . . . The wave releases me—

Don't die, don't die!

—I'm falling toward the rocks below.

There you go, there you go . . . Urgent whispers slicing through the precious silence.

Hands tugging me.

Darkness tugging me, holding me.

Come on. Sharp voice.

My cheeks sting.

Something cold, hard, forced between my lips; thick slimy substance trickling down my throat. Choking me, gagging me. Death and darkness spew from my mouth. Hands shaking me, slapping. *Come on, come on* . . . Waves of darkness, waves of sickness breaking over my head. My body, unresisting, flung by the waves, sinking, resurfacing.

"Come on!"

The storm abates, the waves diminish. The darkness loosens its hold. I float.

With a monumental effort, I open my eyes. A thousand years have passed. I'm in my hospital room; the pillow under my head is wet and foul-smelling.

I try to raise my head; my body is convulsed with exhaustion; my throat is lacerated; pain beats in my temples and in my chest.

"Hi."

Jenny. The girl next door. She's sitting cross-legged on my bed watching me with her silver-button eyes.

"How ya feeling?" She grins, sly, conspiratorial, amused. "You look awful. But I think you got most of your pills out. I gave you shampoo to drink."

232

Beyond her the room is dark, except for a silvery patch on the floor between the bed and the window. The rain has stopped, but a low, growling wind is whipping the trees.

"You're lucky," she says in a laconic drawl. "I came by to bum a cig. If they'd found you . . ." She rolls her eyes. "You'd be up shit creek, lady. You're lucky."

My mind is still, silent, frozen—a wasteland of slush and mud.

"They'd a pumped you out and slapped you on the locked ward." She leans toward me. "No bed sheets, no cigarettes, no doors on the rooms, no knives and forks, only spoons," she says with relish. "That's where you'd a been if it wasn't for me."

I search for some appropriate word, some correct emotion.

A cracked, ruined whisper emerges. "Thanks."

"Don't mention it." Satisfied, she slides off the bed. "Maybe you'll do the same for me one day."

At the door she turns and grins her conspirator's grin. "Next time, though, if you really wanna *do* it, cop an Exacto knife from art therapy. But be sure you cut the long way. If you cut across, they can stitch that." She holds up her arms. Jagged red scars bisect her wrists. "Drink a lotta water tonight. And don't tell anyone you tried this or they'll keep you here forever. They're *never* gonna let me out." She peers cautiously out the door. "See ya!" She tiptoes away, closing the door noiselessly behind her.

I squeeze my eyes shut. I touch my abdomen with my fingertips. The place where my baby had lain, nested in lies and despair.

I call experimentally to the red-haired woman. Echoing silence.

233

"I nearly died," I whisper. I ought to creep from my bed to the window and look out at the starry sky and the moon and the moving trees, and feel my heart open with gratitude and wonder. But the frozen stillness blankets me, and my heart and my mind are numb and aching with cold.

I sleep and wake, sleep and wake. I see *my* house. Flames leap from every window, the roof collapses. Violent winds fan the fire. The ground gives way. The circular front porch slides into the sea. Furniture, books, paintings, all my treasures thrown by the wind into the sea.

In the dream I stand watching at the edge of the water, crying silently. A woman's voice surrounds me, sheltering and strong. Don't be afraid, she says, we'll save the house. I turn to face her, but the woman is myself.

Michael is visiting me in the music room, a small alcove off the dayroom that boasts a scratchy phonograph and a battered upright piano.

His gaze is cautious. "You seem much better today," he says.

"Yes. I'm feeling better now."

He folds his hands. "Dr. McShay says you acknowledge that there's no baby."

The swift, familiar stab of loss. "Yes," I answer obediently. "There was no baby." I look beyond him at the stack of worn albums arranged on a metal shelf. "I wish there had been. A baby would have changed everything."

Michael's mouth compresses into a thin line. He says nothing.

"Things are going okay, then, with you and the doctor?" He rises from his chair.

"Yes."

"What have you been talking about with him?"

"This and that. My childhood, my work."

"You haven't said anything?"

"About what?"

"You haven't told him about David?"

"No."

"Good."

A canopy of silence hangs above us.

Michael shifts in his chair. His eyes glance surreptitiously at his watch.

"When is David moving?"

"Moving?" His face is blank.

"You told me he was thinking about moving. Up north."

Alarm lights Michael's eyes. "Oh, yes, I forgot." He shrugs with his old boyish appeal. "His plans changed."

"Oh." Something moves just below the surface of my mind. Barely recognizable, black and coiled. "Maggie says he's spending a lot of time at our house."

"Yes, he's there a lot." Michael has arranged his face to look piteous and virtuous. "I've needed him. It's been very hard."

"Has he moved in, then?"

"I wouldn't call it moving in—"

"Where does he sleep?"

"Annie, this is—"

"Where does he sleep?" My voice has grown too loud. A burly aide is watching me from the corner, ready to move. Behind the glass partition of the nurses' station, a nurse sits like a miser over her hoard of hypodermic needles and obliterating drugs.

"Where does he sleep?" I whisper.

"On the sofa," Michael says with offended dignity. "What did you think? The kids are right there. . . ."

"I don't want him in the house."

I see the struggle on his face. When he speaks his voice is gentle and tender. "Darling, he's a good friend. You're not around. I need his help. It's as simple as that."

"I don't want him there."

Michael stands and embraces me as if I'd just said something wonderfully kind.

"Did you hear what I said? I want him out."

He puts his hands very gently over my mouth. "Sweetheart," he says, "I don't want you to get yourself upset. I only want you to get well and come home. I love you. David loves you. Soon you'll be home and everything will be fine." He kisses my forehead. "I have to go. Take care of yourself." He gives me a sweet, regretful smile and strides quickly away toward the locked door at the end of the passage that leads to the outside.

I remain standing in the music room.

Blue twilight comes through the music-room window. Beyond the hospital grounds, lights are coming on in the houses on the hill. Husbands and wives who will eat together with their children, laugh or quarrel, do the dishes, watch TV, and go to bed, where they will turn to each other in passion or relief or boredom, but always with some sense—deeper than their sense of themselves—of belonging.

"The resident on duty said you wanted to see me, that it was urgent."

Dr. McShay has the disgruntled, disoriented look of someone interrupted in the midst of a fierce argument. Or a sexual encounter.

He makes a tent of his fingers on the desk and composes himself into blandness.

I can't imagine him making love to anyone, I can't picture his face transformed by passion.

"What seems to be the problem?"

"It's not a problem. It's something I haven't told you before."

He lifts his eyebrows questioningly. "Yes?"

I take a deep breath. His eyes will widen with shock. He'll leap from his chair. *How terrible for you. Now I understand.* He might take my hands, or hug me. In his arms I might stop shivering.

"My husband is homosexual."

The terrible words tremble in the air above us. I clasp my hands.

"I see." His face doesn't alter. It's as if I'd thrown a rock into a pond only to see it float like a leaf on the unbroken surface.

"Go on." The same toneless, modulated voice.

"I can't." I gasp. I feel as if a huge beast, trapped somewhere inside me, were struggling to wrench itself free. "*You* have to say something . . . tell me how to feel. . . ." I hunch my body around the violent, tearing pain.

"That's not my job," he says. "You have to tell me."

My ear caught it, just before he snatched it back: the smallest, and therefore most precious, trace of tenderness. What if, behind the thick convex lenses of his glasses, his eyes were kind?

With the slow, thorough patience of an artisan, Dr. McShay is trying to reconstruct, shard by shard, my smashed life. I supply him with facts; he turns them this way and that, trying to find where they fit.

He says that when he's finished I will be intact and capable.

But I know that I will be run through with a thousand tiny cracks and fissures; that nothing will ever be the same.

I pace the dayroom counting my steps. Robbed of the protective fog of my madness, I'm left clear-eyed, "sane," with nothing to divert me from the gnawing sadness and hopelessness that live in me.

The hours pass, seeping one by one into a pool of stagnant days. Patients are admitted, others released. Meals are delivered, eaten in silence. Dr. McShay is absorbed in his work of reconstruction. His earnest dedication is at least worthy of respect. I try, for his sake, to find some source of light, some small signal of hope.

I pace the dayroom counting my steps.

Maggie strides down the corridor toward me. She carries a large, paper-wrapped bundle, which I know has been searched by the apologetic nurse's aide at the front desk.

"Hello, love." She's brisk, determinedly cheerful. "How are you feeling?"

"Better, thank you." The sadness deepens around me. She studies my face. "Mmm," she says, one eyebrow raised.

In my room she sets her bundle on the bed and perches beside it, one hand resting on its flat surface.

"What's going on? Michael says your doctor's told him not to visit you for a while."

"Did Michael ask you to come here and plead his case?" My attempt at banter fails, my voice emerges ragged.

"No," she says quietly. "I just wondered. You both seem upset."

"Too many secrets. There were too many secrets. I'm trying to clear the air." Only the truth from now on. But I already knew that. The red-haired woman's treachery taught me that. . . .

I lift my head to meet Maggie's. "I have something to

tell you." I brace my shoulders against the back of my chair. "Michael's lover . . . was David."

Maggie returns my gaze; her eyes are cool and steady. "So I gathered."

I stare at her.

"It wasn't hard to figure out. Especially when you see them together."

My heart begins to race dangerously. I clench my hands to quiet myself. "How could you have known and still . . . My house, my kids! . . . Why didn't you say something? Why didn't you tell him to get out!"

"Annie," she says in a voice of indulgent protest, "Michael doesn't know I know. If his secret is so important to him, why upset him? You can't blame David for what happened. I'm sure you know that. If Michael hadn't found him, he would have found someone else. Maybe someone not so nice, who didn't give a damn about you and the kids. . . ."

"You're supposed to be my friend!"

She reaches over and takes my hand. "I am your friend. Don't look at me like that. You'e got to accept Michael the way he is. Just like I've got to accept Oliver. Or we'll both wind up alone."

"Alone! Something worse than death . . ."

"Don't get upset. Come on," she soothes, stroking my hand. "You've gone all pale. Let's not talk about this anymore. You have plenty of time to work all this out later. When you're strong and well and out of here. Look"—she holds the parcel toward me—"I've brought you something."

She tears off the brown paper and spreads on my bed, next to her, a box of watercolors, a sketch pad, fine brushes, drawing pencils.

I stare at the array as if they were mysterious artifacts belonging to a lost civilization.

"It was Michael's idea," she says, smiling, pleased. She opens the box of paints and arranges the silver tubes with their colored labels across my pillow.

"I can't paint," I say flatly. I've given the art therapy class a wide berth, refusing to participate, choosing instead to labor listlessly over a bit of bedraggled, hideous needlepoint. "I don't want to," I whisper.

Maggie's pleasure fades into disappointment. "These are the very best brushes. The man in the art store said so. Real camel hair." She places one in my hand.

"No!" I drop it onto the bed as if it has scalded me.

"Why not?" Her voice is edged with exasperation.

How can I explain to Maggie? Painting in this place would destroy painting for me forever; my art would become tainted with misery and disease, inextricably woven into the nightmare. . . . "Later. When I'm home."

Maggie shakes her head. "I'll leave them. You might change your mind."

"I won't."

"I'll leave them anyway."

We sit together in silence. Maggie's long finger taps her knee.

The food cart makes its rattling entrance onto the ward, accompanied by the thick, unsavory smell of hospital cooking.

Maggie stands uncertainly. "I suppose I'd better go."

"Yes." I stare at my hands. New depths of loneliness seem to have opened inside me.

Maggie twists the straps of her pale leather purse. "I really miss you," she says, husky-voiced.

"Why? You've got Michael and David to play with." I hear my voice, as cold and dead as the hours, days, years facing me.

"Don't," she whispers. Her eyes are filled with tears. "I'd better go."

I remain at the window, my back to her, until I'm sure she's passed through the locked door at the end of the corridor. The truth will heal all your wounds. Dr. McShay said so. Another lie. Maggie is lost to me.

I stand over my bed in the fading light, reading the names on the silver tubes. "Cadmium yellow, burnt umber, rose madder, Prussian blue . . ." I whisper. The sounds fall into the silence like an ancient benediction. I pick up one of the tubes—vermilion. I unscrew the cap, squeeze a minuscule dab onto my finger, run my finger across the thick, knobby watercolor paper. A brilliant smear of green, vibrant and alive. Underwater green. I moisten the tip of the thinnest brush between my lips, draw it slowly through the massed green. The color spreads, shapes itself into the horizon line of an evening sea. I close my eyes.

My house, the white curtains blowing in the breeze from the ocean, the circular front porch dappled with blue-green light, rises in front of me.

I had forgotten my house. Since the night of the pills, the night that my baby and the red-haired woman ceased to exist, I have not let myself think about my house.

A tiny pinprick of light pierces the darkness surrounding me.

I take the pad onto my knees and begin, with faint, frightened pencil lines, to sketch my house.

22

Now I spend every day in my house. I make dozens of detailed paintings. The house from every angle. The house at dawn. The sea at twilight with small boats making for port.

Life on the ward goes on around me, swirls over my head like smog. I breathe it in, but otherwise it leaves me unaffected. I am in my house, standing at my easel on the wide porch overlooking the sea. Slowly, brushstroke by cautious brushstroke, I am painting myself back to life. My palette softens and brightens; zinc gray gives way to rose madder, cadmium yellow, vermilion. Day by day, I layer hope onto the canvas.

"We're making progress," Dr. McShay says. Inside his beard, his mouth pulls into a strained, uncomfortable smile, as if it were unaccustomed to being used for that purpose. "I'm quite encouraged," he says stiffly. But his eyes behind their thick glasses are almost pleased.

"Thank you." The blinds on his windows cast thin shadows on the pale carpet. I'll paint the floors in my house white. No carpets to impede the shifting patterns of light thrown by the sun on the ocean. . . .

The doctor's voice obliterates the vision. ". . . Let's talk about your children. . . ."

"Robin and Emily . . ."

"Yes," he echoes, "your children."

I catch my breath. Why hadn't I seen it before? They'll live there too. The three of us together. My heart lifts with a surge of excitement. They'll each have a room. . . .

As soon as my session is over I race back to my drawing pad. I add two more rooms onto my house, one on either side of the turret. Two small rockers added to the front porch . . . How could I have imagined my house without my children in it?

Now I begin to draw the inside of the house. Room by room. I take slow pleasure in the placement of furniture and books, painting each object in minute detail.

Dr. McShay smiles more often now. The nurses have grown friendlier. I've been given permission to paint in my room. Like van Gogh at St. Rémy. The thought makes me smile.

The nurses admire my work. "Your house?" they ask.

"Yes." I exhibit my sketches with cautious pride.

I'm given a pass to wander the grounds unsupervised. My medication is reduced.

"You can't put it off indefinitely," Dr. McShay says.

His confidence reassures me.

"There's nothing to be afraid of," he says. "You can handle it now." He's dropped his usual tone of chilly condescension. He speaks to me almost as if we were friends. For the first time, I smile at him. "All right."

On the morning of the visit, I put on a blouse dotted with pink rosebuds and a pale pink skirt. I haven't worn

243

these clothes since the trip to San Francisco. I brush my hair and apply lipstick and rouge. In an effort to quell my anxiety I begin to sketch, filling in the tiny intricate pattern of the wallpaper in Emily's room.

Michael arrives shortly before noon. He taps tentatively on my open door.

We stare into each other's eyes. His are guarded; mine must be too. He has also taken some care over how he looks. His hair is newly cut; he wears a pale blue shirt and dark blue crewneck sweater—neither of which I recognize.

"Hi." I hold out my hand to him.

He bends to kiss my cheek. "You look great."

"Thanks."

He sits opposite me, folding his hands like a schoolboy. "The doctor says you're making a lot of progress. You could be getting out soon."

"So he says."

He shifts in his chair and clears his throat. "So—I'm glad the ban was finally lifted." His jocularity is forced; behind his smile, his eyes are frightened. "What was all that about, anyway?"

I closed the sketchbook and lay it on my knee, keeping one hand on it, as if it were a talisman guaranteeing courage.

"I told him."

I see the startled look in his eyes, but he keeps his voice pleasant and steady. "Told who what?"

"Told McShay. About you and David."

"I see." He retreats behind his icy silence; his face is closed. He waits for me to speak, to defend myself, to apologize, to dissolve.

The realization forms like a bubble rising to the surface of a pond: this silence, which has always terrified me, which Michael has wielded expertly, which has held me in an unbreakable spell, has no magic, no destructive powers. It's only Michael being very clever.

I want to shout with laughter!

I match his silence, folding my arms across my chest and watching him, my face carefully blank.

He twists in his chair. He leaps up and begins to pace the room.

"I asked you not to. I had good reason. You gave your word."

I shake my head, sitting, unmoving. "No more secrets, Michael."

"I see, I see." His mouth is tight, his eyes are darkening. "We've been all over this before. I can't make you understand. We're talking about me, now, not you. What I do in bed is nobody's business. It doesn't affect anyone but me."

"How can you say that? It affects me, it affects the kids."

A spasm of pain crosses his face. "And of course you feel you should tell the kids too."

"Yes, I do."

"You think it's important for them to know who their father is sleeping—"

"The *truth* is important."

"That's bullshit, Annie. When are you planning to tell them? Right away? Or do you think you should wait till they're old enough to know where babies come from?"

"They have to know—"

"This is crazy."

"Telling the truth is not crazy."

"Listen to me, Annie." He comes very close to me. I think he's going to grab me, but instead he folds his arms tightly around himself. "For the past eight weeks I've worked my ass off trying to keep the news about you from

245

your parents. It's been harder than hell, but I've managed. I've even got the kids cooperating—"

"You've got them lying for you?"

"No. Not for me. For you. Or did you want your parents to know that you've just spent two months in the bin, raving, claiming to be pregnant—"

"I don't want my children to learn how to lie."

"I thought *I'd* go nuts too. My mother's been calling wanting to know when you're coming back from your visit to your parents." His voice has risen. His hands clutch each other, the knuckles showing gray under the stretched skin. "This has been very hard on me, Annie. *Very* hard. Christ." He paces the room. "Can you understand at all what I'm saying?"

"I don't want the children to be liars. I want them to be braver than we've been."

"Brave? It has nothing to do with bravery. You're almost well now. Do you want me to phone your folks and tell them every detail of your breakdown? I don't call that being brave, I call that sabotage."

"No. It's not, it's always better. Even if it feels terrible at first—"

"Is this part of your sickness or are you just trying to get back at me?"

"I don't want to lie for you anymore, Michael."

"Fine. Then I'll call your father and tell him his clever, beautiful daughter went crazy."

"You won't have to. I'll tell him myself."

Michael whirls on me. His eyes look ravaged behind their ferocity. "That's a great idea—especially in his current state. I suppose you're going to tell him about San Francisco too?"

I stand unsteadily. "What about San Francisco?"

"Your 'old college friend.' "

246

"Claire—"

"Maggie told me. She thinks that's what made you so crazy."

"What . . . ?" I whisper. My breath catches in my throat.

"You know." His pale face grows paler. "You slept with that woman. Claire."

I hear a roar in my head like a waterfall, pure and powerful. I feel it lifting me up, carrying me along, sweeping me over the edge of my fear.

"Claire was because you were off somewhere fucking David!"

Michael recoils.

"Claire was because you left me alone. Because you've been leaving me alone for months and months. Because you never want to make love to me anymore—"

"That's not true—"

"You're a liar. You've been lying all your life. Because you're a coward."

He grips the chair. His narrowed eyes are green as a cat's; a vein pulses in his neck. "You don't know what it's like," he hisses. "You have no understanding. Some people can't take the truth. They have to be protected."

"Like you protected me? Liar! Coward!"

"I told you the truth. Finally. Look what it did to us."

"Because you lied first. Because you married me knowing you were lying to me."

His jaw tightens. "I loved you. I didn't want to lose you."

"How do you know you would have lost me? You didn't even give me a chance to decide—"

"All right. You want to know what it feels like? Go call your father. Tell him about your little fling. Come on. Let's go to the phone right now. You can be brave and love the truth—tell your dad that you fucked a woman in

San Francisco." He takes my hand, tries to pull me to my feet. "Come on." I try to pull away from him but he holds me.

"I didn't sleep with her, Michael," I shout. "Nothing happened. But even if it had, that's not about me, that's not who I am."

"Exactly!"

He drops my arm.

I rub where he gripped me. My eyes fill with tears.

"Sleeping with men isn't who I am either, Annie. It's just one part of me. And there are certain people who don't need to know. You have to respect my right not to tell, and their right not to hear. You can't—" His voice breaks. He turns away, moves to the window. A slanted beam of afternoon sunlight falls across his cheeks, pointing up the presence of deep furrows of anguish. He runs his hands through his hair. "Jesus," he says. "I've been missing you so much. Why are we fighting?"

I look beyond him at one of my sketches of the house taped to the dresser mirror. Moonlight makes silver squares on the front porch, the empty rockers stir in the wind off the ocean. I can hear the sound of waves breaking over the rocks, I can smell the salty scent of marsh grass. . . .

"We're fighting to become happy."

He shakes his head, sinks into the metal chair. "It's all gotten so tangled. It used to be fine. We *were* happy."

"No," I say softly, "*you* were happy."

He stares at his hands. "I'm sorry," he says. "I never meant to make you suffer. Never."

"I know." Suddenly, agonizingly, I want to hold him, make love to him. . . .

"How's David?" I ask hoarsely.

"Okay."

248

"Maggie came to see me. She brought the art supplies. Tell her I've started using them."

"Have you? That's good." His voice is flat, empty.

"Want to—" I was going to offer to show him my sketches. But a wave of something—self-protection? shyness? possessiveness?—sweeps over me, and I keep quiet.

His eyes move listlessly around the room. They pass over the sketch on the mirror without taking it in. "I'm glad you're painting again. Maggie bought some art things for the kids too. Emily's been drawing a lot lately. She's getting good at it."

"I wish I was there to help her. Robin too."

Michael glances at me. He's seen the flash of jealousy in my eyes, he feels my longing. "They wish you were too."

"They've got you. And David. And Maggie."

He nods.

"Michael . . . ?" The thought has just asserted itself. "Have you told Maggie? About you and David?"

He stiffens. "No. Of course not."

"Suppose she knew. What do you think she'd do?"

"I don't know. But I'm not about to put her to the test."

"I think you should. I think it will make a big difference in your life."

"No, Annie. You, me, and David. As long as we keep our secret, we'll be safe." He looks at me with anxious eyes. "What did McShay say when you told him?" He looks at me like a small, frightened child.

"He said we have to tell the truth to each other and then decide what we want."

Relief floods Michael's face. "That's all? That's all he said?" He stands and moves to me. "It's going to be all right, then." He puts his arms around me. "Thank God. I was sure he was going to make you leave me." He buries his face in my hair.

I hold him, trembling with love and anger.

"It's so good to touch you," Michael murmurs. "I love you."

I press my lips against the smooth hard skin of his neck, and breathe in the warm, familiar scent of soap and sun-warmed earth.

"There's a way for us to be happy," he tells me. "I know there is."

I hold him tighter.

October 1973

23

IN ACKNOWLEDGMENT of my impending freedom, Dr. McShay knocks on my door and waits to be admitted.

"Today's the big day, eh?" He smiles his rigid smile.

"Yes." For the hundredth time I check myself in the mirror, smooth my hair, my dress.

He shifts from one foot to the other. His eye lights on my crammed suitcase. "Need a hand closing that?"

"Thanks."

He leans his weight on the suitcase and I snap shut the locks. Deprived of the safety of his desk and file folders, Dr. McShay seems as awkward as a shy teenager. A sudden gust of unexpected warmth surfaces in me. I extend my hand to him.

"Thank you for everything."

He frowns; a faint blush rises above his beard. He shakes my hand. "Good luck."

I look into his worried, severe, earnest eyes.

"Good luck to you too." I found my way through the maze, back to reason and balance. I've been declared sane. But what mysteries have I unearthed? What questions have I answered?

I don't know.

I know I've altered. The red-haired woman is banished; my baby-that-never-was is gone. My passion for Michael has changed its form, transmogrified into an unquenchable longing to live—not just to live, but to live happily.

And I know what has to happen now.

Michael must leave David. He must stand by his choice to be my husband.

What will he do when I tell him?

If he says no, will I be strong enough . . . ?

Dr. McShay releases my hand. "The day nurse will sign you out," he says. He nods, flashes his stiff smile, and moves off down the corridor, his obligatory tweed jacket flapping against his bony hips, back to his office fortress, where he'll shuffle his cards, consult his books, dispense his formulas and potions.

A cheerful orderly pokes his head around my door. "Ready?" He hefts my suitcases onto a cart and leads the way through the heavy locked steel door, down the elevator, into the hospital lobby, where Michael is waiting.

We drive through sleepy Sunday-afternoon streets. My hands are trembling, my eyes burn in the unaccustomed brightness. The air is heavy, languid, sweet with the scent of orange blossoms. Browny-green palm trees, red bougainvillea, white stuccoed houses, cobalt-blue sky, chrome-hard sunlight, cars, children on roller skates, supermarkets, billboards, buses . . . everything throbbing with real-world color, bold, brilliant, actual; everything dazzles.

"Today even Los Angeles looks beautiful."

Michael grins and squeezes my hand. "I'm so happy to have you home," he says. He turns off the main road into the streets of our neighborhood. "The kids are so excited, they didn't sleep all night."

I press my hands to my chest to quiet the turmoil of anticipation. "Me too. I've been counting the minutes."

"They'll be home by dinnertime."

"What do you mean? They're not there?"

"I sent them over to play with Melanie. I thought you'd want a few minutes to settle in before you saw them. . . ."

"Oh, no!"

Michael's face furrows with dismay. "Darling, I'm sorry. I thought you'd want to take things slowly, get your bearings. . . ."

How could he not know how desperately I've been missing the children, how could he imagine I'd want to put off seeing them?

"They've decorated the house," he says, as though that might compensate for their absence. "They worked all morning."

"I'll make a big fuss."

He adjusts his rearview mirror. "I have a bit of news," he says in a different voice, hushed and heavy. "I thought I'd better tell you. I don't think she will, she won't want to spoil your homecoming— Everyone's all right," he says quickly in response to my fearful look. "It's only that Oliver's filed for divorce."

"Oh, really? I'm not surprised. How does Maggie feel about it?"

"She's pretending to be relieved, very jolly and all that. But I know she's suffering." His voice softens. "Poor kid."

"She'll be better off without him."

Michael starts at the bitterness in my voice. "I don't like to see a marriage break up."

"He's a bastard."

"I thought you liked Oliver."

"I hate what he's done."

"There are always two sides," he says, with an air of righteousness. "You're getting upset. Maybe I shouldn't have told you." He turns onto our street. He slows the car, pulls into our driveway. "Here we are. We're home."

Our house. Our real house, not a drawing of a fantasy. . . .

I step from the car while Michael is unloading my suitcases. The front door is unlocked, the living room is empty. The stereo is on, tuned to a lively jazz station. Pinned across the archway separating the living room from the dining room is a large crayoned poster: "Welcome Home Mommy." Crepe-paper flowers and red balloons wave from its corners.

From the kitchen comes the sound of voices.

Maggie, in my chef's apron, is standing at the open screen door. On the threshold, laughing, waving a long loaf of French bread like a baton, is David.

They both turn at the same instant; they stare at me with startled eyes.

Maggie recovers first. "Darling." She rushes at me, her arms spread wide. "You're early! Michael said four or four-thirty . . . You look absolutely marvelous. . . . It's so wonderful to see you. . . ."

My gaze remains fastened on David. He stands rigid, his hand on the doorframe, his eyes avoiding mine.

"I've cooked a gorgeous welcome-home dinner. . . ." Maggie's words tremble in a breathless rush. "I just couldn't wait to see you. . . . It will be grand to have you home. . . ."

David's face is closed and tight. I hear Michael's steps behind me.

"Annie, darling, I've put your— Oh." Michael stops short beside me, his face pale with alarm.

"David just came by to drop off the bread for dinner," Maggie says quickly, conciliatory. "We thought you weren't arriving till four. It's all right. . . . He's not staying. . . ."

David raises his eyes to mine. His look is full of trepidation and remorse. "Welcome home," he says.

Michael makes a small cautionary movement of his hand.

David's eyes sweep Michael's face. He sets the bread on the counter. "See you," he says.

Michael frowns.

"Thanks so much for the delivery service, it was lovely of you." Maggie grasps David's arm and propels him gently through the screen door.

The three of us are suspended, frozen. Confusion, desolation, anger swirl around us.

Maggie breaks the spell. "Champagne!" she warbles. "We need to toast your homecoming." I lean heavily against the table. David's presence has chilled and tainted the fragrant warmth of the kitchen.

"I feel like an intruder." I try to make my voice light and teasing, but they've both seen the look in my eyes.

"To you, to you." The champagne cork explodes across the kitchen. Maggie pours. "Our Annie is home!"

"Welcome home, darling." Michael raises his glass. "To Annie. To good times." His hand on my shoulder feels uneasy.

"Hear, hear." Maggie drains her glass. "Now, I think I should let you two have a few minutes alone." She takes off the apron and drapes it over a chair. "I'll be back when it's time for dinner." She blows me a kiss.

Michael watches her leave, his face tense.

I move around the kitchen, touching the stove, the sink, the potted basil plant on the windowsill. An unfamiliar cookbook lies open on the counter. A new white teapot has replaced our old chipped brown one.

Michael follows me with his eyes.

"I didn't expect to find Maggie here. I thought it would be just us and the kids."

"She was so eager to welcome you back. She's been cooking for hours."

"With David's help."

Michael says nothing. I move through the house, from room to room, Michael trailing behind me.

We come to our bedroom. I sit on the bed, running my hands over the old blue quilt, trying to reawaken remembrance in the touch of the worn soft silk.

"How are you feeling?" He sits beside me.

Nothing seems real. As if the reality and familiarity of this house had been siphoned off and poured into my imaginary house by the sea.

"I feel a little odd. Everything seems strange. . . ."

"You've been gone a long time."

I search his eyes, looking for answers, reassurances. But, as always, behind his warmth something is hiding.

"Lie down. Rest for a minute." He pushes me gently back against the pillows.

My eyes roam the room, linger over the family photographs on the dresser, the thumbed paperbacks on the shelf above the window, clothes hanging in the open closet. . . .

"What's that?" A corner of pale, soft silk sandwiched between my tweed coat and my terry-cloth bathrobe.

His glance follows mine. "Oh, that's Maggie's. She keeps a few things here. She's been spending the night sometimes. Ever since Oliver filed, she's been very lonely."

"Where does she sleep? Between you and David?" The venom escapes before I have a chance to snatch it back.

Michael recoils as if I'd slapped him.

"David doesn't sleep here," he says with wounded eyes.

"I thought you'd know that. And since you ask, when Maggie does spend the night, I sleep on the couch."

"I'm sorry."

He puts his arms around me, brushes my lips with his. "That's all right, darling." He sits up abruptly, his face breaking into a grin. "The kids! I hear a car on the drive."

The front door slams, feet clatter. The children, warm, damp, boisterous, hurl themselves onto the bed, into my arms.

I hold them as tight as I can, trying not to cry.

"Let me see you." I thrust them away at arm's length, still clutching their hands.

"Are you better, Mom?" Emily searches my face.

"Yes, my angel. All better."

"You were gone so long, Mommy." Robin buries his head in my lap.

I stroke their perfect skin, their soft hair, kiss their eyes, their grubby hands. "I'll never go away again." I look up at Michael's face. "Never again."

Maggie comes back at dinnertime; the children greet her with raucous delight. She puts the finishing touches on the meal, Emily serves. Michael, acting the patriarch at the head of the table, beams at all of us in turn.

In Maggie's presence the children seem to grow shy of me. They direct their remarks to Maggie or Michael.

"Wasn't that the coolest, that homer Steve hit last time?" Robin asks Maggie, his new Little League fan.

"I told you Tiffany would get grounded for what she did at Kim's birthday party," Emily says to Maggie. "And she did."

"Tell me about it," I say repeatedly. "Fill me in."

The childen's faces grow recalcitrant, weary.

"It was nothing," they say. "No big deal."

"I'll make it up to you," I blurt. "All that time I spent away . . ."

"It's okay, Mommy." Their glances are embarrassed. Maggie bustles with the food. The conversation flows with easy intimacy between her, the children, and Michael.

The darkness that keeps me separate grows deeper.

"It's almost bedtime," Maggie says, gathering the dessert plates.

"I'll put them to bed." I stand.

The faces around the table stare at me.

I lead the children upstairs, tuck them into their beds.

"Is David coming over tonight? He was going to finish reading me this story," Robin says pouting.

"Not tonight." I bend stiffly to kiss him.

He turns over on his side, disgruntled.

"Good night, my darling." I press my lips against his cheek.

He turns back to face me . . . forgiving. "I'm glad you're home, Mommy." His small hand touches my face.

"Me too."

Downstairs in the kitchen, Maggie and Michael are washing the dishes. I take an apron off the hook and tie it around my waist.

"What are you doing? You're the guest of honor." Maggie snatches it off.

"I want to help."

Michael puts an arm around us both. "I'll do the clean-up. Why don't you two go inside and have a talk?"

"A wonderful idea." Maggie's smile is reluctant.

"Go on." Michael gives us a playful push. "Off you go."

I sit on the living-room sofa. Maggie slides into the armchair opposite.

She looks at me, then glances quickly away. "It's really

good to have you back." She plucks a thread off the chair arm.

"It's good to be out of that place."

"And you're all better now?"

"Yes. All better."

Maggie's eyes move restlessly toward the kitchen. She gives me a too-bright smile. "I guess my tour of duty here is over."

"Thank you for everything. Michael said you've been an enormous help."

"I've quite enjoyed it. Cooking, looking after the kiddies . . ." She lowers her eyes. "Actually, it's been a bit of a lifesaver . . . given me something to do."

"Michael told me. About Oliver."

She raises her head; her face is clouded with pain, her mouth is defiant. "That prick. I should have guessed. Still, it took me by surprise. All that rubbish he talked, I was the center of his life, all the others were just flings, he'd die before he left me. . . . All lies."

"Is it the playwright?"

"No." She emits a short, abrasive laugh. "He dumped her too. This is someone new. She's nothing, nobody. Just a girl. With a baby. Not even his." Her face twists. "I'll fight it, though. I'll bleed him dry. He'll be left with nothing."

"I'm really sorry, Maggie."

She shrugs elaborately. "Not to worry. I'll manage. I'll find someone else. If he thinks I'm going to spend the rest of my life alone, pining over my lost love, he's out of his mind."

She runs her hands through her hair, shakes her head so the coppery curls fan out over her shoulder. "I am awfully grateful, though, to Michael," she says. "The last few weeks have been pretty awful. He's been wonderful to me." She leans forward, her hands balled into fists on her knees. "I hope you know how lucky you are," she says fiercely. "You have the kindest, the best, the most loving husband in the world."

"He's also gay." My words hang suspended on the thick air between us.

Maggie's eyes widen. She frowns. "So what?"

"Not much, if you're just his friend. You'd feel different if you were married to him."

She leans back and looks at me, her face solemn. "I don't think so," she says. "I used to feel sorry for you, your situation. But now I'm not sure. I think you make too much of it. You don't appreciate what's good about him. His loyalty. So what if he has a little romp with his pal now and again? You should have looked the other way, pretended you didn't know."

"Like you," I mutter.

"What?"

"You. Michael has no idea you know about him and David, has he?"

"No," she says. "There's no point to it. It would only make him guilty and anxious. Maybe not trust me." Challenge rises in her eyes. "And don't you tell him, either. If you want to muck up your relationship with him, that's your business. But keep away from mine."

"We're talking about my husband!"

Maggie stiffens, then sags against the cushion. She shakes her head slowly. "Of course, of course," she murmurs. "I'm sorry. I only meant he needs a friend. Someone outside of this great messy love triangle. I want to be that for him." Her eyes plead. "That's all right, isn't it?" Her voice trembles. "Christ, I need friends too. I've been feeling so wretchedly alone. . . ." She covers her face with her hands and cries.

I sit watching her. From the kitchen come the sounds of plates clinking, Michael singing. I feel myself sinking under a vast ocean of weariness.

"Nothing's changed. Nothing will change," I whisper.

Maggie lifts her head, dries her tears on the back of her hand. "What a bloody fool I am." She smiles crookedly. "Such a lot of rot. You're right. Nothing's changed. We're all still pals. We'll all have good times together." She stands shakily. "I'd better go. It's late."

She stands, hesitating, waiting for me to say something. I stare at the floor, the meticulously vacuumed rug. "You've taken good care of things while I was gone," I say hoarsely. "I appreciate it."

Maggie lowers her head. "Welcome home," she whispers. I watch her turn and slip silently out the front door. I can hear the retreating tap-tap of her high-heeled sandals on our gravel driveway.

Michael turns off the lights in the dining room, then locks the front door. He picks up a few scattered magazines and lays them on the coffee table.

"Bedtime, I think." He caresses my knee.

"Not yet."

"All right." He sits beside me on the sofa. "What's up?"

"It would work out well, wouldn't it?" My voice trembles.

He puts a solicitous arm around me. He rubs my back. "What is *it*?"

"You and Maggie."

"What are you talking about?"

"Maggie. She'd be perfect. She doesn't know about you and David. This time you'd keep it like that. . . ."

"What is this?"

"She's not having my kids!" The words erupt in a raw shout.

"What is this? Maggie loves you, you're her friend."

"That's what you told me about David."

"Annie. Stop, please. This is crazy."

I pull away from him. "Could you do it? Go through this whole thing all over again, all the deceit, the lying . . . ?"

"Do what? I don't know what—"

"Live with Maggie. And lie to her."

"That's a meaningless question."

"You could. I see it in your face. And it would be easier. So much easier with her. Because she wouldn't care, even if she knew."

"Please, darling, please . . . you're upset. It's been a long day. You've got to calm down." He's gripping my hands as though he were drowning.

I study him, the fear in his eyes, the anxious furrows along his mouth, his trembling lips. I close my eyes. The darkness inside me breaks, begins to roll away like spent storm clouds. I open my eyes. Gently I pull my hands away from him. "There's no other way, Michael. I can't live like this anymore. You have to leave David. Once and for all. Forever."

His eyes look deep into mine; they shimmer with sorrow and resolve. "I can't."

I nod. Outside, a car passes on the silent street, its headlights sweep the darkened wall of the dining room. "I almost died, Michael. In the hospital. I tried to kill myself."

His mouth gapes in horror. "McShay never told me that."

"He never knew. A patient found me. She saved me."

Michael sags against the couch. "Did I do that to you?"

"No. I did it. And I won't ever allow myself to feel that way again."

Maggie's words, like the voices of taunting children, fill

my head: *You make too much of it. . . . You don't appreciate him.* I stand. "It's over, Michael."

"Over. What d'you mean, over?" His jocularity is forced; fear has started to seize his eyes.

"I want a divorce." The words fall between us like an iron gate.

"What are you talking about? This is nonsense." He stands to face me.

I cover my mouth with my hands. *Everything could be the way it was if I only stop now.* "I don't want to live this way."

"But you have been living this way, and you stayed. Why did you stay?" I can feel the growing panic under his logical argument.

"I stayed because I loved you."

"And you don't now?"

"Yes . . ."

"There." Relief floods his face. "You love me, we love each other. I told you the doctor would try to interfere, put ideas in your mind."

"It wasn't the doctor." The sour, soapy taste in my mouth . . . Jenny's hands shaking me . . . *next time . . . cut the long way. . . .* "I want you to go."

"Go?" He looks dazed.

"Leave." My voice breaks. "Pack all of your things." Michael's image seems to blur. "Tomorrow I'm going to see a lawyer." The words tastes like steel.

His mouth is drawn back as if for a scream. But then it hardens into a sneer. His eyes ice over. "A divorce. I guess that would leave Maggie and me in the same position. . . ." He lets the implication of his words seep in.

I close my eyes against the pain and turn away. "You'll need a lawyer, too, to work out the details, visiting rights and so on."

Rage tears across his face. "The kids! You're not getting the kids. . . . You've just been in a mental hospital—that makes you unfit!"

"And I'll tell the court that your life-style sets an unhealthy example for children." I speak in a voice I've never heard before.

Michael's face blanches. He sinks into the sofa. "You wouldn't do that." His voice is stunned, muffled, hushed with sorrow. He shakes his head. "I won't let you. I'll fight you. I have friends. I'll find a lawyer. . . ." He stops as if he's lost the thread of his argument.

"I don't want it to be like that. Lawyers and ugliness. That would destroy the kids."

He stared at me as though I were a stranger. "Why should I move out?" he hurls. "I pay the rent. You don't even know how to run a house. All your life someone's taken care of you." His face is distorted now with loathing. "If that's how you want it, *you* get out. You'll see soon enough."

I hug myself tight. The look on his face rips me open. I can't believe this is us. Saying these words, looking at each other with this naked hatred. The floor seems to tilt under my feet. Still, I'm borne along by a force I know is good. "We stay here. The kids and me. You leave. Now." The words emerge calm, unshakeable.

"You won't have any friends," he spits. "Forget about Maggie and David. They'll never forgive you. Just like you won't forgive Oliver."

"I'll make new friends," I whisper.

He stands, lurching. He throws me a look of wild-eyed anguish, races for the kitchen. I hear the screen door slam.

Silence.

I sit, rigid, my hands clasped in my lap.

A slight movement on the stairs. My heart contracts. Was that the pale face of a child watching? Or only the shifting reflection of the moon, shining through the window on the landing?

A sadness beyond tears envelops me. I sit motionless on the sofa.

After a long time I'm aware of a small, rhythmical sound; it penetrates my sorrow, bores a tiny opening of healing sweetness and hope. I go to the window, lift the shade. Outside, a gentle, fresh rain is falling.

24

THE DOORBELL rings its three ascending notes. The echo of dinner parties, Michael shouting from the bathroom, *They're here already? Mix the margaritas. . . . Don't let them say anything good till I come out. . . .*

"Hi." He stands on the front porch, nervous, guarded. "I'm not too early, am I?"

"No. Come in." He's here to pick up the last of his belongings—books, fishing rod, typewriter. He moves with the stiff formality of a guest uncertain of his welcome. "The living room looks different." He glances at the rice-paper shades, the new wicker armchair. "What's that painting? Did you do it?"

"Yes. It's a house I once saw."

"Nice." He sits awkwardly on the sofa.

"Like a drink?"

"Please." He wipes his forehead and smoothes his hair. For the past month we've seen each other only in lawyers' offices and in court. The changes in his face stun me. Sadness lines his mouth. A battle is being fought in the depths of his eyes.

The old impulse—to hold him, to bury my face in his

shoulder—rises in me with unexpected force. I hand him his scotch.

"How have you been?"

"All right." His terse answer resonates with accusation, bitterness, loneliness.

"Are you still staying with Maggie?"

"No." A muscle moves in his jaw.

"Why not?" I ask the question brashly, knowing I have no more rights to his private life.

He makes a vague waving gesture. "It wasn't working." I see the longing in his eyes to confide, to make me his ally.

"Did she find out about you and David?" I make my voice kind, but my probing comes from another source—I need to know if any of what we went through has made any difference in him. "Did you tell her?"

In his clamped silence I hear my answer.

"You ought to tell her."

"That's my decision."

"I suppose it is." I haven't seen or spoken to Maggie since the night I sent Michael away. I had a note from her—brief, apologetic, but unyielding: *Annie, You've been a good friend. And I've tried. But this is beyond me. I can't side with both of you. You have the kids; Michael needs me. I'll miss you. Maggie.* Her absence is a chronic, deep ache.

"Where are you staying now? With David?"

"No. I'm not ready for that." His mouth is grim.

"I thought when we split up it would all be easier. . . ."

He shrugs, irritated. "It's not. Not for me." His eyes move toward the staircase. "The kids sleeping?"

"Yes. School tomorrow."

He nods, his face a mask of pain. "They're all I think about."

"They miss you too. They're pretty angry at me, especially Emily."

He looks at me, his eyes filled with the old question.

"All I've told them is that we need to live apart, but that we both love them. They're mystified. And hurt."

He nods, staring at the bare, bleached floor.

"I'm going to have to tell them, Michael. I can't let them go on thinking I threw you out and destroyed our family on a whim."

"You don't want the blame, in other words," he says softly, bitterly.

"I want us to share the responsibility. If you don't tell them, it means you don't trust them."

He runs his finger around the rim of his glass. He swallows the remainder of his drink.

"I have no control over what you tell anyone else," he says quietly. "But they're my kids too. I have rights. It's my place to tell them. You're right, they'll need to know, but you have to let me decide when." His face is touched with dignity and suffering. He looks more beautiful than he ever has. The old love, colored with sadness and loss, sweeps over me. I want to applaud his courage, but all I can say is, "When?"

"When the time is right. They don't even know what sex is yet—let alone what it means to be gay. Except that it's something to be despised for, or at least made fun of."

"How old is old enough?" I press him, struggling against the rising tenderness, the desire to protect him from his pain.

"I'll know when the time is right."

"I want an outside limit. . . ."

He looks off toward the window, into the night. "When Emily turns thirteen."

270

We look at each other across a vast distance, a space made up of all the linked moments of our life together.

"All right," I say, "I'll consider it a promise."

He stands. "Can I see them?"

"You won't wake them?"

I wait for him at the bottom of the stairs, listening to the small, safe sounds filtering through the open window, a neighbor's TV, a solitary car, the chatter of mockingbirds. Outside, the blossoms of the jacaranda tree lie like black velvet against the purple night sky.

When he descends his face is locked against his emotions.

"You'll be here on Sunday?"

"Yes, the usual time."

"I'll have them dressed and ready."

"Thanks."

At the door he hesitates. My arms raise reflexively to embrace him. I push them back, press them tight against my sides, relinquishing finally and forever the feel of him in my arms.

"Sunday, then."

When the front door has closed behind him, I stand gazing for a long time at my painting. The wide, welcoming white house, the curving porch suspended over the cliff, the Michaelmas daisies, the spiky marsh grass, the dark, beautiful prismatic surfaces of the rocks. Beyond it all, the sea, shimmering, a bright, broad promise.

SANTA CRUZ, CALIFORNIA

June 1977

25

Japanese lanterns hidden in the trees throw lacy shadows on the darkened lawn. I can hear the music as soon as I pull my car into the sandy driveway. Through the windows I can see the dancing figures of Emily's friends.

Pink balloons bob on pink ribbons tied to the balcony rail. Behind my house, where the lawn drops off to the pebbled beach, the ocean glistens in the moonlight.

Letting myself in the back door, I fling my coat and shoes into the hall closet and push open the shuttered dining-room doors. The pottery vase on the pine table holds thirteen perfect white roses. Beside it looms the cake—three-layered, swirled and flowered, sugar-pink, the candles already in place. I prop my present to Emily against the sideboard, which is heaped with wrapped and ribboned packages.

I contemplate my gift anxiously.

Is it the height of vanity to give your daughter your self-portrait as a birthday present? She'd probably prefer something to wear, or a new stereo. . . .

No. She *has* to have this. I was thinking of her when I painted it; the love in my face is unmistakable. So is the pain. And some courage. I study myself on the canvas. Not young anymore. Or pretty. But strong now. Will she see that? Will she finally know me? Forgive me?

Michael pokes his head around the study door. "There you are." He kisses me lightly on the cheek. "Private reserve . . ." He holds up a bottle of champagne and two glasses. He bustles nervously, opening the champagne, pouring drinks. "Your place looks great, I like what you did with the studio."

"Thanks. How's your house coming along?"

"David finally finished laying the tile in his bedroom. All we have left to do is one section of the roof and terrace."

"I can't wait to see it."

"He's working like a madman. In fact, he'll be late tonight. As usual . . ." He rearranges the stack of presents on the sideboard.

The ease of our conversation, the gentle, sweetly regretful friendship that has evolved from our pain is an unexpected, precious gift.

"What's that?" He points to my self-portrait.

"My present to her. What do you think?"

He frowns. "It doesn't look like you."

"It does."

"No. You're prettier."

"It looks the way I feel." I laugh.

"Dad?" Robin's round, eager face appears in the door. He hoists a cocktail shaker. The bartender's apron he wears reaches almost to his high-top sneakers. "What goes in a Harvey Wallbanger besides vermouth and Chartreuse?"

"What are *you* doing fixing drinks?"

"Mom said I could. What else goes in?"

"Pepto-Bismol."

"Dad." His ten-year-old scorn is monumental.

276

"Maybe we'd better go inside and chaperone if Harvey Wallbangers are cropping up." Michael starts for the living room.

"Wait." I lay my hand on Michael's arm. "We'll be right there, sweetie. Close the door. . . . Michael, let's talk a minute."

He looks at me, then glances away.

He moves to the window, stands staring out. Waiting.

"Tomorrow's the day," I say quietly.

"Yes." The old pain has resurfaced in his eyes. He turns his face away. "Don't you think she's guessed by now?" There's a note of pleading in his voice.

"I don't know. She's never mentioned it. But it doesn't matter," I say firmly. "She needs to hear it from you. She'll have questions. You have to answer her."

He thrusts his hands into his jacket pockets.

"You promised."

"I'm frightened," he says.

"Daddy!" The door flies open. Emily comes toward us, sure, graceful, grinning with childish excitement, her eyes shining with power. She has a white camelia fastened in her long brown hair; her white silk dress moves with her body in a way that I know thrills her.

"You look sensational," I say.

She dismisses my compliment with an airy wave, but her eyes devour it greedily. "You're late," she scolds.

"There was a muddle at the printer's. . . ."

Her gaze returns to her father. "Will you dance with me, Daddy? The kids all love to watch you dance."

Michael smiles, delighted. He snaps his fingers and moves his feet to the music. Emily laughs and pulls him behind her into the living room. As always, I'm struck by the sameness of their features—the secretive green eyes, the uncompromising nose, the beautiful, petulant mouth.

I watch them dancing, Emily's cool sexy glide, and I'm filled with pride and wonder at her assurance and strength. And awe at her determined effort to be happy.

The music ends. Emily stands inside a circle of rapt, adoring boys, talking, laughing. Her hands dart like starlings, her slender body sways and bends like a young tree.

Outside the circle, Michael watches, his eyes luminous with pride and love and fear.